KILLER IN THE OUTBACK

THE DREAMTIME AND A DEADLY KISS

A Diana Daniels Mystery

DIANE DEMETRE

LUMINOSITY PUBLISHING LLP

KILLER IN THE OUTBACK
The Dreamtime and a Deadly Kiss

A Diana Daniels Mystery

Paperback ISBN: 978-1-8383183-0-7

Cover Art by Poppy Designs

DEDICATION

For Agatha Christie, the greatest mystery writer of all time, whose classic whodunnits filled my young imagination with mystery, murder and mayhem.

I am from the never never, a long time gone by
The Dreaming is my creation, I am at home when I die.
— *Stephen Clayton*

CHAPTER ONE

WHAT STRIKES ME FIRST IS the sunlight. Not your ordinary kind of sunlight, but the extraordinary kind that's brighter than a dozen summer's days rolled into one. Surreal, yet somehow commonplace for this faraway land. Before me on the bed, diamond-faceted shards of light slant and slide in a hypnotic rhythm, carrying me to a distant time when life was far simpler. The Beatles classic *Lucy in the Sky with Diamonds* pops into my head, and I hum along while the light teases me to join it in a boat on the river. Although I long to do just that, I know this isn't the time to be swept away by the song's mystical mood or the light's playful antics. Instead, I revert to my unpacking. But like an excited child on Christmas morning, my elation gives me pause once more.

Tucked away in a luxury cliffside retreat atop the Chamberlain Gorge in the Kimberley region of Western Australia, I can finally tick this vacation off my bucket list. Being here in one of the most ancient places in Australia, in fact, the world is the fulfillment of a lifelong dream to connect with the cultural heritage, isolation, and primitive harmony of the vast country I call home. Hugging some T-shirts to my chest, I stare spellbound outside. *What a place.* A slight pang nips at my heart. Tom would have loved this adventure. He's been dead now two years and though I've grown accustomed to being a single woman, there are times, like this, when I miss him. With a soft sigh, I shake off the melancholy and return my full attention to the vast landscape. Except, my appreciation of the spectacular vista is short-lived because smack-bang in the middle of it is the back of my sister-in-law's head.

"I could use a little help in here, Mimi?" I call as a joke.

She doesn't answer, but that's not unusual. Mimi's immersion in her surroundings is oftentimes to the abandonment of her five senses. An endearing, yet irritating quality. I wander outside onto the open, timber-decked balcony, cantilevered over the red, rugged rock a few steps below. The unfenced edge of a sheer escarpment, only a couple of meters beyond the retreat, is an accident waiting to happen. However, I remind myself, this is a holiday, not one of my risk assessment consultancies.

Mimi sits cross-legged on the wooden deck chair, humming softly, her hands on her thighs, palms upward with index fingers and thumbs touching. I lean close to her ear, my voice a brusque whisper. "Mimi."

She doesn't stir but prizes open one glittering gray eye which scrutinizes me with mock displeasure. "Can't you see I'm meditating? I'm connecting with the Dreamtime." Her lips curve upward in a serene, yet cheeky smile.

Mimi's the funniest person I know. With the rare knack for finding humor in just about every situation, she can be either hilarious or so politically incorrect she makes me want to cringe. Currently, she's neither. Just a little annoying. I check my watch. "There's plenty of time to meditate later," I scold. "We're meeting the manager in ten minutes for the orientation. So, let's get a move on please."

She unfolds her legs with a groan, stands and faces me. "Seriously, Diana, you need to ditch the watch while we're here." Her glance of disdain catches my wrist.

I disagree with a scowl.

Not to be thwarted, she flourishes a wide sweep of her arm toward the dramatic landscape across the river. "El Kwestro is seven hundred thousand acres of pure magic. Listen to it."

She closes her eyes, and I do the same. Of course, she's right. Aside from the incessant rustle of millions of leaves as the wind gusts through paperbark and eucalypt trees, and the intermittent shrieks of birdlife, there's nothing but blissful silence. This is what we came away for, peace and quiet. I exhale a deep breath and the knot of tension in my shoulder eases its grip.

Yet despite my best efforts to stay in the moment, my punctual nature prevails, and my eyelids snap open. "I know this place is magic. But let's at least be on time to begin with. Come on." I stride into my room with Mimi tutting behind. "I can't believe you unpacked so fast," I say over my shoulder.

"I didn't. I just dumped my bag and came down to you."

That's Mimi. I smile to myself careful to hide my amusement.

She's booked into Woolybutt, the furthest retreat from the homestead, while I'm next in Kurrajong, and the third is Pandanus. Named after well-known Australian plant species, they're the only three, luxury, free-standing retreats at El Kwestro. Their namesakes can be found growing risk-free on the property, whereas our accommodation is built precariously on the top of the gorge. I figure my fear of heights is a little price to pay for the breathtaking views.

"Sometimes I wish I could be more like you," I say, stacking my T-shirts neatly into the closet. "But I like to unpack, get everything organized, and settle in straight away."

"Each to their own. Personally, I like a little bit of mess." To make her point, she drops my jeans onto the floor.

Tossing her a glare, I bend down and clip them onto a hanger. "And that's precisely why we're not sharing a retreat."

We laugh at our differences, knowing they make our relationship stronger. When Tom died, it was Mimi who'd been there for me. She may have been Tom's biological sister, but she's my spiritual sister. With her love and support, I made a new start in life, and now with her chaotic assistance, we finish unpacking my clothes and are out the door with a couple of minutes to spare.

Arm in arm, we stroll down the snaking pathway, past Pandanus, and toward the main homestead. On our right lies a sprawling, irrigated lawn the size of two football fields boasting luscious green grass and bordered by well-maintained, colorful gardens. Beyond the homestead's two-meter high, chain-linked-fenced boundary, the turmeric-colored earth speaks of the true nature of this place. Like an oasis in the desert, El Kwestro homestead is a remote sanctuary in a parched landscape sucked dry of visible life. Many might say this northern tip of Western Australia is a god-forsaken place, but beneath its inhospitable facade, lies a land that's sustained the most ancient civilization on the planet for over fifty-thousand years.

Shattering the silence, a sleek black helicopter buzzes overhead. Its rotating blades blur against a vivid blue sky, reminding me of a giant honeybee, readying itself to land. We veer left and up a few timber steps onto the long, wide-planked veranda of the main homestead. Built in the mid-twentieth century, the homestead has changed hands several times before being converted into its present incarnation of exclusive accommodation. And it's pleasing to note nothing of its authenticity has been lost in the conversion.

In the garden beside the veranda, a fresh-faced young man rakes fallen frangipani leaves into small piles. He works by the rule of no leaf is left behind, and I marvel at the care he takes. On hearing our steps on the wooden floorboards, he glances up. "G'day."

We slow to a stop. "Morning."

I return his sunny smile. "And you are?"

He breaks from his chore, swipes his tattered Akubra hat across his damp brow, and rests on his rake. "Andrew, ma'am." His flushed face wears the unblemished expression of contentment.

"You enjoy your work," I say more as a question than a fact.

"Yes, ma'am. I do. I love this top end of the country. I'd rather be raking leaves in the boiling heat than stuck in one of those smoggy cities trussed up in a suit and tie." He laughs, tips his hat, and returns to the tedious task.

"Well, you're doing a fine job, Andrew. Thank you."

Once out of earshot, Mimi giggles. "He's not one of your employees, you know."

"I know, but he seems such an industrious, likable young man. A little encouragement goes a long way."

The veranda flanking the homestead's six guest rooms on our left stretches like a long fashion runway. I recall from reading the brochure that three of the rooms lead out onto leafy gardens at the rear while the other three have spectacular Chamberlain Gorge views. I point down another long veranda to our right. "I think the great room's this way."

After passing the kitchen and office, we enter a spacious, well-appointed room. With its vaulting cantilevered ceiling, open walls screened to prevent the entry of bothersome insects, and an impressive shoulder-high stone fireplace, it's reminiscent of Karen Blixen's homestead from the movie *Out of Africa*. Only much larger. A few glass-paneled armoires line the walls, their contents a selection of Aboriginal artifacts and stunning pearl jewelry. Charmed by the cozy atmosphere, I'm keen to grab a good book, snuggle into one of the sofas, and while away my days.

A tall, red-headed woman in her mid-thirties strides toward us, pale-skinned hand out-stretched. "Hello, Diana, Mimi, I'm Amy Gillis, the homestead's manager. Welcome." Her black pencil skirt, black pumps, and fitted white blouse accentuate her trim, taut body, though she seems more suited to a board meeting than an orientation tour. She'd be described as a stunning woman, except she possesses a long, hatchet face with a severe underbite. Yet the warmth of her greeting draws attention away from her excessive genes. "Did you settle in okay?"

I shake her hand. "Yes, thank you. The cliffside retreats are spectacular."

Mimi glances past her. "I can't wait to see the rest of the place."

"Well, let's get to it. Follow me." We flank her as she heads outside onto another veranda, part of which is roofed, and part uncovered. She points to the long table under the covered section. "This is where lunch is served every day at one, while dinner is served on this section under the stars at night." She moves to the furthest section banked by a lush garden teeming with semi-tropical shrubs and trees. The outlook from both settings is splendid, with nothing but the gorge and virgin Australian bush beyond.

A young waitress folding and setting linen napkins for lunch glances up. "Hello."

"This is Nellie," Amy says. "You'll probably be seeing a lot of her at lunch and dinner." She redirects to Nellie. "This is Mrs. Daniels and Mrs. Kramer."

"Diana and Mimi," I correct. When the young girl smiles, it's like she has sun in her eyes, and when she returns to her work, it's with the same care as the young gardener. *They'd make a good couple.*

Amy guides Mimi and me down four wide timber stairs, and when we step onto the crisp, manicured lawn, my mind congratulates Andrew once more on his meticulous work.

"Is Nellie bi-racial?" I ask Amy.

"Yes, she's part Aborigine. When her mother died, her father took off and left her with her Aboriginal grandfather who raised her. She's had a tough life."

"That's sad," Mimi says. "She's such a beautiful looking girl."

"And a fine worker too." Amy stops in front of another splendid sight. "This is the pool. It's not heated and can be quite chilly because of the lower night-time temperatures. But after a day hiking the gorges, it's refreshing."

"Great." Mimi beams. "This is where I'll be every afternoon."

I shiver at the thought of plunging into the icy water of the lagoon-shaped swimming pool, but the dozen deck chairs and six umbrellas on top of its sprawling deck give me hope. *That's where I'll be. Sipping a cocktail under the umbrella while Mimi challenges her resolve in the water.*

We wander further down the gently sloping lawn until we come to the grass's edge. The only barrier preventing someone from walking off the edge and falling down the gorge into the Chamberlain River below is a low rock wall, no higher than my knees. I instinctively step back. "My goodness, isn't this dangerous?"

Mimi peers over the spine-chilling drop. "You certainly wouldn't want your guests to drink too much and tumble over, would you?"

Amy appears unconcerned. "That's why we don't allow children at the homestead."

"But haven't you had instances of people falling off?" I lean over and shudder. The chance of survival is slim. If you didn't break your neck on the protruding rocks on the way down, the fall to the massive rock shelf fifteen meters below would certainly kill you. Or at least, put you in hospital for a long time.

"No, we haven't. The guests who stay here aren't normally the types who get drunk." She winks and gives us a shrewd smirk.

I recall the cost of this all-inclusive holiday, understanding her inference. "Still it seems risky."

"Don't mind my sister-in-law . . ." Mimi wraps an affectionate arm around my shoulders and squeezes. "She's a management and specialist recruitment consultant. She's always on the look-out for the right people for the right job with the minimum of risk. The risk here is way out of her comfort zone." She laughs.

I shrug off her arm with a mock sneer. "Maybe so, but I for one, will be careful particularly at night if I come down this way."

"It's well-lit and the staff always have eyes on the guests. There's no cause for alarm. Look, here's the private dining ledge where you can have dinner under the blanket of billions of stars." Amy steps down a narrow staircase of three uneven stairs and onto a rock ledge no more than four meters long and two meters wide. A square table with two chairs balances unsteadily in the middle. "This is the best spot to have dinner, away from everyone else."

"This is even more dangerous." I shudder and hug the back of the low ledge, not daring to even look over.

"Once you're at the table, it's a wonderful dining experience." She lowers her voice. "To be honest, when I was serving here once, I stepped back a little too far and fell off."

Mimi and I gasp. "Did you hurt yourself?"

"Just a few scratches. There's another ledge below that broke my fall." She motions us over and points to a wider ledge a couple of meters further down.

I'm stunned at how casually she speaks of her accident. "You're lucky you didn't kill yourself."

She shrugs. "I'm sure I would have if the ledge hadn't been there. But don't worry, ladies, you're perfectly safe here at El Kwestro. That's why we do the orientation as soon as you arrive, so you know the lay of the land."

"Literally," I murmur, still unsettled.

Amy strides back up the stairs, while we follow with less assurance, until our feet feel the squishy security of the lawn. Onward she marches, regaling us with the layout and highlights of the homestead. "We've two resident crocodiles in the Chamberlain River. You may be lucky enough to see them from your retreat, sunning themselves in the afternoon on the opposite bank."

Not sharing her enthusiasm for the reptiles' proximity, I decide there'll be no self-drive boating alone on the river. That up-close-and-personal connection to the Outback isn't what I'm looking for.

"John and Sylvia Torrens from Melbourne are already here. And Tony and Trish Wilson from America just came in on the chopper."

I did the math, remembering the homestead accommodates eighteen guests at full occupancy. "Not a full house yet?"

"Not yet, but we've more arriving tomorrow." Amy flicks her ponytail over her shoulder and quickens the pace back into the great room. She marches to the tall fridges and flings open both doors with great drama. "It's a twenty-four-hour open bar, so help yourself. Champagne, beer, wine, soft drinks, whatever you like. And the staff can make all sorts of cocktails."

"Terrific." Mimi wanders over to inspect the variety of wines and champagnes on offer.

"Now, if you'll excuse me, I have to greet the Wilsons. Nellie will be able to assist you. If you need anything, I'm usually in the office. Have a lovely day. I'll see you here tonight for sundowners." Pivoting a sharp turn, she walks off, her ponytail swishing behind her.

Mimi leans across the waist-high timber bar, watching the manager's brisk exit. "She's certainly one smart cookie."

"What I call a human dynamo. I wonder why she's way out here. She seems far more suited to a high-flying job in the city."

"Maybe she's like Andrew. She just loves the Kimberley. They say once the Outback gets in your blood, it's hard to leave. Who knows?" With a shrug, she tosses her hands in the air and returns to the fridges. "It's time for a drink. I'm parched. What do you want?"

"I'm not sure." I twist my mouth, waiting for it to tell me what I'd like. "Something really cold."

"Perhaps I can help?" The sweet childlike voice belongs to Nellie.

Mimi was right when she'd called her beautiful. There's an innocent sexuality to her. Probably in her mid-twenties, she shines with the glow of flawless youth, amplified in her big, brown eyes, charming smile, and generous lips. "What do you normally like to drink, Diana?"

"I love dry martinis, but I think it might be a little early for one of them. We've been up since the crack of dawn." What with the hour flight from Darwin to Kununurra, followed by a one-and-a-half-hour road trip to El Kwestro, half of it on an unpaved road, I'm not sure alcohol is a good idea.

"For god's sake, Diana. You're on vacation. Relax. Have a drink." Mimi upends a white wine bottle, filling her oversize glass past half.

Nellie's face shines jewel-bright. "I can make you a deadly kiss, if you like." *The girl with kaleidoscope eyes.*

I drag myself back from my musical musings. "What's in it?"

"It's a martini cocktail with vodka and rose and violet liqueurs." She cocks a brow, waiting for my decision.

I relent with a nod. "Okay. A deadly kiss it is. But not too strong." I settle onto a barstool while she sets to work. "How long have you been here?"

"About a year." She selects three bottles.

"Do you enjoy it?" I watch her stir rose liqueur and ice cubes into a mixing glass.

"Mostly. You know how it is. Because all the staff live and work together there's a bit of friction. Like in a family." She tosses the ice and liqueur away and stirs the vodka into the mixing glass.

"Do you live here, on-site?"

"Gillian and Christopher Richards do. She's the General Manager for the entire El Kwestro property including the station, camping grounds, and tented cabins. He's the Executive Chef for the homestead. They live in the unmarked room at the far end of the homestead veranda."

I recall passing it earlier when we stopped and spoke to Andrew.

"But the rest of us live down at the station in staff quarters." Into a mixing glass, she adds the violet liqueur, pours in the vodka, strains it into a chilled martini glass, and slides it toward me. "A deadly kiss."

"It looks amazing." Tipping the frosty glass to my lips, I take a gentle sip. The floral liqueurs subdue the hit of vodka, bringing a grateful smile to my lips and a warm glow to my throat. "It's heavenly."

Nellie giggles. "No, it's a deadly kiss."

"It may start off as heavenly, but I bet it's got a deadly kick to it," Mimi warns.

"I'm sure you're right. I better go easy." I take another sip. "Just out of curiosity, Nellie, since you're so far away from family and friends, does El Kwestro have a policy about staff fraternizing with each other?" I glance at Mimi not to interject.

Nellie's eyes dart from side to side before she leans forward over the bar. "Even though management doesn't allow it, the staff have a saying . . . don't screw the crew. We only have sex with staff from different departments, not our own."

"So hypothetically, someone from front-of-house could have a relationship with someone from gardens and maintenance?" I flash her a half-smile.

Her eyes widen. "How do you know about me and Andrew?"

Ah. I was right. "Just a hunch. You two seem a perfect fit for each other."

Mimi huffs. "Don't mind her. She's got a gift, or so she likes to think." She twitches me a cheeky smirk. "Diana gets hunches about things, about people. It's terribly tiring being around her because she's usually right." She salutes me with her glass before taking a hefty slurp of wine.

"Oh, you're like my grandfather, Tommy George," Nellie says. "He's an Aboriginal elder. He knows things too. He sees them in the sand." Deep affection floods her face as she talks about her grandfather's gift and the Dreaming—the Aboriginal stories and beliefs behind creation.

"I'd like to meet your grandfather while I'm here, if he agrees."

"He doesn't take visitors, but I'll see what I can do." Before I have a chance to ask more, another couple enters the great room. "Hello, Mr. and Mrs. Torrens, what can I get you?"

Mimi and I smile in their direction and allow Nellie to serve them uninterrupted.

Crooking my arm, Mimi bundles me outside to the veranda. "I can't believe it. We've only just arrived and you're already on the scent. What is it?"

"I'm not onto anything. We came here to get in touch with ourselves and connect to nature. Meeting an Aboriginal elder will enhance that experience." I sip my deadly kiss, feeling it creep into my brain.

Mimi faces me, frowning and smiling at the same time. "I know you too well, Diana Daniels. You're picking up on something. What is it?"

I stare past her to the cloudless blue sky. More luminescent than any sky I've seen before. Even more than the sky at the Galapagos Islands, where I exposed a jewel thief and caught a murderer. Then it hits me. The sensation squirming in my gut is the same as it had been back then. An insistent nagging to dig deeper into things, to ask seemingly random questions, for no apparent reason. A ragged breath rushes into my lungs. *Not again.*

Light-headed, but not from the alcohol, I sense something's brewing here at El Kwestro, and I'm the only one aware of it.

CHAPTER TWO

FROM THE CORNER OF MY eye, I glimpse Tony Wilson fork the last of his grilled barramundi into his mouth, like a sea lion swallowing a whole mackerel.

He burps and pardons himself. "The fish was awesome."

Beside him, his embarrassed wife arranges her cutlery indicating she's finished. Though Tony's plate is dish-washer clean, Trish's is still laden with food. She's barely taken more than a few mouthfuls, which gauging by her underweight appearance, appears to be her normal eating pattern.

He frowns at her plate. "Aren't you going to eat more than that?" She ignores him.

Sylvia Torrens clears her throat and raises her plate to Nellie. "Yes. It was delicious." She's a striking woman in her forties. With pixie-cut, brunette hair, and polished alabaster skin, she reminds me of one of those cover models on a high-end lifestyle magazine. The sort who gaze out to sea from their beach-side apartments, dressed in understated, designer-chic clothes and oozing sophistication. John, her equally handsome and stylish husband, nods a silent thank-you when Nellie clears his plate.

Mimi reclines in her chair, and catching Nellie's attention, points to her wine glass for a top-up. "Tell us a bit about this art gallery you own back in the states, Tony." Mimi loves painting. In fact, she loves all art. Her husband, Aaron, built a small studio in their back yard where she paints most days. Her works feature mainly abstracts, which I joke are representative of her eccentric personality. But now, as I examine her well-scrubbed face and hands, the persistent traces of paint which have become her trademark over the years are missing. And I suspect, she's craving her creative fix.

"It's called the Wilson Art Gallery." Tony's drawling Californian accent reminds me of Detective John Nash who I worked with on the *Silver Galapagos* expedition ship. It's easy on the ear, though John was a lot easier on the eye. Tony's a big barrel of a man, overflowing with his own importance. "Trish majored in art at college, while I did business management. When we married, we decided we wanted a business in the art world. The gallery came up, so we bought it."

"Business must be good, then?" I ask, interested in more detail.

"It has been since Aboriginal art became popular in America."

"That's why we're here at El Kwestro," Trish says. Though she's a bird-like woman, she speaks with commanding fervor. She wears no makeup, her mousey-brown hair is pulled back in a low bun, and her pale blue eyes glisten with intellect. There's a sincerity and authenticity about her I like. "We've come for the annual Kimberley Art and Culture Festival."

Mimi straightens, sending the wine in her glass swirling. "When's the festival?"

"This weekend in Kununurra. But there's a special dinner here at El Kwestro on Friday night for the art sellers and buyers. The Kimberley Under the Stars art event."

Mimi turns to me with unrestrained excitement. "I'd love to go."

"Maybe there's a couple of tickets left. We'll ask Amy."

She turns her attention to Sylvia and John Torrens. "And what about you? What line of business are you in?" The wine, the Outback heat, and the topic of art have made Mimi even more chatty, nearly to the point of pushy.

I notice Sylvia glance sideways at her husband. "Ah . . . we sold our antique business in Sydney recently and moved to Melbourne. We decided to take some time off and travel a bit." She clasps his hand which is wrapped around the stem of his wine glass, his knuckles whitening. For an instant, I wonder if he'll snap it clean in two.

"*Ooh*, antiques. I love antiques." The slightest of slurs laces Mimi's voice.

I give her a discreet nudge. "Well, if you'll excuse us, we're going to unpack. Maybe we'll see you on the Chamberlain River Gorge cruise this afternoon?"

Tony and Trish affirm they'll be going, while Sylvia glances at John who merely shrugs. Mimi murmurs her disappointment at my insistence to leave but eventually relents, bringing her glass with her.

"Why did you do that?" she grumbles, as we stroll back through the great room.

"I think you need to go a little easy on the wine out here."

"But I haven't had that much."

"I know, but the heat makes the effect of the alcohol worse. Besides, I'll help you unpack so we can go on the gorge cruise this afternoon." I hook my arm through hers and smile away her pout.

"Okay," she says with reluctance and tosses the last of the wine onto the lawn. She does a slow turn on the spot. "It is beautiful, isn't it?"

"Stunning. And we've only seen the homestead property. Wait until we get out into the gorges and do the hikes." My workload for the past year has consumed most of my time and energy. Though non-stop work has been a preferable alternative to loneliness since losing Tom, it's had health consequences, which I intend to rectify with loads of R & R on this trip.

Mimi wraps her hand over mine. "So . . ." Her mischievous voice matches the gleam in her eye. "What do you think of the Torrens and the Wilsons?"

"The Wilsons seem nice enough, although I suspect Trish uses her weight to control him."

"What do you mean? She doesn't have a weight problem."

"Oh, yes she does. She's emaciated, and she drinks. She eats like a bird because the alcohol suppresses her appetite. And because he hates it. Tony probably controls everything else in the marriage and the business, but she controls what she eats. I suspect it drives him mad."

She laughs. "My god, the things you see. I thought they were a happily married couple in business together."

"If there's one thing I've learned is that nothing is what it seems. There's always something going on below the surface."

"And what about the Torrens? What's going on there?" She wags her empty wine glass under my mouth like a paparazzi reporter's microphone.

"There's something sad and angry about him. Sylvia's the good wife. She'll stand by him, whatever it is." A glint from the garden to our right catches my eye. "Look, there." In a ground nest of twigs and small broken branches, the aluminum bases of tea light candles glisten in the sunlight.

Mimi moves to the edge of the path where it veers off to my retreat. "What is it?"

"I think it's a bower bird's nest." Being as quiet as possible, we step onto the ground about a meter from the nest. "The male bird collects bright objects and scatters them around the bower, trying to attract a mate to the nest," I whisper.

She tilts her head backward, looking up at the trees. "I can't see him anywhere."

"He's probably off finding more swag to add to his collection." I bend down and take a couple of photos. "It's our first encounter with Australian wildlife."

"Oh, god. Don't go all David Attenborough on me."

"I promise I'll go easy on the natural world if you promise to go easy on the wine during the day."

She raises her empty glass in an oath. "I promise."

"Good. Now let's get you unpacked, we'll put on our hiking gear and grab a coffee before the gorge cruise."

★ ★ ★ ★

BY THE TIME WE SETTLE into the old tin dingy with our naturalist guide, a gentle giant of a man named Bob, the sun's begun its slow descent in the western sky. Steering the rusty boat's two-stroke engine, Bob heads down the bark-brown tinted Chamberlain River through the towering gorge. On either side, giant cliffs of millions-of-years-old stacked sandstone dazzle us with their fiery colors while the sun blazes into each nook and cranny as if searching for ancient hidden treasure.

"The colors are intensified at sunrise and sunset," Bob says, while we *ooh* and *ahh* at the terracotta oranges, burnished golds, and flaming reds.

In front of me, Mimi chats to Trish and Tony about how renowned artists, both Aboriginal and Western, capture this natural spectacle. They're so enthralled in their art discussion that I take the opportunity to chat with Sylvia.

"Didn't John want to come on the cruise?" I don't want to pry, but his reluctance at lunch to converse tweaked my interest.

"He isn't feeling well." She sounds casual, but I notice her fingers fidget at the mention of his name.

My sideways glance catches her pale green eyes scrutinizing me. "That's a shame."

With a voice as smooth as the Chamberlain River, Bob continues his commentary. "The mountains, gorges, and plains of El Kwestro are the product of volcanic eruptions, fracturing of rock, layering of sediment, and constant erosion. This geology sets the Kimberley apart from the rest of the country and gives it its unique character."

I take advantage of his hiatus. "You mentioned you and your husband decided to travel. Have you been anywhere else?"

"Not yet. We thought we'd get away from everything for a while. That's why we came here. Then, we'll go across to Broome and then down to Perth."

"That's quite a trip. How long will you be gone for?" I purposely keep my conversation light while my sixth sense nudges me to dig deeper.

"To be honest, we haven't decided. It'll depend on John."

"Isn't he well?" I face her, concerned that her husband might be seriously ill.

"No, he's fine . . ." Her lips lift in an unconvincing smile.

"Are you sure? You're a long way from medical care out here."

She heaves a heavy breath. "He has a few mental health issues."

"I see. Don't we all?" I smile, not with sympathy but with humor, and she relaxes a little.

"What is it that you do, Diana?"

"I have my own management consultancy business. Companies hire me as a recruitment and management specialist. My primary role is to find the best person for the job."

"That must be tricky?"

"It can be, but the Myer Briggs personality test helps. It works as an indicator of a candidate's psychological preferences in how they perceive the world and make decisions. Sixteen different personality types come from the four principle psychological functions of sensation, intuition, feeling, and thinking."

"It sounds complicated, being able to pick the right person every time." Her face hardens. "It's difficult to know who to trust these days."

"That's true, but having done it for so many years, I've acquired a pretty good insight into people and human behavior."

"That's the sort of insight we could all use." Her words hold a trace of bitterness.

"And you? Now that you don't have the antique business anymore, do you still work?"

"No. I volunteer at our local church. They were good to us after . . ." She clamps down on the rest of the sentence.

I suspected that the Torrens had suffered some great upheaval in their lives, and her abrupt stop confirms it.

Whatever it was, it probably forced them to sell their business, leave Sydney, and move to Melbourne.

"'Hope smiles from the threshold of the year to come, whispering, 'It will be happier,'" I say. "It's Tennyson. I read his poems whenever I need to unwind."

Her mood turns pensive, and she stares past me at the massive cliffs. "Yes. That's what we'd hoped for. That it'd be happier." When her gaze returns, I notice her eyes are swamped with tears.

"Would you like to talk about it?"

She hesitates. Her pale, forlorn face stamps itself on the fractured backdrop of ancient red beauty. Both speak of trials and tribulations. "No. I'm fine. Thanks." She wipes away a tear from the corner of her eye and straightens. Her tight smile marks the end of our conversation, and her focus returns to Bob who points out a small rock wallaby on the ledge to our right. I half-listen while he circles the boat in the river's waterhole. Two languid, meter-long barramundi swim around the dingy, as do dozens of small, seven-spotted archer fish, who lift their heads and squirt water at us in demand of food.

"Cheeky things," Mimi complains, wiping water from her forehead.

We cover our faces, trying to avoid their determined and accurate aim.

"If you all look over this side." Bob waves us to one side of the dinghy and it dips perilously downwards. He then sticks his finger in the water, wriggles it like a worm and the archer fish disperse. Smack! We all scream and holler. One of the barramundi clamps onto his finger, and as he lifts her high from the water, she hangs on valiantly. The fish lets go, and Bob's finger is no worse for the attack.

He laughs at the fright he's orchestrated. "Barramundi have no teeth," he explains. A true showman, his act is well-rehearsed, and he delights in his audience's applause. While Mimi, Tony, and Trish plead for him to do it again, beside me Sylvia's face has turned a whiter shade of pale. She sucks in a slow, deep breath obviously trying to control her anxiety.

Whatever the Torrens' have been through, it isn't just John who struggles with its aftermath. Sylvia's close to shattering into a thousand pieces like a delicate crystal ornament with a hairline fault.

★ ★ ★ ★

WHEN WE ENTER THE GREAT room, Nellie greets us with an engaging smile. "Would you like a deadly kiss, Diana? And a white wine for you, Mimi?"

Mimi holds up two fingers. "Make it two deadly kisses please, Nellie."

"I'll bring them out to you on the veranda if you like."

"Thanks."

When we wander outside and say hello to the others who've already arrived for sundowners, there's a prickly tension in the air. The type that arises when strangers try to act like friends because of social convention and forced proximity. It strikes me that Tony, who is used to playing alpha male has been holding court without objection.

He lifts his beer in the air toward us. "Mimi. Diana. I was just telling John he missed a helluva cruise this afternoon . . ." His condescending tone grates.

Sylvia slides her hand into her husband's and squeezes.

"Yes, it was lovely," I say. "But I'm sure the cruise happens each day. There'll be another chance for John to see the river gorge."

"Indeed, there will. Good evening everyone." Amy claims the veranda and is greeted by a chorus of hellos. "How's everything going? Everyone happy?" Enthusiastic answers in the affirmative ring out. "If I might suggest, the full impact of sunset is best seen down on the bottom of the lawn. We're so far north here at El Kwestro, that at sunset the sun looks like it falls from the sky. You'll get the best vantage point on the edge of the property. Follow me."

Like a gaggle of geese, we jostle behind her and file onto the lawn, drinks in hand. While she gives a quick commentary, we watch the sun paint the scenery on the other side of the gorge with sweeping strokes of crackling color before dropping like a stone, leaving the sky bathed in purple.

"Spectacular," I murmur.

"Certainly is," John Torrens says.

Having edged in beside me without my noticing, he's staring at the darkening vista as if hypnotized. I follow his gaze. "Coming here's been on my bucket list for a long time. I'm pleased I made it," I say.

"Sylvia and I needed to get away. The further, the better. When we heard about El Kwestro, we thought this was about as far away as we could get without leaving Australia." He speaks in a calm, even manner while his attention stays fixed on the landscape beyond.

"Yes, your wife told me—"

"Sylvia didn't tell you everything, but she did say she liked you." Deliberately, he turns to face me, his gaze fusing with mine. "It's been a long time since she felt she could trust anyone."

"She strikes me as a resourceful woman, and she clearly loves you."

"Sylvia's been my rock. I'm not sure whether I could've survived without her." He hesitates. An abiding sense of grief lingers on him, reminding me of how I felt just after Tom died.

I draw a deep breath. "Forgive me for asking, but did you and Sylvia lose someone close to you?"

"Why would you say that?" He turns defensive.

"I'm sorry if I intruded. I sense you've suffered some great loss. And there's nothing as sad as losing someone you love."

"Yes, there is. Losing your only daughter to suicide." His face falls.

"Oh, I'm terribly sorry. That's heart-breaking."

"It was a few years ago now. Sylvia handles Stephanie's suicide better than me. It got big media coverage. In the end, we had to change our name from Campbell to Torrens to escape the media."

The clapping of hands shatters our private tête-à-tête. Standing to our right, Amy herds the guests together. "Everyone, if you'd like to make your way to the long table, we're about to serve dinner."

Sylvia steps next to John and hooks her arm through his, while I move closer to Mimi.

"I wish I'd brought my painting gear. This place is too beautiful not to paint."

"Yes, a shame." My response is merely a polite aside. I usually find Mimi's joyous enthusiasm contagious, but this evening my mind lingers on my conversation with John. The cracks in his soul are as deep as the fissures of the Kimberley and have been inflicted just as violently. I doubt whether he and Sylvia even register the beauty surrounding them, let alone experience any joy since Stephanie's suicide. *A sad business.* And one my sixth sense urges me to pursue.

CHAPTER THREE

"I FOUND IT," I SAY to Mimi, who's pouring us each an orange juice. My laptop is propped open on the bar in the great room, the only place at the homestead with connectivity. It's unreasonably early for a Wednesday morning, particularly for holidaymakers, which suits our need for privacy. All sensible guests are asleep. The only staff around is the chef, who's cloistered away in the kitchen doing breakfast prep, leaving Mimi and me to our own devices.

She leans over my shoulder and reads the headline. "'Father suspected of daughter's death.' Shit. That's John Torrens." She points to the distraught face of the man on the front page of the article.

"'John Campbell was arrested for allegedly killing his daughter, Stephanie Campbell . . .' I read on silently and then flick to the next article. The story proceeds with lots of suspicion, allegations, unsubstantiated evidence, and articles blaming him for his daughter's death.

"Do you think he did it?" She hands me a glass of juice.

"Don't know. But there's more here." We read on, sipping in silence until the last article on the story identifies there'd been new evidence found. A suicide letter from Stephanie was discovered behind the mirror in her bedroom. "'In the letter, Miss Campbell writes of an unknown lover who jilted her and sites this as the reason she took her own life.'"

Mimi shakes her head. "The poor man. Bad enough your daughter commits suicide, but to be accused of her death would be unbearable."

I close the lid of my laptop, saddened by our discovery. "Indeed, it would. Stephanie Campbell was an eighteen-year-old architecture student at Sydney University. She obviously had a passionate affair, probably with someone at uni, fell in love, and then, when her lover called it off, Stephanie ended her life."

"No wonder they changed their name and moved cities. I wonder if they ever found out who the lover was?"

I stare into my empty glass. The last film of juice clinging to the sides remind me of the heartache gripping John and Sylvia. "I doubt it."

"Well, if I'd been Stephanie's lover, I sure as hell wouldn't have admitted it. Who wants to be blamed for your ex-girlfriend's suicide?" Mimi collects our glasses and pops them in the sink.

"Which means, if the lover was never discovered, John and Sylvia never got closure . . ."

Sliding onto the stool beside me, she says, "How awful."

I doodle my fingertips over the top of my laptop. "This explains the Torrens' anxiety."

"Yes, but does it satisfy you?" She tilts her head, pinning me with her cool, powder-gray gaze. "I can tell by that faraway look in your eyes that your brain is formulating scenarios. You're going to ask them, aren't you?"

I act innocent. "Ask them what?"

"Whether they know who the lover was?"

"I don't want to intrude."

"Oh, *puh-lease.* You can't help yourself. When those hunches of yours start, nothing stops you until you get the answers. I've seen it before."

There's no point arguing. It's the same sense of foreboding that forced me to get involved in a mystery on the *Silver Galapagos* cruise twelve months ago. I couldn't ignore it then, and I can't ignore it now.

She slants me a shrewd look. "You know you're supposed to be on holiday?"

"I know, and I am. Maybe there's nothing sinister going on. It's just that . . ."

She holds up her hand. "Stop. I don't want to know. If you need a Watson to your Sherlock, I'm not your man. I'm available to bounce ideas off, but don't ask me to go snooping where I don't belong. I'm no good at subterfuge." She spins off her stool.

"Deal." I stand and tuck my laptop under my arm. "I'll do the investigating, and you do the listening and reporting back."

"But why would anyone tell me anything important?"

"Because you possess one of those bright, dizzy personalities that people like. They don't think you have a brain to bless yourself with."

With a loud *harrumph*, she knuckles her hands on her hips and pouts a full stop. "I resent that."

"Sorry. But I've discovered that people with criminal persuasions tend to brag about themselves and their endeavors. And who better to do that to than someone they underestimate as an airhead."

"Well. If anyone thinks I'm an airhead, they'd better think twice."

"Exactly. So, if my hunch is correct, and there's something not quite right here, you may be just the person I need to ferret out information without even trying." I squeeze her hand.

"Okay." Reluctance rings in her voice. "But I hope you're wrong."

"Me, too." *But I know I'm not.*

★ ★ ★ ★

THE SIX OF US PILE INTO the 'tripi', short for troop carrier, the name which the staff affectionately call the windowless, six-person land cruiser. Although it's only eight o'clock in the morning, the sun's already scorching land and sky. I'm outfitted in true Australian outback gear of Wrangler jeans, patterned shirt, and hiking boots, complete with Akubra hat and sunglasses. On the other hand, Mimi's bundled her long, gray, un-dyed hair atop her head in a bright gypsy scarf which matches her floating long sleeve blouse. At least she's wearing a pair of cheesecloth pants and not a skirt, and what barely pass for a pair of sandals. She's more befitting a flower-power music festival from the early 1970s than an outback excursion.

I eye her up and down with undisguised concern. "I sincerely hope you've brought proper hiking gear for when we do the gorge hikes?"

"I did. But I thought since we're just staying in the tripi, I'll come comfortable."

"And what happens if we break-down, and you have to walk. You're not properly attired, you know."

She leans her lips close to my ear. "Listen, if you want me to play the ditzy creative type, you have to cut me some slack."

I laugh out loud. The Torrens and Wilsons sitting in front of us in silence, swivel around, obviously curious as to our high spirits, and smile politely.

A muscular young woman kitted out in khaki shirt and shorts, and heavy-duty hiking boots springs onto the driver's running board. When I dig Mimi in the ribs and point to the young woman's boots, indicating the correct footwear for this morning's tour, she turns up her nose and ignores me. *She'll be sorry.*

"Good morning everyone, my name is Hayley. I'll be your driver and guide this morning for the bush culture and history tour." She slides into the driver's seat, knocks the tripi into gear, and sets a slow crawl along the gravel driveway leading from the homestead to the property gates. I glance back at the historic weather-board homestead, set in its artificial emerald sea of green against a sky of Delphinium blue, and wonder what today will bring. Will we return victorious or vanquished? With no idea where the thought comes from, I face forward in the hope of finding out. Once the tripi hits the dirt road outside the gates, Hayley hits the gas. The wheels kick up billowing clouds of red dust, which become our constant companions for the next few hours.

"We'll be driving through the savannah bushland this morning and stopping at different places of interest where we might see egrets, herons, and ibis as well as wallabies." Though she speaks into her headset, we can barely hear her above the road noise. Deep corrugations in the dirt road caused by last wet season's torrential rains make an almighty racket under the wheels and bounce us around like wayward tennis balls. We grip onto whatever we can in the tripi to survive the bucking ride. Unable to converse due to the noise and clouds of dust, we watch the endless acres of bleached blond spear grass whiz past in a blur. This land is dry, brittle, and blanketed with fine, powdery dust, in the absurdist colors from sizzling paprika-red through to sunny, saffron-yellow. After thirty minutes of this monotonous, yet compelling landscape Hayley stops the tripi and we stumble out, happy to be standing upright and still.

Once our land-legs return, she herds us toward a swollen, silvery-barked tree that looks like it's been yanked from the ground and turned upside down. Its gargantuan branches resemble displaced roots stretching skyward in search of safety. "This is the famous Durack tree. It's estimated to be about five-hundred-years old. It's named after the first family in these parts . . ." She stops in her eloquent commentary, and lowering her voice, says, "What are you doing here?"

Looking flushed and apologetic, Nellie steps from behind the tree into full view. "Sorry. I didn't mean to scare you. I need to see Diana for a moment."

Before Hayley has a chance to speak, Nellie quicksteps over to me. "He said yes."

I blink. "Who said yes?"

"My grandfather, Tommy George. He's willing to see you, but you must come now."

I scan around, unable to see another vehicle. "How?"

"We walk. He lives over that ridge." She points to a craggy hillock about a kilometer away. Or it could be more. Because of the light haze, distance is difficult to calculate up here.

"Are you kidding me?" Mimi's eyebrows lift high on her forehead. "Aside from the walk, how are we going to get back to the homestead?"

"I'll get Hayley to come back this way on the return. She can pick you up then."

I incline my head, targeting Mimi with a hopeful stare.

She tuts and blows out a breath. "Okay. I'm up for it."

"Good." I clap my hands together and tell Nellie to organize it with Hayley.

When my eyes travel to Mimi's feet, she wags a finger at me. "And not a word from you."

I hold up both hands. "Not a word." I chuckle quietly to myself, knowing Mimi's feet are about to be very hot and sore.

"It's all sorted," Nellie says, on her return. "Hayley will come through this way in about two hours."

I check my watch, and when I catch Mimi scowling at it, I crinkle my nose in defiance of still wearing it. "Okay. Lead on."

Nellie glances at Mimi's feet, but Mimi speaks first. "Don't worry. I'll be fine."

"Okay then." But she looks uncertain. "Let's go." She sets off at a brisk pace.

The three of us traipse, and at times slide, down a sloping dirt track, until we reach a small, flowing tributary of the Chamberlain River. A crossing of slippery, uneven river rocks about fifty meters long, and a couple of meters wide is the only way to the other side. When Nellie stops, we move in beside her. "Keep an eye out for crocodiles." She speaks with the same ease as if offering to make us a drink at the bar.

"What? You mean they'll be here, at the crossing?" Mimi looks ready to bolt, so I grab her hand.

"No, but if they see you, they'll hang around, hoping you'll venture deeper into their territory."

"Well, there's nothing to see here," I call to the unseen crocs. "Move along." I wave my hand like a traffic cop, hoping to calm Mimi.

"There's nothing to worry about. They won't spring up and grab you. Just stay on the rocks in the middle of the crossing, and you'll be fine," Nellie says.

Mimi regards the uneven, rocky path before us, her eyes wide with worry. "I've seen what they do to the zebras in Africa at the Masai Mara River crossing. And it's not pretty."

Nellie laughs a clear, sweet sound. "That's not going to happen. Follow me." With the advantage of youth and the balance of a cat, she steps onto the exposed, river stones and is on the other side in no time.

We step off with far more caution, one slow footfall after the other.

I glance over my shoulder, concerned that Mimi might slip and fall because of her unsuitable shoes and become croc bait in an instant. "Are you okay?"

She doesn't lift her head. "I'll be fine. You go first, and I'll step where you do."

Her confidence in my agility is commendable, if not a little ill-advised. Taking far longer than Nellie, we make it to the other side, dry, uninjured, and without sighting a crocodile.

We heave a thankful breath, and Nellie sets the pace once more. "It's dry land walking from here on."

Thank goodness.

Ahead of us lies remote wilderness and behind us, our transportation has departed. Mimi casts me a nervous glance which I reciprocate with an encouraging smile. But I know what she's thinking. Here we are utterly alone, traipsing off with a girl we've only just met into one of the most isolated, uninhabited places in the world. With no other recourse, we square our shoulders, exchange a wink, and step off.

After a few moments, I open a new conversation. "Your grandfather lives out here?"

"Yes, he's the only Aborigine who still lives on El Kwestro property. All the others moved on years ago."

"What does he do out here all alone?" Mimi's attempt at casual conversation doesn't fool me, but it's good enough for Nellie.

"He lives the old ways. He could move to Kununurra, but he prefers life here." She picks her way between the patches of spear grass. "Be careful not to touch the grass or it'll cut you."

We maneuver between the clumps of tall, razor-edged grass, wary of her instruction.

I pause and breathe in the serenity. "I can understand why he stays out here. There's a magic to this place." *The magic I hoped to find on this trip.*

With each step, our feet crackle on the parched ground, creating a strange harmony with the earth. Lulled by its intoxicating effect, we trudge in silence across the low-lying plains dotted with baobab, paperbark, and eucalypt trees. The air sucks the moisture from our bodies, replacing it with a furnace of dry heat. Like an infrared sauna, the effects are both exhausting and invigorating.

Nellie points to what looks like a ruined castle towering upward in the distance. "They're the Cockburn Ranges. Grandfather often brought me out here on a walkabout in the school holidays. We'd spend days, sometimes weeks just walking the land, and he'd tell me the stories of the Dreamtime." Her face glows with the happy memories.

"You've been fortunate to have such a wonderful man in your life." I remember how much I loved my grandfather. Kind, protective, and intelligent. What more could a young girl want in a male mentor.

"Yes. He taught me a lot about myself and life."

Mimi winces. "How much further?" Her feet must be killing her.

"We're nearly there. Grandfather will have some bush medicine for your feet."

After another fifteen minutes of hiking, and muffled sounds of pain from Mimi, Nellie steers us up a steep, low ridge. The terrain is riddled with loose gravel and risk. One slip could mean disaster. I take my time, mindful of how dangerous the outback is without the right guide and equipment.

Suddenly, a small Aboriginal man dressed in a pair of thongs, scraggy navy shorts, and a tattered blue cotton shirt appears in front of us. His bewhiskered, smiling face is topped with an old blue cap, sporting a Darwin Sailing Club insignia. The only indication of his age are the wisps of graying hair that his cap fails to hide. Despite being an original inhabitant of this land, he looks incongruous out here in his shop-bought clothes.

Panting and drenched in sweat, Mimi and I finally reach Nellie who waits at the top next to her grandfather.

"Grandfather, this is Diana Daniels, the lady I told you about. And this is Mimi." She turns to us. "And this is my grandfather, Tommy George."

Struggling to catch my breath, I hold out my hand. "A pleasure to meet you, Tommy George." In an instant, he wraps me in a bear hug, his sinewy arms squeezing tight. That he welcomes me with such enthusiasm without any thought of my sweaty, smelly body says much of his sincerity.

After releasing me, he captures Mimi in his arms. "Good to meet you," she manages on regaining her breath.

"Come inside. I've got tea."

Tommy George's modest living quarters are snugged under the overhanging ledge of a massive rust-colored boulder, with little protection from the elements. An old swag to sleep in lies on the ground, a change of crinkled clothes hangs pegless on a twine line, and a battered ice chest in which I suspect he keeps a few necessities like butter and milk rests in the shade. He motions us to sit on rickety tea chests gathered around a small open fire. Respite slackens Mimi's face the moment she elevates her feet that now resemble boiled lobsters.

Tommy George eyes her feet then fishes out an old Nivea hand cream tin from a nearby shopping bag. "Rub that on. It will help."

Mimi nods her thanks, opens the tin, and after discarding her sandals, scoops out a generous fingerful of an opaque, orange ointment and does as instructed. When she closes her eyes and moans in relief, I wonder whether the old man's medicine has magic in the tincture.

"Nearly ready," he says, drawing our attention to the fire. Suspended on a cross structure of crooked branches, a tin-can threaded with a heavy wire handle and filled with water, begins to boil. It's the proverbial boiling billy from the story of *Waltzing Matilda*.

He regards us, his searching eyes finally coming to rest on me. "Nellie tells me you dream?"

"I'm not sure I'd call it dreaming exactly. I have hunches about things, about people."

He nods, sagely. "That's dreaming. Great Spirit whispers to you."

"I guess you could say that . . ." I squirm a little under his gaze. He gives the impression he sees right through me. "Nellie says you're a master of dreaming. Would you share some of your stories with us?"

He inclines his head, his lips twitching a crafty smile. "We drink first." He nods at Nellie.

Wrapping her hand in a tattered tea towel as protection, she removes the boiling billy from the fire and spoons in a hefty measure of black tea leaves. Suddenly, with the strength and speed of an Olympic athlete, she spins the billy around and around in arm-length circles. Mimi and I duck unnerved that the scolding water will rain down on us, but the centrifugal force keeps the brewing tea in the billy. By the time she's finished, the tea has steeped to the color of tar. She liberally spoons sugar into four tin cups and pours us each a strong black tea.

I blow on it to cool it down, then take a tentative sip of the muddy, sweet brew to be pleasantly surprised. "This tastes wonderful. Thank you."

"Agreed." Mimi licks her lips.

With eyes as black as tea, Tommy George studies us over the rim of his cup. It's the same expression I use when I want to unsettle candidates in interviews. He's waiting to see how we react under his scrutiny. What are our motives? Can we be trusted?

When I meet his challenge, he slips off his tea chest and places his cup on the dusty earth. Squat on his haunches, he stretches out a gnarled finger and draws what looks like the image of a long-legged bird.

"Brolga . . ." He begins the story of a beautiful young girl, named Brolga who was the best dancer in her tribe. "One day an evil spirit, Waiwera decided he wanted her, and in a willy-willy wind, he took her away." His finger swirls circles in the fine red soil, kicking dust in the air, just like the wind. "After days of searching, the tribe found her. They threw spears and boomerangs at Waiwera to get him to release Brolga. But the evil spirit decided that if he couldn't have her, then her tribe couldn't either. Waiwera vanished in a willy-willy" —more soil swirling— "and a tall, gray bird appeared, dancing long hopping steps, and stretching its wings. The tribe knew Waiwera had changed Brolga into a bird. The bird we know as the brolga."

He springs to his feet and imitates the dance of the brolga. I can't believe my good fortune. To witness this ancient story being told by a tribal elder framed against his ancestors' backdrop sends shivers over my body. I want to applaud but refrain from doing so in case I insult him or the story.

But Mimi claps loudly. "Tommy George, that was fabulous." She's beaming.

"Thank you," he says, obviously enjoying her effusive appreciation.

I join in the applause. "Thank you for sharing that story with us."

He drops to the ground, his hand hovering above the earth as if he's about to tell another story. But his body stiffens. His black eyes dart up and meet mine, and in them flashes fear. He rubs the patch of soil as if afraid to read its message and returns to his tea chest. Beckoning to his granddaughter, he draws her beside him, encircling her waist with an affectionate squeeze. "My Nellie reminds me of Brolga. A beautiful girl whose dancing is so graceful and special."

She blushes. "Grandfather. Stop."

"It's true." He fixes me in his gaze and pauses. "But you, Diana, you know." His eyes narrow.

"Know what?" An uneasy feeling flutters in my gut. *Please, don't go there.*

"You have seen evil spirit, haven't you?"

I shudder, remembering what happened on the *Silver Galapagos* expedition ship. "Yes. I've seen evil."

He lifts his gaze to Nellie. "See. You must be careful my beautiful girl. There is evil who hungers for beauty. You must be careful, or you will end up like Brolga."

I watch as Nellie dismisses his warning as silly, but I sense the old man isn't trying to terrorize her. He's dreamed her future in the red earth of his ancestors.

★ ★ ★ ★

HAVING SURVIVED THE TREK BACK from Tommy George's and after ridding ourselves of the clinging red dust in the retreat's deluxe showers, Mimi and I hurry to lunch. "I must say whatever the ointment was that Tommy George gave me has worked wonders." Beside me, Mimi dances a couple of high-stepping brolga moves on our way down to the homestead. "I'm starving. I wonder what Chef has for us today?"

"I don't care what it is. I'm with you. I'm famished."

We arrive in time for Amy's introduction of the new guests. "Diana, Mimi, come meet our newlyweds, Mr. and Mrs. Pullman. They're staying next to you in Pandanus."

"Peter and Kristen, please." An athletic young man with smoldering good looks shakes our hands. Next to him, a pretty, young woman in her twenties, says hello while affectionately rubbing circles on his back. She reminds me of how much in love I was with Tom on our honeymoon.

"And this is Maria Loukas and Jo Arnold from Melbourne." Amy introduces a dark-haired, olive-skinned vivacious woman of obvious European descent and a striking, elfin-faced woman with short, shaggy blonde hair. Dressed in jeans and sneakers, and holding each other's hand, they possess an easy confidence in themselves and each other.

After hellos, we adjourn to the long table for lunch.

Maria and Jo interest me the most, so I sit next to them. "What brings you to El Kwestro?"

"We're here for the Kimberley Under the Stars art event." Maria's sultry, dark eyes light up with excitement.

"And for a break," Jo says, dampening her lover's enthusiasm a little.

Maria turns down her passion a notch or two. "I'm the struggling artist, and Jo's the successful lawyer."

"Rubbish. You're a successful artist. It's just that not enough people know it. But they will." Jo rubs against Maria's arm like a devoted pet.

"Every artist needs a cheer squad like Jo." Although there's genuine appreciation in Maria's voice, I wonder if she doesn't feel a little intimidated by Jo's high-profile job and financial success. Perhaps even indebted to her.

"This place is something else, isn't it?" Jo says. "We're in the Chamberlain Suite on the far end of the homestead veranda. The balcony overhangs the river. Like being on top of the world."

"I'm pleased I brought some of my painting gear with me. The light here is stunning." Maria tilts her head, squinting at the sun.

"My sister-in-law, Mimi, loves to paint. She's bemoaning the fact she didn't bring her gear."

"Maybe she'd like to join me sometime, and we can do some sketching from our balcony?" Maria's face lights up once more to match the day.

"I'm sure she'd love that. Why not talk to her after lunch?"

"I will. Thanks."

While Maria and Jo speak to Sylvia on their left, Peter and Kristen Pullman chat with Mimi further down the table. We number ten guests in six rooms, leaving three rooms currently vacant. I wonder how many others are yet to arrive.

Nellie reaches down to retrieve my plate. "My grandfather enjoyed meeting you both today."

"And I thoroughly enjoyed meeting him. He's an amazing man."

"I think so." She lingers, her eyes darting side to side. "But I think he worries about me too much. He has a house in Kununurra where he lives during the wet. But he stays out here in the dry season to keep an eye on me."

"Don't begrudge him for loving you. He just wants to protect you."

"I know, but I worry about him out there all alone."

"From what I saw he's more than capable of looking after himself."

She shrugs. "I guess you're right. Anyway, he said that if you wanted to visit again, he'd like that."

"That's wonderful. Tell him I'll definitely see him again before we leave."

"I will."

After lunch, everyone disperses to afternoon excursions or leisure time. I notice Maria talking to Mimi and by her overjoyed expression, she's accepted her offer of sketching together. The three women walk off toward the Chamberlain Suite, leaving me to my own devices.

Down by the pool, I spy a sun lounge under the shade of a sprawling tree that has my name on it. *Perfect!* After ordering a deadly kiss from Nellie, I wander down, glad to have some time on my own. Within minutes, I recline, eyes closed, tuning into the Dreamtime energy which Tommy George spoke about this morning.

Just as I'm about to drift back in time, a meek voice disturbs me. "Do you mind if I join you?"

I return from my dreaming and peer up over my sunglasses to see Sylvia's expectant face smiling down at me. "Of course not. Please . . ."

Removing her wide-brimmed sunhat, she slips onto the lounge beside me. "I think you found the best place of all down here at the pool."

"I tend to agree. It's so peaceful." I glance sideways at her. "John resting?"

"Yes. Being with people makes him anxious. He's lying down in the room." Her fingers curl and uncurl the edges of her hat, an unconscious behavior to channel her anxiety.

I soften my voice to ease the tension. "John told me about your daughter's suicide. I'm so sorry."

"I expect you know everything about it, thanks to the internet." She rolls her eyes, but her incessant fidgeting slows to a stop.

"I admit I did look up the case. You've been to hell and back." She nods. "Do you mind if I ask you a question?"

"Go ahead." She releases her hat, her hands finally still.

"Did you ever find out who Stephanie's lover was that jilted her and broke her heart?"

A tortured expression pulls at her face. "No. We tried everything, but none of Steph's friends knew. She didn't tell a soul about it."

"And she didn't keep a journal?"

"She did. But the only entry we couldn't make sense of was Ace—A–C–E. We figured the guy's name was Ace, but neither the police nor us could find anyone with the name of Ace anywhere. We just kept coming up to dead ends."

"Excuse me, ladies, here are your drinks." Nellie places them on the table between us, adorned with a linen napkin each. "Is there anything else I can get you?"

I glance at Sylvia who shakes her head. "No thanks."

When Nellie leaves, I pick up the thread. "Then John was arrested?"

"Yes. It was terrible. By the time he was released, we decided to leave Sydney. Our lives had been ruined. We sold the business for whatever we could get, changed our surname, and moved to Melbourne. I don't think John will ever recover." Emotion chokes her voice.

"And you?"

"Someone has to stay strong. I fly back to Sydney from time to time to visit Steph's grave and see the police in person in case they've found anything and" —she swallows hard— "but what can I do? My daughter is dead, and my husband is alive. His health must come first, or I'll lose him as well." Her hand trembles when she raises the wine glass to her lips.

I swing my legs over the lounge to face her. "I can't tell you how sorry I am for you both. If there's anything I can do, please let me know."

"Just being able to talk about it helps." She gives me a thankful half-smile.

"I'm happy to listen anytime you want." I reach over and pat her knee. "Why don't we talk about happier things."

While we chat about our plans for the next few days, I marvel at Sylvia's resolve and resilience. She's a remarkable woman. But in the back of my mind, the name Ace loops on a reel, mocking me.

CHAPTER FOUR

I SLIDE OPEN THE DOOR to Mimi's retreat and stick my head in. "You back?"

"Out here."

Even though I can't see her, I walk through the open sliding doors and onto the back deck. There, on my left, Mimi frolics in the outdoor bath like a nature nymph, bubbles frothing under her chin.

"Isn't this the best?" She sloshes around sending water spilling everywhere.

I perch on the side of the bath and flap my hand in the water. "I think I'll take a bath before dinner tonight. It's certainly a magical setting." Cleverly designed so no other guests can see onto your deck, the retreats give the impression of total isolation. With a clear view across the gorge, the outdoor bath adds a luxurious touch to the intimacy with Mother Nature and the Dreamtime energy. "How did the sketching go with Maria?"

"Wonderful. It's over there." She points a soapy arm toward the outdoor table.

I wander over, open the sketch pad, and study her work. "This is terrific. Maybe it's time you gave up the abstracts and started painting landscapes."

Her happy laugh joins those of nearby birds. "Let's not get ahead of ourselves. I love painting abstracts. They're liberating."

"But these sketches are really good," I persist.

"Maria thought so too." She throws a handful of foam into the air. "Anyway, it was fun, and we're going to catch up again. Maybe one morning."

"What did you think of Maria and Jo?"

As I turn, Mimi executes a full death roll like a crocodile sending frothy water in big waves over the sides. In one swift recovery move, she clamps her hands on the side of the bath and rises in a long, soapy streak.

I laugh. "You may be a wonderful artist, but you're no Birth of Venus."

She pokes out her tongue and wraps one of the plush olive-green bath sheets around her sudsy body. Leaving puddles of lacy foam behind her, she pads over and drops in the deck chair next to me.

"The only thing this place lacks is room service. I'd kill for a glass of wine." Her right leg shoots into the air where she gives it a brisk rub.

"I'm sure you can wait until you get dressed." I sharpen my tone and repeat, "So . . . what did you think of Maria and Jo?" Mimi's left leg swiftly replaces her right and receives an even brisker rub. I know she's purposely stalling but I play along. "Well?"

She drops her leg. "They're lovely girls. Maria is an amazing artist. Really gifted. And she's so full of life. We talked and laughed. It was great." Her gray eyes dance. "We had the best time."

"Sounds like you met a kindred spirit."

"Yes. That's what Maria is, a kindred spirit."

"That would make her an ESFP then."

"There you go again. With your Myer Briggs crap. Why can't you just say I'm fun-loving and super energized." She leaps to her feet and does a turn, towel flapping.

"Because that's what ESFPs are."

"*Pfft.* I prefer my description." She drops into the chair, curling her legs beneath her. "Anyway, Maria's a damn fine artist. She's entering the Hadley's Art Prize this year."

"What's that?"

"It's Australia's newest leading landscape art prize with a $100,000 prize for first place."

"Winning that would certainly set her up financially."

"She's also studied with some leading Aboriginal artists at various art galleries across the country. That's why they're up here for the Kimberley Under the Stars event. She's hoping to reconnect with some of the artists and do more study if she can."

"And Jo? What about her?"

"From what I see, she adores Maria. She obviously bankrolls her art career."

"And?" I raise my eyebrows, waiting for more.

Mimi frowns. "Oh, I don't know. They seem such an odd match. I don't think Jo has a creative bone in her body. She's got a plan for everything."

"What do you mean?"

"She's got Maria's entire career mapped out. When's she going to paint, what contests she should enter, where she should go to do more study. For a moment I thought she was going to tell her how to improve her sketching. She's not demeaning, but she's certainly bossy."

I nod my understanding. "I bet she'd make a great chess partner."

"Oh my god. How did you know? She brought a chess set with her. Out in the most beautiful part of the country and she wants to play with black and white statuettes. Unbelievable." Throwing her arms in the air, Mimi marches inside to get dressed.

"Everyone's different," I call over my shoulder. "Sometimes those differences make a relationship stronger."

"Maybe. But she'd drive me mad."

While I wait, I wonder if Jo drives Maria mad. I'm sure she does at times, but Maria's ambition probably outranks her irritation with Jo's perfectionism. She could rightly or wrongly surmise that without Jo, she might never become a successful artist.

"Ready." Mimi fluffs her purple gypsy skirt complete with tiny hem bells which she has teamed with a magenta cheesecloth blouse cinched at her trim waist with a tan leather belt. Her damp, gray hair is swirled on top of her head with a lacquered chopstick jammed through the loose bun, while a pair of oversize hoop earrings dangle from her ears. She's the poster child for a forty-seven-year-old hippie. A wild earthy goddess, and I adore her eccentricities.

"Listen, you go down and have your wine. I'm going to take a bath and get changed. I'll meet you down there in about thirty minutes."

"Okay. I'll take the sketch pad and pencils Maria gave me. I'll be around the pool."

★ ★ ★ ★

AFTER A DELICIOUS BATH INFUSED with nature's sights, sounds, and essences, I decide on a pair of white cotton slacks and T-shirt. Even as my hand goes to the obvious lack of color, I know my choice is deliberately complementary to Mimi's colorful clothing. I *tut* out loud. It's a habit I developed with Tom, ingrained over thirty years. Choose garments that complement rather than contrast. My hand shoves into the drawer and grabs a long cotton tie-dyed scarf sporting every color of the rainbow. I wrap it twice around my neck and eye myself in the mirror. *That's better.* A knock at the door interrupts my self-appraisal. "Just a minute."

On opening it, I'm surprised to see Nellie. "Can I come in?"

"Of course."

She edges inside and stops. "I'm sorry. I know it's against the rules for me to do this, but I wanted to speak with you about something." The frown wrinkling her brow seems at odds with her smooth skin.

I point to the window seat, while I sit opposite on the bed. "Please sit. How can I help?"

"Grandfather taught me a long time ago to listen. Listen to nature, listen to what is going on around me, but most importantly to listen to myself."

"He's a wise man."

"I overheard something, something that probably means nothing, but I can't get it out of my mind."

I know the feeling well. "Go on."

"And I don't know what to do about it?"

50

"Would you like to tell me?" Alarm stabs at the base of my skull. *I don't like this.*

Her lips twist, and she exhales a sharp breath. She hesitates. "I, eh . . . No. It's all right. I'm just being silly." She springs to her feet. "I better go."

With no less force than if someone pushed me in the middle of my back, I lurch forward and clasp her hands. "Are you sure? If you have a hunch about something, it's better to share it." I know this from experience.

"I think I'll tell grandfather tomorrow."

As she moves to the door, my sixth sense sends up warning flares. *Stop her.* With more urgency, I say, "Nellie, your hunch brought you here *now*. Are you sure you don't want to tell me?" I lock her in a hard stare while my gut twists and squirms.

"Thanks. I shouldn't have bothered you." Her mood changes to sunshine. "I'll have a deadly kiss waiting for you when you come down." She pivots and scampers away, like a mystical creature of the bush while I'm left prickling with panic.

★ ★ ★ ★

WHEN THE SUN VANISHES FROM the sky uttering its last vibrant red breath, Mimi and I stroll back from the pool into the great room. A tall, bearded man with shaggy, collar-length hair and bushy eyebrows hovers between Tony and Trish Wilson. His serious expression is barely discernible through his encircling russet-red mane.

Mimi giggles. "He certainly blends in out here, with all that red hair."

I scowl, but there's no denying Mimi's humor, and we giggle to ourselves.

Tony waves us over. "Come meet Dale Baker, the newest arrival."

We exchange hellos. "Where are you from, Dale?" I ask, curious to know the young man's background.

"I live in Kununurra." He speaks in a practical, no-nonsense tone.

"What do you do there?" Mimi asks.

"I'm a helicopter pilot."

Duly impressed, the four of us wait for more, but that's all Dale offers. Predictably, Mimi persists. "Who do you fly for?"

"I'm contracted to fly for mining and tourism companies."

"How interesting. You must know every inch of the Kimberley," Trish says.

"Yes, I guess I do." He sounds indifferent and an awkward silence descends.

I try a new direction. "What brings you to El Kwestro?"

"They contract me during the festival to fly VIP guests in and out."

"Obviously, we weren't important enough?" Tony says, a note of sarcasm in his voice.

Dale shrugs, again indifferent. "I just do what Amy tells me."

"Of course. Don't mind my husband." When Trish touches Dale's forearm, he flinches away.

I press on. "So, you'll be here for the next few days then?"

"Yes." He raises a packet of cigarettes. "If you'll excuse me . . ." and heads outside.

We watch his retreating figure making its escape from four nosy guests. At least, that's what I expect he's thinking.

I redirect a smile to the Wilsons. "What did you get up to this afternoon?"

"We went on a guided gorge walk," Tony says. "It's rated as easy to moderate, but there was a helluva lot of climbing over rocks."

Trish interrupts her husband. "It was wonderful, though a little challenging."

I shift my gaze outside. "Looks like it's time for dinner."

With Mimi beside me, we head toward the long table. "That Dale Baker is an odd character," she says in my ear.

I notice the glow from his cigarette where he stands alone down on the lawn. "He's introverted. They don't feel comfortable in social situations, particularly if they're the center of attention. I suspect his smoking addiction has saved him on numerous occasions from having to deal with extroverts like you and me."

"Still . . ."

★ ★ ★ ★

ALTHOUGH DALE JOINS US FOR dinner, he gravitates to the end of the table where he only has to tolerate one guest, which is John Torrens. A perfect situation for both men who dislike gregarious people. Mimi and I sit at the other end, opposite Maria and Jo with Peter and Kristen next to them. Tony chats about himself to Kristen most of the time, leaving Trish outcast at the end across from Dale and John, neither of whom she engages in much conversation. I notice she sculls her wine while playing with her food. A tell-tale sign of an alcoholic. I watch, wondering if Tony's got any idea of his wife's addiction. If so, does he care? He strikes me as a classic ESTJ— someone who takes charge, possesses an organized, systematic approach to life, and has little sympathy for anyone who doesn't agree with his tough-minded views.

Though conversations flow during dinner, one of those uncomfortable lulls hugs the table while we wait for desserts. An uneasy sensation flutters in my stomach. Thankfully, Nellie arrives, all smiles and service. She expertly balances four servings of individual pavlovas topped with fresh passionfruit pulp and house-made raspberry ice-cream and delivers the first two to Maria and Jo to a chorus of appreciation. When she swivels to deliver the third to Peter, he pushes back in his chair and collides with her. The creamy dessert flies upwards and upends in a flurry onto his lap.

Nellie gasps. "I'm so sorry . . ."

Peter launches from his chair, scrubbing the front of his trousers with his napkin. "What is wrong with you, girl." His vicious tone stuns everyone.

"I'm sorry, sir. Here let me—"

He slaps her hand away and glares. "Don't touch me."

Nellie recoils, as do all of us watching.

"Get me the manager," he demands, and she scurries off.

"She didn't mean—"

But before I could finish, he turns on me like a rabid dog. "I suggest you mind your own business."

"Peter, that's enough," Kristen pleads, tugging at his sleeve. Tension crackles through the night like a looming electric storm while we await the deluge.

Amy strides up, full of authority. "How can I be of assistance?" On seeing his trousers, she goes straight into damage control. "I'm so sorry, Mr. Pullman. We'll attend to the cleaning of your trousers immediately."

He points an accusatory finger at Nellie who trembles off to our left. "I don't want her serving me again."

Amy's expression toughens. "She didn't mean to. It was an accident, Mr. Pullman."

"I said I don't want that little black abo—"

We all gasp, appalled.

John Torrens springs to his feet. "Now listen here, she's just a young girl trying to do her job."

Kristen leaps up beside her husband and crooks his arm with a firm tug. "I'm sorry, everyone." She shares a desperate glance, her face reddening.

"Please, Mr. Pullman, let me help you." An undeniable edge of command underlies Amy's conciliatory tone. She's going to handle the matter before it gets any worse. Flanked by his wife and the manager, Peter Pullman is led from the table, cursing under his breath. I notice when he passes Nellie, he glowers at her. An unwarranted reaction to an innocent accident.

While the rest of the guests exchange horrified opinions, I go to Nellie and wrap my arm around her shoulders. "Are you all right?"

Her brown eyes swim in tears. "I guess so."

"It's hard being blamed for something that wasn't your fault."

"I didn't mean to spill his dessert." Her voice chokes.

"I know you didn't, but that's not what I meant. Peter Pullman is a racist. He's blaming you for your ethnicity. His behavior was unacceptable and hurtful." I pin her in my gaze. "Are you sure you're all right?"

"Yes. Thank you. I've never had that before. I thought he was going to hit me."

"If he did, I doubt it would've been the first time he's hit someone."

She rubs her hands up and down on her apron. "I better get on with the rest of the desserts."

"Maybe you should go home? Isn't there someone else who could finish up for you?"

She shakes her head. "Only me. My shift finishes in an hour. I'll go home then."

I hold her at arm's length. "Well, if you need anything, you know where I am."

"Thanks." She heads toward the kitchen, and I return to the gob-smacked guests.

★ ★ ★ ★

I KNOCK ON THE OFFICE door and wait. No answer, but I'm sure I can hear voices. I knock again and just as I'm about to stick my head in, Amy steps out of the office and onto the veranda. "Diana, how can I help you?"

"I just wanted to make sure Nellie was all right. After dessert, I didn't see her again. But she said she still had another hour of her shift to go."

"I told her to knock off early after that terrible scene with Mr. Pullman."

"I see. Is she on lunch shift tomorrow?"

"Yes. She comes in around eleven."

"Thanks. I'll catch up with her then. Good night."

"Good night."

I catch up with Mimi who's waiting for me on the veranda.

"So?" she asks.

"Amy said she knocked off early. I hope Nellie's all right."

Mimi murmurs a curse. "That Pullman bloke needs a kick up the arse."

"I agree with you on that one."

"You have to wonder why Kristen married such a pig."

"People do strange things for love."

With the chill of the outback night nipping our skin, we wrap our pashminas tighter around our shoulders as we stroll up the pathway leading to our retreats. Nearing Pandanus where the Pullmans are staying, we slow, noting that the lights are still on.

"All quiet at home." Mimi sneers. "I don't know how she's in the same bed as him."

I stop, alert to something sinister in the surrounding darkness. A shiver darts up my spine like a long-legged spider. A spontaneous moan escapes my lips. "I don't like it, Mimi."

She inclines her head, and in the filtered moonlight through the leaves, I watch her frown deepen. "Don't like what?"

"Whatever's going on here."

"But what *is* going on here, aside from that incident tonight?"

"I don't know yet, but my gut tells me there's something." I gaze over her shoulder into the night, hoping I'm wrong. But I'm not. Whenever my sixth sense squirms in my stomach with this much insistence, it means there's danger. Except I never know where the danger's coming from until it's too late. That's when I'm left to pick up the pieces. It was the same when Tom died, and I knew he had cancer before he was diagnosed. The same happened onboard the *Silver Galapagos* expedition ship with Celeste. There have been so many instances when I knew, but I didn't know what I knew. Now, it's happening again.

When Mimi clasps my hands, mine are clammy and cold compared to hers. "Come on. Let's have a cup of tea at your place before bed." She threads her arm through mine, and with her on one side and my gloomy portents on the other, we amble up the small rise toward our retreats.

CHAPTER FIVE

There's something different about Andrew this morning. His body lacks its lively, youthful manner, and the stray frangipani leaves prove that he's not concentrating. Though I'm sure he heard my steps on the veranda, he doesn't raise his head. "How are things this morning, Andrew?" I ask, upbeat. When he looks up, I'm alarmed by the anguish on his face. "Whatever's the matter?"

"It's Nellie." His voice sounds brittle.

My heart picks up speed. "What about her?"

"She didn't come home last night."

"Oh no." My stomach somersaults. "Tell me."

"She usually pops in to see me when she finishes her shift, but she didn't. I went to see her this morning and her roomies told me she hadn't come home."

"Has anyone seen her?"

"Not that I can find. I asked Amy, and she told me she let Nellie off shift a little earlier last night after some kerfuffle with a guest. From what I can make out, no one's seen her since."

"Has she ever done this before?"

"No. She's like clockwork. She finishes shift and comes back to the staff quarters with the night chef. But he said she'd already gone when he knocked off."

"How would she get back?" Concentric circles of dread radiate out from my gut.

"I guess she'd walk, but that's not like her. I'm worried about her."

I am too. "Have you spoken to Gillian?"

"No, just Amy. We're not supposed to bother Gillian with homestead matters."

I wave a dismissive hand. "I'm a guest. I can bother anyone I like. Leave it with me, and I'll see what I can find out."

It's just after seven. Not early in the tourism industry. I backtrack along the veranda to the unmarked room at the far end and knock. The face of a surprised woman in her late thirties peeks through the cracked door. "Can I help you?"

"I hope so. I'm Diana Daniels. I'm staying in Kurrajong. I'm hoping I might have a word with you."

Surprise shifts to suspicion on her face. "Isn't Amy about?"

"Actually, Gillian, as the general manager of the El Kwestro property, I think this matter falls under your auspices." I make the matter sound grave and urgent, which I intuitively know it is.

"Very well. Come in." She opens the door and indicates to a small kitchen table, crammed into a corner of the sparsely furnished room.

"I'm sorry, Mrs. Daniels, but guests don't normally wish to see me so urgently or early." After smoothing back her short, blunt-cut hair, she sits opposite me and laces her fingers on the laminate-topped table.

"I'm sorry to disturb you, but it's important." I proceed to detail last night's episode with Nellie and Peter Pullman, my discussion with Amy afterward, and Andrew's account of Nellie's absence. "To be honest, I'm worried about her."

"Forgive me, Mrs. Daniels, but as a guest, why should this concern you?"

"My professional work entails reading human behavior and getting a sense of people and situations. As strange as it sounds, I've a strong feeling that we need to treat Nellie's disappearance as serious." My mouth goes dry.

"But she's only been missing, if in fact she *is* missing, for under twelve hours. Perhaps she's visiting friends or family. If she's doing the lunch roster, she's not due in until" —she glances at her phone— "eleven." She tilts her head and regards me closely.

I know what she's thinking. From a logical perspective, she's correct. I'm jumping the gun, so to speak, in assuming Nellie won't show up for her shift. "Is there any way we can track her down? Call the station and ask them to try and find her at the staff quarters?"

"I guess we could do that. Why don't you leave it with me? I'll see what I can do." Rising from her chair, she gives me a look I've seen before. As much as she tries not to appear or sound condescending, it's obvious. She thinks I'm crazy. Some middle-aged woman with an over-active imagination trying to get noticed. "Just one more thing . . ." I lift a finger and lock eyes with her. "You mentioned Nellie might be visiting family. I met her grandfather, Tommy George yesterday."

Gillian's eyes widen. "You did?"

"Yes. We walked out past the Durack tree to his home."

"Really? No one's ever met Tommy George. He's quite a legend in these parts." Her words are tinged with admiration.

"I'd like someone to drive me out there now to see if Nellie is with him. Can you arrange it?"

She drags her fingers through her black hair, disrupting it further. "Let me check with Amy and see if we've got a tripi available."

"Excellent. I'll be in the great room. If someone could let me know as soon as possible, I'd appreciate it." I'd just given the general manager an order, subtle though it was, but I suspect there's no time to lose.

"Of course. Thank you, Mrs. Daniels, for your concern." She ushers me to the door.

After making a pit stop to tell Andrew about my meeting with Gillian, I race up to Mimi's retreat and charge in. "Right, put on your walking gear. We going to see Tommy George."

"What? Again?" She's propped up in bed, sketching the scenery across the river gorge.

"Come on. Up." I grab her pencil and close the sketch pad. "I'll tell you all about it while you get dressed."

★ ★ ★ ★

GILLIAN MAKES GOOD ON THE tripi, and Hayley our guide from yesterday. I jump in the front next to her while Mimi sits behind, her head thrust between the bucket seats, so as not to miss any of the conversation.

Once out of the homestead property, Hayley turns a worried face to me. "What's all this about?"

"What did management tell you?" I ask as the vehicle bounces on the dusty, corrugated road.

"Amy just said I needed to drive you to the Durack tree and wait. Then drive you back."

"Have you seen Nellie since yesterday?" I watch Hayley's bronzed brow wrinkle.

"No. Why?"

"She didn't come home last night, and Andrew's worried about her."

She screws up her nose. "She didn't? That's odd."

"Were you and Nellie good friends?" Mimi shouts over the road noise.

"Sort of, but Nellie never got really close to anyone. Except Andrew. He knew her the best."

"Did management know they were a couple?"

Hayley angles me a sideways glance. "They might have suspected it. They usually turn a blind eye as long as the staff doesn't let it interfere with their jobs."

The noise worsens, and we fall silent, alone with our thoughts. Mine turn somber along with the urgency building in my gut, the harbinger of dark deeds.

Within half an hour, we arrive at the Durack tree, and Mimi and I prepare to set off.

"Are you sure you know where you're going?" Hayley sounds worried. Unsurprising since she's leaving two city-slickers to walk the outback by themselves.

Mimi turns to me, her face pinched with apprehension. "Yes, are you sure?"

"I'm sure. We were only here yesterday. Things can't have changed since then."

"Maybe, maybe not." Hayley shakes her head. "But the outback is a dangerous place. It's easy to lose your bearings. Here, take my compass." She digs it out of her pocket and hands it to me.

Mimi's anxiety ratchets up a notch. "Do you even know how to use a compass, Diana?"

"Of course," I lie.

"Here, this is where we are." Hayley points to the directional marking on the compass face. "If you get lost just keep the arrow pointing here and keep walking. If you're not back in an hour, I'll blast the horn every five minutes."

"Okay. Got it." I fist the compass into my shirt pocket, knowing it won't be used.

"I'll stand up on the bonnet and watch you, just to get a ground bearing." She clambers onto the tripi.

I point to where we're headed. "It's not that far. It's just over that ridge." To Mimi, I give a rallying smile. "Right. Let's go."

She mumbles something under her breath, before falling in beside me.

We double-time down the rocky track and halt. After a cursory sweep for the resident crocodiles, we tiptoe across the exposed rocks in the tributary without incident. The thought of my being on a wild goose chase crashes into my mind, but I've no time to argue with it. We must press on. Once on the other side, I set a steady pace, which Mimi matches. "Are you going to tell me what's going on?"

"I wish I knew for certain. I'm hoping that Nellie's with her grandfather and everything is all right."

"And if she's not?"

"We have a problem."

"Meaning?"

"If she doesn't turn up for her shift this morning, I have a terrible feeling she'll never turn up again."

I hear Mimi suck in air, but I don't dare look at her. There's nothing more I can add.

By the time we traipse across enough rugged, red earth to coat us in a fine dusting of powder, I glimpse Tommy George in the distance standing on the top of his ridge. Leaning on his spear and with one leg tucked under him, he reminds me of the brolga, at once graceful and alone. When our eyes meet, I force a half-smile, but he doesn't respond. My blood runs cold. Does he know the reason for our unannounced visit? Puffing and panting, we trudge up the small slope, until we come face to face.

I offer him my hand. "I'm sorry to barge in on you like this Tommy George, but—"

Anxiety narrows his eyes. "Where's Nellie?"

"That's why we've come. I'm hoping she's here with you." But I know she's not.

"I haven't seen her since you were here." He gestures for us to follow. "What's happened?"

We sit next to him on the tea chests and scull some water from our bottles, while I explain what happened last night and that Nellie didn't arrive back at the staff quarters. Beneath Tommy George's bristled skin, I watch his color pale. He slides to the ground on his haunches, knees high next to his ears. With eyes closed and murmuring a soft chant, he traces his bony fingers in the fine red dirt. In that instant, millions of years condense into a present moment when an Aboriginal elder calls upon his ancestors for help. His hands still, and we lean forward, trying to work out the meaning of the swirls, circles, and lines in the sand.

"This is a waterhole. This is bush tucker, and this is a meeting place." His voice is nothing but a croaky whisper. "Nellie is here."

I shudder at the thought of questioning whether she's safe. "Can you be more specific than that? I mean that could be anywhere in El Kwestro."

"She's here." He inclines his head up at me, and I notice his silent tears have left muddy tracks on his cheeks. "She's here."

My heart clenches. *She's not safe.* "Very well. I'll do my best. A waterhole, bush tucker, and a meeting place." I stand, resolute.

He clambers to his feet, and reaching down, lifts a crooked walking stick hand-carved from an old branch. "Take this."

"Thank you, but I can't possibly . . ."

He thrusts it toward me with insistence. "Take it. Keep it with you. It will help."

When I wrap my hand around its twine-wrapped nub, it snugs into my palm as if fashioned for my size and height. "Thank you," I say, humbled by his gift.

"Find Nellie. Bring her home." He speaks not so much a request, but a command.

"I'll do my best."

Under the blazing sun, Mimi and I set off, retracing our steps to the Durack tree. There's no need for the compass or conversation. The one thing we need is time. But I fear we're already out of that.

★ ★ ★ ★

HAYLEY SWITCHES ON THE IGNITION and revs the engine. "Where to now?"

"I've no idea. All I know is that we're looking for a waterhole, bush tucker, and a meeting place."

She rubs a hand across her mouth. "The only place nearby that fits those three things is Jackaroo's Waterhole."

I exchange an urgent look with her. "Let's go."

Leaving a cloud of red dust behind, and under Hayley's expert guidance, the tripi heads off at a smart speed. "It's a waterhole where we sometimes have morning tea at the end of the bush culture and history tour. It's a pretty place, not far from the homestead."

"Is it on the way from the homestead to the staff quarters?" I ask.

"Not really. It's a bit of a detour."

"Do the staff go there?"

"You mean to hang out or swim?"

I nod.

"Sometimes. But only if guests aren't there."

"When were you there last?"

"Yesterday after the tour. We had morning tea there before we came back and picked you guys up."

She turns off the main road and onto a sidetrack which snakes around a couple of bends. As the tripi slows, an unexpected oasis materializes like a mirage before us.

"It's beautiful," Mimi says. "Who would've thought this existed out here."

We jump out of the vehicle, our shoes puffing out residual red dust. The rich, brown earth now under our feet and the thick, verdant vegetation fringing the waterhole exists only because of an underground aquifer. My eyes sip the refreshing visual cocktail, while my mouth longs for a long, cool drink. Nevertheless, this semi-tropical paradise is merely a brief respite in a desolate landscape. For wherever the sun blasts the earth that's beyond the aquifer's reach or not under the protection of the gum trees' canopies, swathes of tall, bleached spear grass still rule supreme. But now is not the time to appreciate the natural world. I wave my stick in the air. "Right. Let's look around."

Hayley lifts her Akubra and swipes her forehead. "What are we looking for?"

"Anything out of the norm." I point my stick to the left. "How about you go that way, Hayley."

"Okay." She nods and begins her investigation.

"Mimi, you concentrate around this area. I'll go further down in that direction." I indicate to the right.

"Okay, but don't get lost."

I stride along the bank of the waterhole, using my stick to poke and push at the shrubs and undergrowth. Why on earth would Nellie come out here? And why did she leave the homestead last night by herself? I linger for a moment, casting my gaze further ahead. A narrow track contours off along the water's edge. Glancing back over my shoulder, I take my bearings and then head down the path. Though the emerald green water is enticing, I half-expect to see a pair of crocodile eyes sizing me up from the middle of the waterhole. There'll be little chance of escape if one of the prehistoric lizards is lying in wait on the bank ahead. *Maybe this isn't such a good idea.*

"Shit." Not watching where I'm walking, I stub my foot on an exposed rock and stumble forward. Thank goodness for Tommy's George's insistence. My stick saves me from face-diving into the ground. Ready to curse the wretched rock, I spin around. A small neat foot protrudes from the spear grass and my heart sinks. "Oh no. Nellie." Barely a whisper, but it sounds like a scream renting the tranquility of Jackaroo's Waterhole.

I edge the grasses aside. Her limp body lies as if asleep, except her soft brown eyes aren't closed. They stare sightlessly upward to the heavens, while her chestnut hair fans out around her head. "Oh, Nellie, what's happened to you?" Swallowing hard, I collect myself. Such a young, vibrant girl snatched from a promising life.

I scan the area for clues, taking a mental note of everything. The fall of the grasses, how she lies on the ground, her clothes, the expression on her face. Everything has a story to tell about what happened here. My stomach clutches with an odd combination of despair and determination. Though I can't tell how she died, I know this is no accident. Somehow, Nellie had become a target. But why, and most importantly, by who?

CHAPTER SIX

WHILE HAYLEY CALLS THE HOMESTEAD on the tripi's two-way radio to advise them of my gruesome discovery, Mimi shadows me back to Nellie's body. Around us, the world assumes a different resonance. Instead of whispering a soothing lullaby, the leaves hiss a brittle, mocking tune. Colors glare with razor-sharp edges, pungent smells assault my nostrils, and my sixth sense becomes more acute, more adamant. For me, everything changes when death pays a visit.

"I can't believe it." Mimi sounds tired and strung out.

I point my stick to the uneven ground and move aside. "Watch your step." I catch her gaze and her eyes follow mine.

"Oh god." She slumps and her flushed face drains of its blush.

Even though I discovered Nellie's body and knew what to expect, my disbelief is still raw. "Nothing prepares you for seeing something like this," I say, heavy with regret.

Mimi drags her gaze back to me. "What do you think happened?"

"I think she was either lured or forced here by someone who then killed her."

"But why? Why would anyone want to kill Nellie? She's so sweet and innocent."

"That's what we have to find out."

Mimi retreats a step. "Wait a minute. What do you mean? We? This is a police matter. We can't go sticking our nose into this." Her head moves side to side, insistent.

"Funny, I've been told before not to stick my nose into business that doesn't concern me, but I ignored it and solved a murder."

"But this is different. I'm here," she reminds me.

"Exactly. We're both involved, whether you like it or not." I pause, and she presses her lips tight in acceptance. "Good. Now, once the police get here, I'll get Hayley to drive me back to the Durack tree. I have to tell Tommy George."

"Oh god, that poor man." Sympathy replaces Mimi's prior reluctance.

"You go back to the homestead. Freshen up. Once I get back, I'll come and get you. Don't say anything to anyone, understand?"

She frowns. "You don't think . . .?"

"Listen. My original hunch about something being wrong at El Kwestro was right. And if my second hunch about Nellie being intentionally murdered and not randomly killed is also true, then I don't want the killer getting you in his or her sights. The lower the profile you keep, the better. Understand?"

Eyes wide open, she bobs her head in tentative nods.

"Good. Now let's go back to the tripi and wait for the police."

★ ★ ★ ★

MY LONE HIKE BACK TO Tommy George's can only be described as a funeral dirge. Though there are no wailing or sobbing mourners accompanying me, I'm acutely aware of the solemn nature of my visit. I'm the proverbial bearer of bad news and my heart aches at the role. Balancing on one leg and clutching his spear in the opposite hand, his silhouette greets me long before I arrive. As I climb the slope to the ledge on which he props, he stares at the faraway horizon. Even when I stand beside him, his gaze remains unwavering. I inhale a deep breath and scrub a hand across my brow.

"We found Nellie."

He nods.

"She's been killed."

He nods again, and I sense his heart break into pieces of unutterable grief. I wait, respecting his silence. Eventually, his tormented face turns to me. "It was evil spirit, Waiwera. He came and took my Nellie from me."

Unsure of what to say, I revert to our previous conversation. "You were right about the meeting place, the bush tucker, and the waterhole. I found her at Jackaroo's Waterhole. The police are there now. They will take care of everything."

His expression implodes. "They will take care of nothing. They don't care about an Aboriginal girl. She's dead to them already." He spits at the ground. "A white man killed my Nellie and no white-man police will find him. But you will." His eyes flash, and he clutches my hand and squeezes. For a moment, I think he'll squeeze the life out of it, out of me. But I don't pull away. We're bound together now on the same mission. Nellie.

"I will do whatever I can to help, but I've no authority here."

He stares at me, hard and watchful. "You have *my* authority. You have the authority of my ancestors." He opens his scrawny arms skywards in a large sweeping circle. "We will help you find Waiwera."

I incline my head upwards into the blinding sunlit sky, half-expecting giant Aboriginal faces to appear like gods from a long-ago past. Even though the temperature soars toward its noonday maximum, clammy chills chase each other over my skin. "I'll do my best."

"Good. Now go and find the evil spirit. Don't come back until you've found Nellie's killer." He resumes his stillness and horizon gazing, like a stone statue.

I don't utter another word. Whether I want to or not, he's commissioned me to find his granddaughter's killer. And who am I to deny the decree of an Aboriginal elder? With nothing else to say, I dig my stick into the ground, lean my weight into it and make my way back down the slope. All the while, ancient voices whisper stories in my head, stories I don't understand.

★ ★ ★ ★

BY THE TIME MIMI AND I enter the great room, it's abuzz with staff, guests, and three police officers. Removed from the group, Gillian and Amy chat with an officer, though not the one who interviewed me at Jackaroo's Waterhole. This fellow is older, with an amenable, sun-tanned face and an air of authority about him. I sneak closer to overhear their conversation, but Sylvia dashes up to us. "Do you know what's going on?'

I avoid a direct answer. "Hasn't anyone said anything yet?"

"No. We were just told to assemble here. All this police presence makes John very nervous." She glances toward her husband who's tucked into the corner of a lounge chair, his face distorted with anxiety.

"I'm sure they'll explain shortly." Excusing ourselves, Mimi and I claim a couple of vacant bar stools at the bar. I search for Nellie to make me a deadly kiss. Then I remember. Emotion rushes into my throat, but I suppress it. I'll channel it later in finding her killer.

"Everyone, if I could have your attention please." Gillian hushes the room. "This is Senior Constable Geoff Mitchell. He'll explain why we've asked you all here."

Though short in stature, the Senior Constable is a bear of a man, solid and strong, with a powerful physical presence. When he steps forward, everyone's respectful attention centers on him, except Peter Pullman. He leans on the fireplace mantle with the demeanor of an insolent teenager. His obvious dislike and disrespect for authority, coupled with last night's abusive performance, places him on the aggressive fringes of the ENTJ personality type. He's a bully, ready to wage war against anyone he believes poses a threat to his power.

"Thank you for coming." Mitchell sounds more youthful than his lined face implies. "I've some unfortunate news to deliver. This morning, the body of one of the El Kwestro staff, Miss Nellie Walker, was found at Jackaroo's Waterhole."

Amid the gasps and murmurs, Andrew wails out. Gillian, who's angled herself next to him, wraps her arm around his shoulders and guides him to one side.

Mitchell continues, "Based on our preliminary investigation, we're treating Miss Walker's death as suspicious." He pauses, allowing everyone time to register the meaning of the last word.

"You mean she was murdered?" Peter says.

"Suspicious, sir." Mitchell curves his lips upwards in a friendly, yet lethal half-smile. It's obvious he's dealt with many Peter Pullmans in his life on the force. "We'll need to interview everyone to ascertain your movements over the past twenty-four hours. As such, no one is permitted to leave the homestead until further notice."

"You've got to be kidding," Tony says. "I mean, Trish and I didn't come all the way from California to end up as suspects in a murder case."

Trish jabs him in the ribs. "*Shh*. The poor girl's dead."

"I understand this is inconvenient for everyone, but it shouldn't take too long. Officers Hamers and Timson will be assisting me." Mitchell nods to the two fresh-faced officers, a woman and a man respectively, who look barely old enough to have graduated high school. "We'll hurry this along as best we can."

Maybe Tommy George was right in thinking that the police will simply fast-track Nellie's death. Move the investigation along to keep the top-paying guests happy.

Mitchell defers to Amy who steps forward with her usual efficiency. "It's nearly one o'clock. Lunch is being served at the long table outside." With a flourish of her arm, she leads the way, while the guests dawdle behind like lost cattle. The staff return to their duties, their faces pale and shocked.

Mimi clutches my arm. "I could use a stiff drink."

"You go ahead. Save me a seat. I want to talk to the Senior Constable first." I sidle in close by, while he instructs Hamers and Timson on the next course of action. I pretend not to listen, but he's decided on the library as the location for the interviews and sends his officers to organize it. "Excuse me, Senior Constable Mitchell?"

He swivels to face me, blasting me with striking blue eyes. I blink. "Oh, I'm awfully sorry, but your eyes . . ."

He holds up a hand. "I know. They're really, really, blue. My mother always told me they'd be an asset, but they've given me nothing but grief. It's hard to be taken seriously in the force with these eyes." His self-deprecating humor makes me smile. "How can I help you . . . Mrs.?"

"Daniels, Diana Daniels."

"Right. You're the lady who found Nellie's body. Timson told me he interviewed you down at the waterhole."

"That's right. But I wondered if I might speak with you in private."

"Of course. But don't you want lunch first?"

"After everything that's happened, I'm not that hungry."

"Very well. Let's see if the library's ready. We'll talk there."

We leave the great room and walk past Andrew, head in hands, slumped next to Gillian. I slow down. "I'm so sorry, Andrew." My hand goes to his shoulder.

He raises his head, his expression pitiful. "My Nellie. Who would do this?"

"I don't know, but we'll find out."

"Does Tommy George know?"

"Yes, I just came from there."

"You have to find whoever did this. You have to." He speaks with the same vehemence as Nellie's grandfather.

"I promise." I pat his shoulder.

"Come on, Andrew. I'll drive you back to the staff quarters." Gillian clasps his hand and pulls him to his feet beside her.

With a last beseeching look at me, he allows Gillian to guide him away.

"That poor young man," I whisper.

"He seems to think a lot of you since he asked you to find Nellie's killer and not the police." There's a hint of irony behind Mitchell's words.

I shrug. "You know how it is with young people. They don't trust the police, what with all the bad press these days."

"I think it's more than that." He cocks a bushy brow. "Particularly since you've met Tommy George." His expression leaves no doubt how impressed he is with my meeting the elusive old Aborigine.

"It's a long story." I flash him one of my 'keep-the-boss-happy' smiles. "How about I tell you all about it?"

He chuckles but says no more as we head to the library. It's a neat, little room, no bigger than an old-fashioned parlor, which is what it probably was before the conversion. Painted in vivid white, three walls are lined in floor-to-ceiling bookshelves, while a vintage fireplace features on the fourth wall. Timson and Hamers have pushed the sofas to one end and set up a desk with chairs, front and back, ready for the formal interviews. They vacate the room when we enter, closing the door behind them.

"Please take a seat." Mitchell offers me the chair in front of the desk while he slips into his, behind. He removes his cap and pulls repeatedly at the damp collar of his police shirt, as if ready to melt. I notice the young officers positioned his chair in the direct line of the air conditioning vent. He's got them well-trained. He tugs at either side of his collar one last time before nailing me with those eyes. "So, you've met Tommy George?"

I recap my three meetings with Nellie's grandfather, while he takes notes on the tablet in front of him. I also describe Nellie's surprise visit to my retreat yesterday afternoon.

"She didn't tell you what bothered her?"

"No. And she was dead before she had a chance to see her grandfather this morning to tell him."

Mitchell reclines in his chair and shoves a hand through his short hair making it stick out like echidna quills on the top of his head. "Any idea at all what she was on about?"

I hesitate, summing him up. His open, friendly face conveys an easy-going nature, but the probing intellect behind the dazzling hue of his eyes indicates more. He mightn't be in the big city working on high-profile crime cases, but he's a shrewd operator. I decide on full disclosure. I'll need his help as much as he'll need mine. Not that he knows that yet. "I have to tell you Senior Constable—"

"Call me Geoff," he says.

"I must tell you, Geoff, I've the distinct impression there's more going on here than the random killing of a young woman."

His brows lift. "And why would you think that?"

I huff out a breath. "Because I have a sense about things."

He eyeballs me—hard. "A sense about things?"

"Hunches. Intuition. A sixth sense. Because of my study in human behavior and my work in specialist recruitment, I've developed a specific skill set when it comes to sensing what's going on with people."

"And?" Though he tries for an impartial expression, I suspect he thinks I'm woo-woo.

"There's something else going on here at El Kwestro aside from Nellie's murder."

"But we haven't confirmed she was murdered."

I tut three times. "Of course, she was murdered. It's because of whatever she overheard, or thought she heard."

"You seem awfully convinced."

"I am. To put it bluntly, I know things. I don't know how I know, but I know. It used to drive my late husband crazy, as it does my sister-in-law, Mimi Kramer, who's here on holiday with me. But it is, what it is. Nellie Walker was murdered, and I'd like to help you find whoever did it."

He folds his ham-hock arms across his chest, twisting his mouth while he considers my offer. "I don't think that's—"

I interrupt him and tell of my involvement on the *Silver Galapagos*. About Detective John Nash from the Monterey County Sheriff's department and his reluctance to believe in my hunches, until I solved the case. "I have John's business card with me, in my room, if you'd like to call him to confirm my story. I'm sure he'll vouch for me."

Geoff rubs his chin, bristled with a crop of sandy brown hair to match his head. "Yes, I would. Just to check your story. You understand, Mrs. Daniels."

"Of course. Please call me Diana."

"Diana, it's most unusual to allow a civilian to participate in a case." He hesitates, regarding me closely. "But my grandmother used to say never look a gift horse in the mouth. I have a feeling you're such an animal."

"I'll take that as a compliment." I smile at him.

"If Detective Nash confirms what you say is true, I look forward to being proven correct in my assessment of your value." He stands and thrusts his hand forward.

"I'm rarely wrong, which makes the likelihood of you being correct a slam-dunk."

We shake hands, and once more, I'm embroiled in another mystery, not by choice, but by circumstance.

CHAPTER SEVEN

"Where did you get to? You missed lunch."

I glance up from my reading and see Mimi picking her way over the rocky ground at the back of my retreat, her hair squirming in the blustery breeze like Medusa's locks. "I wasn't hungry."

She scrambles onto the balcony and sits down. "I thought you'd be joined at the hip with Senior Constable Mitchell by now, off solving Nellie's murder." Subtle isn't a word I use to describe Mimi. "What're you reading?"

"*The Select Poems of Tennyson.*" I wave the little, red book in the air. "Tom gave it to me years ago. Whenever I need to clear my head, I read Tennyson."

"And that helps?" She mocks me with a giggle.

"Yes. It does. In fact, sometimes when I open a page at random, a line in a poem may give me a clue."

Her gray eyes twinkle. "Really. Well, go on then." She leans closer.

I shut and reopen the book, flick the pages, and stop. My eyes scan page twenty-eight searching for anything that might relate to Nellie's death.

"Well?"

I purse my lips. "It doesn't always work."

Her laugh echoes as loud as a kookaburra's. "Seriously, Diana. You're a trick."

"Wait a minute. Here." My finger halts. "'That her fair form may stand and shine, Make bright our days and light our dreams, Turning to scorn with lips divine, the falsehood of extremes.'"

"If you can make any sense of that, you deserve a medal." Another raucous laugh.

"Wait. Don't you see? This poem is called Freedom and this verse describes freedom as a young woman. A fair form who stands and shines." I wait a beat. "That's Nellie."

Mimi frowns. "Go on."

"And that she makes our days bright and lights our dreams. That her divine lips scorn at the falsehood of extremes." I stare off into space. "From Nellie's lips, she wanted to tell me something. Something she knew. Perhaps it was a falsehood, a lie."

I snap the book shut and face Mimi. "Whatever it is that Nellie overheard, she knew it wasn't true."

Mimi regards me with suspicion. "If you ask me, this poem business is a bit of a stretch. Even for you. But what would I know?" She shrugs. "This is your area of expertise, not mine."

"Trust me. It'll become clearer the further the case progresses." I glance at my watch. "Right. Time to see what's going on." I launch to my feet, keen to get started. "You coming?"

"I wouldn't miss it for the world." Twirling her hair and securing it with a clip on top of her head, she readies herself beside me. "What do I need?"

"Nothing. Just your wits. Let's see what Mitchell is up to."

As we head out the front door, I glimpse a movement to our left and pull Mimi back out of sight. "Look," I whisper, holding a finger to my lips.

With an urgent, furtive expression on his face, Andrew scrounges around the bower bird's nest. He rummages through the layers of twigs and knick-knacks like a thief looking for illegal bounty. We flatten against the wall so as not to be seen while straining to watch him. Suddenly, he bends, picks up a glittering object, and palms it into his trousers pocket. A relieved smile spreads across his face. Whatever he pocketed certainly pleases him.

"What's he found?" Mimi whispers.

"I don't know. I couldn't see it."

For a moment, he tenses, his head swiveling left to right, then he bolts down the pathway toward the homestead. After he disappears, we step out onto the walkway.

Mimi bends over to peer in the bower. "I wonder what he found?"

"I've no idea, but it was important enough for him to come back from the staff quarters after Gillian drove him there."

"Very odd."

"Come on." I tip my head toward the homestead. "We'll get to him later."

Before we take another ten steps, Amy rushes up the path to meet us. "Good news," she calls on her approach. "I've been able to secure a couple of seats for tomorrow night's Kimberley Under the Stars art event here at the homestead if you still want to go."

"That's great." Mimi's smile says it all.

"It's going ahead, despite Nellie's death?" I ask, surprised.

"Yes. We can't cancel at this stage, and Geoff has approved it."

"Who's Geoff?" Mimi asks.

"Senior Constable Mitchell," I answer.

"Do you still want to come?"

"Yes, of course, we do," Mimi says.

"I'll send up the details later. See you at sundowners." With a wave of her hand, she dashes off across the lawn.

Mimi skips a little two-step beside me. "That's good luck isn't it?"

"Yes. It is." Even though I'm not that interested in the art, the event offers a good opportunity to delve deeper into Nellie's death. Aside from the guests and staff currently at the homestead, there'll be any number of people who've arranged to be at El Kwestro at this time. Not that we need more suspects. But when grandiose egos, suppressed emotions, and delusions of artistic grandeur combine under the pretense of having a good time, liberally laced with alcohol, home-truths are often unearthed. Truths most people would prefer to keep secret.

When we arrive at the library, Officers Timson and Hamers stand outside the door. "Excuse me, is Senior Constable Mitchell inside?" I ask.

"He'll back shortly, Mrs. Daniels," Timson replies. He's a tall, skinny streak of a man with too many teeth in his mouth.

"Has he conducted any interviews yet?"

The officers exchange a puzzled sideways glance. "I'm sorry, but we're not at liberty to tell you anything about the investigation, Mrs. Daniels." Hamers, on the other hand, is a square-jawed, broad-shouldered, squat young woman. Based on her size, I figure she'd do more damage in a bar fight than Timson. They make an odd couple, but hopefully a good team.

"It's all right, Hamers. Mrs. Daniels will be assisting in our investigations." Mitchell nudges in behind us, and as Hamers and Timson step aside, he motions us into the library.

After introducing Mimi, I listen to him downplay her wide-eyed response to his eyes with his usual spiel. Better suited to a romantic hero than a rural Senior Constable, the rare color of his eyes probably distracts everyone he speaks to. He turns the blast of blue on me.

I hand him Detective Nash's business card. "Here's John's contact details."

"Thanks." He tucks it into his shirt pocket. "I've been thinking about what you said and since there's a spare room here at the homestead, I'm going to stay for a few days. See what I can find out."

I raise a brow. "You're not convinced it's a random killing then?"

"I didn't say that. Random or premeditated, it's too early to say. Anyway, Gillian's offered to put me up in Ghost Gum, the room closest to theirs. If you need me, that's where I'm staying."

"Have you started any interviews?"

"Not yet. I had to organize a couple of things first, but I'd like your help."

"Sure. What do you need?"

"There's an excursion going to Emma Gorge this afternoon. Amy says several of the guests are booked to go. I'd like you to tag along, see what you can find out."

"Happy to help. What time does it leave?"

He glances at his watch. "Thirty minutes."

"Okay, we'll tell Amy, and get changed into our hiking gear. I'll check in with you when we return."

"Thanks. People tend to relax and talk when they're off exploring together."

Smiling my understanding, I turn to leave.

"Diana?"

"Yes?"

"Whether Nellie died at the hands of some random traveler or by an intentional murderer, there's a killer nearby. Possibly staying here as a guest or on the staff. Go easy." He stares at me, hard. "Right?"

I remember how I'd become a target on the *Silver Galapagos* when I got too close to solving the case. "I know how this works."

"Don't worry, I'll be by her side." Sporting a cheeky grin, Mimi flings her arm around my shoulders. "No one would dare bump off two harmless, middle-aged women."

Both Geoff and I exchange an incredulous look and then stare at Mimi, who blinks like an innocent child. With a low groan and a shake of his head, he stalks to his desk, while I bundle her out of the library.

★ ★ ★ ★

WHEN BOB SHUTS OFF THE engine, the six of us clamber out of the tripi, slinging our packs onto our back. He herds us to one side and proceeds with his safety presentation on drinking lots of water, watching our step on the steep, rocky, three-and-a-half-kilometer hike, and keeping an eye out for each other. Mimi chats to Maria and Jo, while Peter and Kristen distance themselves a little from our group.

"Right, let's go." Bob waves us forward and we fall in behind him on the well-maintained gravel path leading from the visitor center's car park into the wilderness. "The Emma Gorge trek offers a unique walk through the Cockburn Range and the massive sandstone and quartz cliff faces. As we hike further in, the trail becomes more difficult to navigate, and we'll need to climb over large boulders. If you need a hand, just give me a hoy." He strides off with Peter and Kristen close behind him, so I pick up speed to catch up.

I fall in beside Kristen. "Isn't this amazing country?" I say with a hint of whimsy, demonstrating I carry no animosity about her husband's outburst last night.

"Yes, it is." She mirrors my tone and smile.

While my gaze travels to the range surrounding us, I notice Peter keeps his eyes riveted straight ahead. He either doesn't hear us or he chooses to ignore our conversation. "You're on your honeymoon. How romantic."

"We've wanted to come here for a while, so what better time than on our honeymoon. Besides, I've been fascinated by Aboriginal rock art for ages. The Kimberley has rock art from the three epochs . . ." While she explains the differences of the Archaic, Erudite, and Aboriginal epochs, my mind teases apart the strange juxtaposition between Peter's obvious disdain for the Aborigine and Kristen's love of Aboriginal art. "We're hoping Dale will take us to some of the sites in his chopper while we're here," she says, drawing me back from my musings.

I lower my voice. "It's a shame about poor Nellie's death, though. Puts a bit of a dampener on your honeymoon."

"Yes, it does," she whispers. "Terrible, isn't it? I hear you found the body?"

"Yes, at Jackaroo's Waterhole."

"How awful for you. Are you all right?" She places a gentle hand on my shoulder.

"I'm fine. Thanks for asking."

"I worked as a nurse with PTSD patients, so I know how distressing these types of situations can be." Her empathy touches me, and I realize it's her sensitivity and compassion that bonds her to Peter, despite his ignorance and arrogance.

"Are you going to continue in your nursing career, now that you're married?"

"No. We're hoping to start a family soon." She flutters a doe-eyed glance in her husband's direction and receives a thin-lipped smile in return.

"I see." I'm desperate to ask about her husband's business, but since he's paying attention to our conversation, I refrain.

We trudge on behind Bob with Mimi, Maria, and Jo in the rear. The oversize clumps of spinifex grass of the savannah bushland which border the beginning of the trail are soon replaced by shallow ravines littered with rocks and boulders of all shapes and sizes. It's as if the earth erupted and spewed its gritty guts out in every direction. Picking a path through the geological debris, we tail Bob, doing our best not to twist an ankle or take a more serious fall.

Unexpectedly, Peter offers his hand to help me cross a treacherous incline. "I must apologize for my outburst last night. I over-reacted, I shouldn't have spoken like that to Nellie or to you."

I force a smile but say nothing to absolve his guilt. "It's unfortunate that Nellie was killed not long after." My voice is as cool as the stare I shoot him.

He hangs his head. "Yes, it is."

Beside him, Kristen rubs his arm in a soothing gesture. She's the classic INFP, introverted, intuitive, feeling, and perceptive. No matter the circumstance, she's a nurturer, first and foremost. I wonder if Peter realizes how fortunate he is to have her in his life. While they move ahead, I take my time and clamber over the rugged terrain, using my hands to steady myself. The last thing I need is an injury. Trying to rescue and haul anyone out of here would be nigh on impossible.

"Are you okay?" Bob's outstretched hand hovers toward me from atop a mammoth boulder.

"Thanks." I grasp his hand, and he instructs me where to put my feet.

After scaling across and sliding down the boulder, we emerge onto a relatively flat, though rocky plateau. Thankfully, without injury. We round a corner and a collective "*ahh*" goes up. "This is Emma Gorge." Pride rings in his voice. And rightly so.

I suck a lungful of air. Not just because of the effort to get here, but because the awe-inspiring scene makes the trek worthwhile. Dotted with vibrant emerald green ferns, the craggy vertical cliffs stretch skywards, creating a natural amphitheater around a vast waterhole. A cascade of water tumbles down two hundred meters from the top, glossing the gray, rust, and ochre palette of the cliff face. Shifting bands of afternoon light play in the waterfall mist, while a crescendo of chatter and laughter from other hikers bounces off the rock.

"Oh my god, this is amazing." Mimi sidles in beside me with Maria and Jo.

Maria inclines her head, marveling at the scene. "Look at the colors."

"And how clear the water is. You can see right to the bottom." Jo points to the millions of ripple rocks, each distinct in its detail, forming the waterhole's bed.

Bob heaves off his backpack. "We'll stop here for about thirty minutes. If you want a swim, you've got time."

"What about crocodiles?" Jo asks the question on my mind, if not everyone else's.

"None here. But the water's pretty chilly."

His warning falls on the deaf ears of Maria and Jo, who peel off their hiking clothes in record time. On hitting the water, their squeals echo through the gorge, followed by our laughter. Kristen tugs at Peter's hand to go in, but he declines. Unfazed, she strips down to her bathers and tiptoes into the waterhole.

Maria splashes around like a happy kid. "Better to just get in quick, Kristen."

"Come on, Kristen. You can do it." Jo waves her in.

With a final glance back at Peter, who smiles and shakes his head, she stiffens and races in with a high-pitched shriek.

Mimi and I find an outcrop on which to sit and watch the fun. "How did you get on with Kristen and Peter?" she asks.

"She's sweet, kind, considerate, and probably far too forgiving of her husband's bad behavior. I doubt she's a valid suspect in Nellie's death."

"And him?"

"I haven't been able to find out much. He keeps to himself. Though he did apologize for his outburst last night."

"So he should." She curses under a breath. "Do you think he killed Nellie?"

"If he did, what's his motive?"

"He's a racist pig."

"Not really a motive to kill someone when you're on your honeymoon." My gaze rests on the back of Peter's head. "But he's capable of violence. That I've no doubt about." The squirming in my gut confirms it. Aggression is his modus operandi. Perhaps Peter Pullman was here for more than a honeymoon. But what that could be, I've no idea . . . yet.

CHAPTER EIGHT

BY MID-AFTERNOON, WE ARRIVE back at the homestead and alight the tripi, tired and dusty. After wiping the dirt from our face and hands complements of the chilled face cloths the staff offer us, I tuck my arm through Mimi's. "Come on."

"Where are we going?" she asks, pulling me in the opposite direction. "I need a shower."

"Just act like we're wandering around the grounds."

"But we are just wandering." She's snippy. "What are you doing?"

I steer her, and her impatience, back along the gravel driveway and onto the lawn on the far side of the property. "When we drove in, I noticed Tony walking into the grounds and maintenance area." I indicate the direction with a subtle incline of my head so as not to draw attention to where we're headed.

"But that's a staff-only area. What's he doing in there?"

"Precisely."

We amble over and when we reach the fenced area, we slink behind one of the nearby African mahogany trees, planted on the property decades earlier.

Mimi cranes her neck out from behind the tree. "I can't see anyone."

"It's Tony, I'm sure. We just have to wait."

She huffs out an irritable breath, while good-natured birds twitter above our heads.

I direct her gaze. "There. At the back. Can you see him?"

"Yes. I think he's talking to someone standing behind the shed."

"By the look of it, he's arguing with whoever's back there." Even from this distance, it's obvious he's angry. His fist waves in the air and he leans menacingly toward whoever we can't see.

"I wonder who it is," she says.

"Since they're in a staff-only area, I assume it must be someone on the staff. Otherwise, why be in there?"

When Tony pivots sharply, we crouch further behind the tree and watch him stomp toward the fence.

"Come on. We better get out of here. This way." I drag her along the line of trees in the opposite direction to where he's headed. Snugged in behind the last tree, we peep around, watching him cross the lawn and stride up the driveway, head bowed. He reminds me of a bull ready to charge. We wait fifteen minutes hoping to see who the other person was, but no one shows.

"Can we go yet?" Mimi sounds as tired as she looks.

"Yes, but only under the pretense of admiring the gardens. I don't want anyone suspecting that we saw anything."

We stroll off along the property fence line like a pair of inconspicuous guests. While I chat casually to Mimi about the shrubs, my mind tries to piece the who, what, and why of Tony's display. Who had he been arguing with? Over what? And why in the grounds and maintenance area? My head rattles like a box of jigsaw pieces. There must be a way these seemingly random events fit together.

★ ★ ★ ★

WITHIN THE HOUR, I'M SHOWERED and changed, and finishing my update on the Emma Gorge hike to Senior Constable Mitchell and what Mimi and I witnessed in the grounds and maintenance area on our return.

He glances at his watch. "There's time to do an interview before dinner."

"I'm keen." In fact, my intuition strains at the leash.

"Let's start with this Peter Pullman character." He sends Timson off to collect our first person of interest. "By the way, I spoke to your mate, John Nash . . ." He slides John's business card toward me. "He sang your praises like a lay preacher.

Reckons you're the real deal when it comes to sniffing out and solving a mystery."

"John's a good man and a terrific cop. It was a team effort."

"I'd be grateful for your insights on this matter. Hopefully, we can get to the bottom of Nellie's death real fast, and you can resume your holiday."

I hope so too, but I doubt there'll be much holidaymaking for a while yet.

A knock at the door signals Peter's arrival. As he's ushered into the room, his surly expression leaves no doubt as to his opinion on being summoned.

Geoff offers him the only chair available. "Please take a seat, Mr. Pullman."

Without uttering a word, he folds into it and crosses his arms in a defiant, defensive gesture. He raises a haughty brow at me but says nothing.

"I need to ascertain everyone's whereabouts over the past twenty-four hours. I understand there was an incident last night between you and Nellie? At dinner?"

His eyes narrow on me. "What's Mrs. Daniels doing here?"

"She's helping us with our investigations."

"Why?"

"Rest assured, Mr. Pullman, nothing you say will be repeated by anyone."

He grunts and curls his lip, obviously displeased that his question wasn't answered.

"Please tell me about last night's incident."

"The waitress dropped the dessert in my lap."

"And then what happened?"

"I told her to get the manager."

I edge tentatively into the conversation. "It was a bit more than that. Wasn't it?"

"Look. I said some things I shouldn't have."

"Like?" Geoff asks.

He hesitates. "I called her a little black abo."

Geoff doesn't visibly flinch, but the ropey muscles in his bare forearms twitch. Maybe they'd like to teach Mr. Pullman some manners. "Did you see Nellie after that?"

"No. Why would I?"

"Perhaps you wanted to teach her a lesson for being so clumsy?" Geoff asks.

"Or being Aboriginal," I say. "You don't like Aborigines, do you?"

"What business is it of yours? But if you must know. No. I don't."

More forearm flinching from Geoff. "That's quite a motive you've got there for killing Nellie, Mr. Pullman."

He cackles. "I'm on my honeymoon. Why would I waste my time killing a little black girl?"

"Since you dislike Aborigines so much, why did you come here?" I ask.

"My wife loves Aboriginal rock art. I love my wife. *Ipso facto*, I'm here for the Kimberley Art and Culture Festival." He opens his hands in feigned submission.

Geoff taps away at his tablet, while I review my notes on my laptop on the ENTJ personality type which I suspect matches Peter.

I ask the question that I wanted to earlier. "What line of business are you in?"

He frowns. "Listen, it's bad enough having to answer his questions" —he scowls at the Senior Constable— "but I don't have to answer yours."

Geoff closes the lid of his tablet and folds his hands on top. "As a matter of fact, you do. Why? Because I'm telling you to." Unveiled sarcasm laces his delivery. "I'll make it easier for you, Mr. Pullman, what line of business are you in?"

He rolls his eyes and concedes. "I'm a stockbroker for small-cap spec shares." It's clear he thinks he's outsmarted us, but since Tom invested in spec shares before his death, I've got enough knowledge to know what Peter does for a living.

I match his smirk with my own. "In other words, apart from the normal trading of shares for clients, you also get unsuspecting mum and dad investors, to invest their hard-earned money in companies that need capital raising from which you get a healthy commission and kickbacks."

A soft, pink blush races up his neck and flushes his face. I sense, rather than see, Geoff smile. *Damn, it's good to be back in the thick of it.*

"I wouldn't put it exactly like that, but close enough." He fidgets. "But what has my business got to do with this dead girl?"

"Just trying to get a helicopter view." Geoff reopens the lid of his tablet, fingers on the keyboard. "What were your movements after the episode with Nellie last night?"

"Amy walked us back to our retreat and waited for my soiled trousers. She left, and Kristen and I relaxed for a while, then went to bed."

"And you didn't go out after that?"

He screws up his nose. "No. Why would I? Where would I go?"

"Do you have a vehicle here with you, Mr. Pullman?"

"Yes. It's a rental. We picked it up at Kununurra airport."

My ears prick at the mention of a car. "So, you drove here from the airport?"

"Yes."

"Most guests come in via chopper or the El Kwestro guest transfer. Why get a rental vehicle?"

"Because Kristen wants to go off the beaten track in search of Aboriginal art. The only way to do that is to self-drive."

"Which means you could have waited for your wife to go to sleep last night, kidnapped and killed Nellie. Dumped her body, drove back to the homestead, slipped into bed and no one was the wiser," Geoff suggests, obviously keen to rattle him.

Peter leans forward, his voice cold. "Yes. I could've. But I didn't. As I said, why would I waste my time? That girl meant nothing to me."

"Where are the keys to your car?" I ask.

"In Pandanus."

"Has anyone else asked for or taken the keys since you and Kristen arrived?"

His eyes shoot upwards, recalling the past twenty-four hours. "No. I'm the only one who's had the keys."

I dip my chin in an abbreviated nod to Geoff, who then obliges. "Right. Thank you for your time, Mr. Pullman. We'll contact you if we need anything else."

Surprise widens Peter's eyes as if he's startled the questioning is finished. "Fine. Thanks." He stands to leave.

"Is there anything else you'd like to say?" I ask, in a warm and friendly manner.

"No, why should there be?"

"You sure there isn't another reason for your stay here at El Kwestro?"

"I told you. It's our honeymoon, Kristen loves Aboriginal art and I love my wife." He adds a nod like a full stop.

"Why?" I ask.

"Why what?" Frustration and impatience climb onto his face.

"Why do you love your wife?"

"Because she's the only one who understands."

Bingo! As I thought. Kristen knows his history and if we want it, she's the one who'll tell us. Not him. "Thank you." I offer a sweet smile and defer to the Senior Constable, who releases him.

Once the door closes, Geoff scrapes back his chair. "What was all that about? With his wife."

"Kristen was a PTSD nurse, so she's worked with trauma patients. I suspect that whatever trauma Peter's experienced brought them together, because he said, 'she's the only one who understands.'"

Geoff shakes his head like a cat teasing a fluffy toy. "Slow down a minute. How did you get all that from one sentence?"

"It's my job to get inside a person's head as quickly as possible. To set the trap without them knowing, and then spring it before they realize they've exposed themselves. That's how I recruit for the major organizations that hire me. Find the right person, at the right price for the job, and make sure they're a keeper."

"Shit." His expression is a mix of respect and disbelief.

"I know it appears a bit mumbo-jumbo. But it's just critical thinking with human behavior and personality types." *And my hunches on the side.*

His face splits into an easy smile. "Glad to have you on the case. What's your take on Peter Pullman, then?"

"He's what the Myer Briggs personality type testing calls an ENTJ—extraverted, intuitive, thinking, and judging. He's a smart strategic thinker, efficient, and a high achiever, hence his ability as a stockbroker. I suspect he's made a pretty fortune for himself and possibly his clients. But if the ENTJ's lust for power, influence, and assertiveness is forced, they become aggressive, even violent."

"Sounds like an accurate profile."

"Why don't we talk to Kristen? I think she'll shed some light on Peter's past."

While Geoff dispatches Timson to find Mrs. Pullman, I wander to the window and stare outside. Nellie's face and her enchanting eyes, flash before me. *Why would anyone want to kill you?* The image fades like a lover's departing whisper. What's the motive? Her body didn't appear to have been sexually interfered with, and there were no signs of a struggle on the ground. Perhaps she was killed elsewhere and carried to the spot at Jackaroo's Waterhole. But that means her killer is someone strong enough, and single-minded enough to execute such a murder. I massage my temples. Planned. It was planned.

"Please come in, Mrs. Pullman." Geoff's welcome interrupts my thoughts.

I turn and smile at Kristen while Geoff indicates her chair. She returns a frown as I move past her to the seat beside the Senior Constable. While Geoff explains the situation, I notice she's trying not to gawk at the intense blue of his eyes. They were probably a great asset in his lone wolf days, but he wears a wedding ring now. Still, they give him an unusual interviewing edge. One he uses to his advantage.

He begins. "Can you tell us what happened last night with Nellie and your husband?"

After Kristen retells the facts of the event, I ask, "Would you say your husband is a racist?"

She lowers her head. "Yes, I would."

"But as someone who appears to love Aboriginal culture and art, why did you marry him?"

She doesn't flinch at the brazenness of my question. Instead, she lifts her head and sighs. "Peter won't tell you, but I will. He was the only child of a middle-class family living in Perth. When he was twelve years old, two men broke into their house late at night. They were loaded up on a cocktail of alcohol and drugs. Gunshots were fired, killing his parents in their bed. Peter hid in the back of his closet, terrified, waiting a similar fate. Instead, the intruders fled downstairs, laughing. Peter ran to the window, hoping to see them. They were Aboriginal boys. The police never found them, and he's lived with crippling survivor guilt and a deep-seated hatred of Aborigines since."

I was right. There's always some past trauma that plays itself out.

"I figure after going through something like that, he'd be damn angry. Wanting his own revenge," Geoff says.

She meets his stare, not wavering under his scrutiny. "I suspect you already know about his juvenile record?"

The Senior Constable smiles. "Yes." He spins the tablet toward me, the recent email open. "It states that Peter was involved in a number of violent attacks on teenage Aboriginal boys."

"It's true. He got into trouble for a while, until he found a good psychiatrist who prescribed him medication to suppress the mood swings. It helped him start a new life."

"But how did you two meet?" I ask.

"Through mutual friends, a few years ago." She pauses. "I know he behaved badly last night, but he'd forgotten to take his meds. The moment that happens, it all comes up again, the horror, the violence, the grief. All of it."

"Don't you ever worry about your own safety?" I ask.

She shakes her head. "Never. I know how to handle him. I understand the trauma and how to reach him. On his meds, he's wonderful. Off his meds, he's hard to manage, but that's where my PTSD nurse training comes in."

"After Amy left the retreat last night, did Peter stay in Pandanus?" Geoff asks.

She shrugs. "Sort of."

Geoff and I exchange a quick frown. "What do you mean?" he asks.

"I lazed in the outdoor bath, reading, for about an hour before going to bed. Peter said he was going for a walk, to calm down."

Bells clang in my head. "But your husband told us, he didn't go out."

"I expect Peter wouldn't call going for a walk, going out. He may have just gone to the edge of the cliff and sat there for a while or wandered along the pathway or the lawn. I don't know. You'll have to ask him."

"But he was back by the time you finished your bath and got ready for bed," Geoff asks, eager to confirm a verifiable timeline.

"Yes. He was already in the shower by the time I stepped out of the bath."

More bell clanging. "Have you had your laundry done today?"

"Yes. It was washed and delivered to our retreat this afternoon."

I meet Geoff's troubled gaze. If there was any evidence on Peter's clothes as to what he got up to last night, it's gone now.

After a few other questions, Geoff releases Kristen and reclines in his chair, hands bracketed behind his head. "It seems Mr. Pullman didn't tell us the full story."

I rise and begin pacing. My best thinking happens when I move. A carry-over from my years of problem solving with Tom. "And he forgot to take his meds last night. We need to find out where he was for that missing hour while Kristen was in the bath." I return to my laptop. "Based on my calculations, the dessert incident happened at approximately nine-thirty, the Pullmans were back in Pandanus by about nine forty-five, Kristen was in the bath maybe by ten. That leaves an hour between ten and eleven that Peter's whereabouts are unaccounted for." I trade a serious look with Geoff. "Do we have a time of death yet for Nellie?"

"At this stage, they reckon she died between ten-thirty and eleven-thirty."

"Cause of death?" A shudder of remorse races through my body for asking, but murder's never fun, especially for the victim.

"Blunt force trauma to the back of the head."

"But she wasn't killed there. She was killed somewhere else. Correct?"

He drops his arms and straightens. "What makes you say that?"

"There was no blood pool when I found her."

"Very observant. You're right. Whoever murdered her did so elsewhere, took her to the waterhole, and dumped her body there."

"So, we're looking for a murder site and a murder weapon."

He nods, and I notice his face has aged since I first met him only a few hours before.

I press on. "If Peter did it, he's a helluva a cool customer. He rushes out of the retreat, while his wife's taking a bath, happens upon and grabs Nellie, kills her and dumps her body at Jackaroo's Waterhole and then races back and into the shower."

Geoff inclines his head. "Most murderers are cool customers."

My frown deepens. "Sorry. It doesn't add up. Too opportunistic."

"I tend to agree, but where was he?"

A familiar nagging stirs in my gut. "I have a hunch that when we find the answer to that, we'll uncover what's really going and the motive for Nellie's murder."

CHAPTER NINE

OFFICER HAMERS KNOCKS AND POKES her head around the door. "Excuse me, Senior Constable, Gillian Richards is here to see you."

"Send her in." Then as an aside to me. "I asked her for some information earlier."

The door opens and Gillian walks in. Though confident in her approach, she's another person who's aged in the few hours since I knocked on her door this morning. Nellie's murder is taking its toll faster than I expected. After taking a seat, Gillian slides a manila folder of papers across to Geoff.

She turns to me, her expression contrite. "Hello, Mrs. Daniels. I'm sorry I was a bit brusque this morning . . ."

I hold up my hand. "That's quite all right. I came on a bit strong."

"But you were right about Nellie. I can't believe she's dead." Shaking her head, she lowers her red-rimmed eyes.

Geoff jumps in all business. "What did you find out?"

She snaps us straight. All business to match. "There were only three vehicles on site yesterday. The Pullman's rental vehicle. The homestead's 4-wheel drive which Amy and any of the designated staff use, and the 4-wheel drive Christopher and I use. Details are in there." She nods to the folder.

"Where are the keys kept for the homestead vehicle?" I ask.

"They hang on a keyboard in the office. If anyone uses the vehicle, they must complete the Vehicle Register with the date, times, their name, the odometer reading, and signatures in and out."

I raise my eyebrows in admiration. "A very efficient system."

She accepts my compliment with a humble smile. "I implemented it to stop personal use of the vehicle."

"I bet it worked."

Her smile widens with pride. "It did."

Geoff pulls the register from the file and studies it. "It says here the last time the vehicle was used yesterday was by someone named Cameron last night at midnight. Who's he?"

"He's last night's chef-on-duty. He took the vehicle back to the staff quarters, handed over the keys to the early-chef-on-duty, who drove it back this morning."

Geoff snatches a pen to take notes on the spreadsheet. "The vehicle remains at the staff quarters all night?"

"Yes. That's why I implemented the Vehicle Register. That way, the staff can't use the vehicle overnight because it'll show on the odometer readings."

He scrutinizes the register again. "Based on this, Cameron drove it to the staff quarters at twelve-oh-five past midnight and Warren drove it back at five-thirty this morning with the odometer readings matching the distances from the homestead to the staff quarters and back."

"Correct, and the only other time the vehicle was used yesterday was by Amy, who drove it into town in the morning and was back by three-thirty. After that, it didn't move until Cameron took it just after midnight."

"Why did Amy go into town?" I ask.

"To get the last supplies for the art event dinner tomorrow night. There's always something that comes up at the last minute."

I recalled the ninety-minute paved-and-dirt road trip from Kununurra to the homestead.

"A long way to go to get last-minute items."

"The joys of being in the outback." More than a touch of irony edges her voice.

Geoff slides out another spreadsheet. "And the Vehicle Register for your car indicates it hasn't been driven since five o'clock yesterday afternoon when you returned to the homestead."

"That's correct. It was our day off. Chris and I went into town. We're permitted to use the homestead vehicle for personal reasons. It's in our contract. That's in there too."

I like Gillian more and more. Her professionalism and commitment to the property are commendable. I'd hire her in a heartbeat.

She continues, "When we got home, Chris cooked dinner and we watched some movies before going to bed around ten. I didn't know anything about this awful business until Mrs. Daniels knocked on my door this morning."

Geoff slips the documents back into the manila folder. "Thanks for this." He pushes it to one side. "Can you think of anyone who'd want to hurt Nellie? Was there tension between her and anyone on staff?"

"I've thought about this all day, and I can't think of a soul. Nellie kept to herself, never had disagreements with anyone. I'm stumped as to who would do this."

"You know she and Andrew were an item?" I ask.

"There was talk on the grapevine, but it never interfered with their jobs, so we didn't pay it any mind. Young love is sweet." A youthful blush replaces the exhausted pallor of her face. "That's why I think it's got to be a random killing. Like the one up here back in 1987 when some deranged German tourist went on a killing spree." Her eyes widen as she trades hopeful looks with Geoff and me.

"At this stage, we need to get a clearer picture. We're not ruling anything out." He stands, and I follow his lead. "Thanks for your help, Mrs. Richards. I know, that as the general manager, you'll keep a tight lid on this."

She rises. "I'm doing my best but with close to one hundred guests landing on the homestead for tomorrow night's event, it won't be easy."

"I'm sure you and your team will manage it without a hitch," I say.

"Thanks, Mrs. Daniels. Fingers crossed."

After she leaves, Geoff slides the folder towards me. "Three different vehicles on the property yesterday and not a chance of matching any of their treads to the patchwork of tire marks at Jackaroo's Waterhole. Timson and Hamers have started searches of the vehicles, but I doubt we'll find anything until the forensic team gives them a thorough going over."

I glance at my watch, only now realizing how late it is. "Dinner's nearly over. How about I get something sent in here and then we'll join the guests for a nightcap?"

"Good idea. We'll do a quick review while we eat."

★ ★ ★ ★

THE MOMENT I STEP OUTSIDE the library after Geoff and I finish up, Mimi grabs me. "Where the helluva you been?"

"In the library." I roll my eyes at the obviousness of the answer. "Why?"

"My god, dinner was a catastrophe." She tugs me toward the great room. "Come on. Let's grab a drink, and I'll fill you in."

When we get there, six haunted faces stare at me. Like store-front mannequins, Maria and Jo sit on one of the upholstered sofas, their posture and faces drawn tight. Sitting opposite them on a matching sofa, blink the Torrens. I suspect they're reliving the worst day of their lives. Stephanie was about the same age as Nellie when she died. Here they are at El Kwestro, trying to get away from the horrors of their past and they land in the middle of a murder case. *Such bad luck.* Equally stunned, the Wilsons hover at the fireplace, pretending to warm themselves in its dying heat. The Pullmans are nowhere to be seen, which is wise, considering his terrible behavior last night. Everyone's got a drink of some sort. From what I see, most are drinking hard liquor. Under the circumstances who can blame them. It's what murder dictates.

I glance at Mimi. "Double vodka on the rocks."

On purpose, Geoff retired for the night, leaving me to do some subtle reconnaissance on the remaining guests. I doubt if anyone will be forthcoming since they know I'm assisting the police now, but it's worth a try. Mimi hands me my drink and together we wander over to the other guests.

I raise mine in the air. "To Nellie."

"To Nellie." While a chorus of seven voices repeats my salute, I study each face in turn, looking for any tell-tale signs. Of what? I'm not sure, but my sixth sense is quickening.

"Do they know what happened yet?" Tony places his glass on the mantle. Scotch, I think, and a full glass. No ice.

"Senior Constable Mitchell and his officers are doing the best they can."

An uncomfortable silence descends, and I notice everyone averts their eyes to their drinks. *Here it comes.*

As usual, Tony puffs up, asserting his perceived leadership position. "I hear you're helping them with their investigation. Why is that?"

"Let's just say I have a special skill set which the police find useful."

"Are you clairvoyant?" A hint of wonder tinges Maria's words. "One of those people the police call in to help find bodies and solve cases?"

Jo swivels a frown at her. "Don't be silly. There's no such thing as clairvoyance."

"I wouldn't be too sure," Mimi says. "We're all here in the outback, searching for some sort of Dreamtime experience, aren't we?"

A hush descends while they consider Mimi's question.

"Granted, but—"

"But what?" Another voice commandeers the conversation and when everyone turns in its direction, a collective gasp goes up.

Like a ghost from the past, Tommy George lingers at the door, his face lined with anger and grief.

I leave Mimi to attend the others and go to him. "What are you doing here?"

"It's been twenty-four hours since Waiwera killed my Nellie."

My eyes automatically check my watch. Ten forty-five. A sharp chill bites my neck. *How did he know?*

His black eyes glint at me. "Have you found him?"

I lower mine, unable to meet his gaze. "Not yet. But we will."

"Where's your stick?" He sounds aggrieved.

"It's in my room."

"Keep it with you. Every day, every night. You will need it to stop Waiwera."

With that, he turns heel and disappears into the night. I marvel at his single-mindedness and the distance he's traveled to the homestead, whether on foot or hitching a ride. I wonder why he came all this way so soon after Nellie's murder. Did he really believe we could've tracked down Nellie's killer by now? Disappointed that his visit was in vain, I return to the group, determined to respect his privacy by not answering the others' questions about him.

I sidle next to Mimi. "Did the Pullmans come to dinner?"

She nods. "But they left straight after dessert. Didn't say much."

"What about Dale? I notice he's not here."

"He had dinner, kept to himself, then Amy called him away to discuss tomorrow's schedule."

I incline my head toward the others. "Any dramas?"

"Nope, but they're like cats on a hot tin roof. Especially Tony. I've watched him all night, hoping to pick who he was arguing with this afternoon." She pouts, frustrated. "I've got no idea. I hope you and the blue-eyed wonder boy got further along than I did."

I let out a soft giggle at Mimi's turn-of-phrase. "Not yet. But it's early days. Lots more people to interview." With that, I top up my drink and address the group. "Is anyone doing excursions tomorrow?"

The Wilsons raise their hands. "We're off to the Bungles for most of the day."

"Mimi and I are painting early to get the morning light," Maria says, pouring herself another double shot of gin at the bar.

Jo wraps an arm around her waist. "Then we're off to Miri Miri Falls for a romantic afternoon." She pecks a kiss on her girlfriend's cheek, making Maria blush.

I turn an expectant face toward the Torrens. "We're not sure yet," Sylvia says. "We'll decide at breakfast."

Indicating to Mimi to finish her drink, I do the same. "Well, good night, everyone. See you tomorrow."

On our way out, I hear the others winding up as well.

"Didn't you want to stay a little longer, do a bit of undercover snooping?" Mimi whispers.

"I think I've done all the snooping, questioning, and thinking I need for one day."

"Aren't you going to tell me about the Pullman interviews?" Her eyes widen with excitement, like my cocker spaniel Berty when he spots a hare in the park across from my apartment.

"Not tonight. I need to sleep and let my subconscious mind take over for a few hours."

"Really?" She sounds disappointed, but I refuse to feel guilty.

"Yes. Really." I bid her good night where the pathway forks off to my retreat. Not bothering to switch on the lights, I stroll outside onto my balcony and gaze at the billions of stars in the blackest of night skies. Stillness creeps in on me, its murmur through the trees hinting at clues. But they remain obscured, like a foggy mirror in a humid bathroom. Tommy George's visit tonight proved one thing though. Evil killed Nellie, no matter what human form it took. Without the help of my hunches, my conscious thinking alone isn't enough to expose the killer. A good night's sleep is what I need. Where, like Tommy George connecting to his Dreamtime, out of the mist, Waiwera might appear.

CHAPTER TEN

SIX A.M. *WHAT IS IT about the police knocking at your door?* For some reason, it sounds more authoritative, more urgent. Rubbing a wonderful night's sleep from my face, I struggle out of bed, throw on my complementary El Kwestro robe and scuff my way to the door.

I was right. The police.

"Sorry, Diana." Geoff strides in without waiting for an invitation.

"Good morning to you too," I remind him with drowsy sarcasm.

"Yeah. Sorry. Good morning." He gives me a perfunctory nod. "It's like grand central station down there." He cocks his head toward the homestead. "Staff everywhere setting up for tonight's Kimberley Under the Stars art event." By his eye-rolling, I gather the Senior Constable is unimpressed.

"And you're here in my retreat at this ungodly hour, because?" I shuffle to the facilities cubbyhole where I pour water into the electric jug and flick it to boil.

"I figure we need to grab the staff before they disappear off into town for more last-minute items if we want to interview them today. This bloody event is throwing a spanner into our investigation." He heads outside onto the balcony.

I empathize with his frustration at having to comply with the homestead's timetable. "Necessity is the mother of all invention."

"Still, it's a bugger."

"How do you like your coffee?" I call louder.

"White, two sugars, thanks."

Why is it women always get stuck with making the coffee? To be honest, playing hostess isn't why I'm miffed. It's because I was woken up and whatever was in my mind about Nellie's murder in that twilight zone between sleep and wakefulness is now gone. With coffees in hand, I wander outside, and together we sip the kick-starter while appreciating the scenery which never fails to calm the spirit. "Who do you want to interview first?" I ask.

"I figure we better talk to Amy, the homestead manager before she hightails it into town."

I cast him a sideways glance and smile. A shame Tommy George didn't meet Senior Constable Mitchell last night. Geoff's doggedness to his duty would have put Nellie's grandfather's mind at rest about the police not caring about an Aboriginal girl's murder. Geoff's no plodding, outback cop. "Good idea interviewing Amy before the day goes pear-shaped. Give me twenty minutes."

He places his half-drunk coffee on the table. "How do you like your coffee?"

"Cappuccino, no sugar."

"I'll have a real coffee waiting for you. A peace offering for waking you so early." He winks one of those piercing blue eyes at me, and I blink.

"Accepted."

He leaves, and I shower.

★ ★ ★ ★

RUDDY FACED, YET UNRUFFLED, AMY appears ready to spring from the interview chair like a jack-in-the-box. Six-thirty in the morning, and she's breaking a sweat. "How can I help?" She glances at her watch with the not-so-subtle implication that she's needed elsewhere.

"We just want to get a clear understanding of your movements on Wednesday night after you intervened with Mr. Pullman over the dessert incident." Geoff's primed at his tablet ready to take notes. The air conditioning blasts in his direction and Amy shuffles her chair over to soak up a little of its cast-off breeze.

She launches in. "I walked the Pullmans back to Pandanus. Once Peter gave me his trousers, I said good night, took them to the laundry, sprayed them with stain remover, and left a note for the staff to attend to them as soon as they arrived in the morning. I went back to my office and wrote an incident report. I let Nellie go early. I told her to finish up and that was the last time I saw her."

"Since the wait staff usually go back to the staff quarters with the night chef in the company vehicle, what was the advantage in letting Nellie go early?" I ask.

"Well, I knew she was upset, so I thought even if she waited for Cameron to finish, she didn't have to work. She could just have a bit of time to herself. Or sometimes, if the staff knock-off early, they call another staff member who has a car and they come up and drive them back." She glances out the window, straining to see how the set-up's progressing without her supervision.

"Where were you when you let Nellie go?" Geoff asks.

"I asked her into my office. She signed off the roster and then left."

"What time was that?" he asks.

"Ten-thirty."

Like an expensive cut of meat, her answers are trimmed of all fat. They leave me wondering if Amy sacrifices empathy in favor of efficiency. "Did you ask her how she was going to get back to the staff quarters?"

"She said she might call someone but intended to begin walking to clear her head."

"Did she say who she was calling?" Geoff asks.

Amy indicates no. "Sorry."

He pulls the Vehicle Register from his folder and regards it. "It states here that at twelve-oh-five past midnight, Cameron drove the company vehicle to the staff quarters and Warren drove it back at five-thirty the next morning."

She nods.

"And that you drove the company vehicle on Wednesday into town and returned at three-thirty in the afternoon. That means the company vehicle wasn't used between three-thirty and twelve-oh-five on Wednesday. Is that correct?"

"If that's what the register shows and the odometer readings match up, then the vehicle wasn't used between those hours."

"But couldn't someone change the readings on the register?" I ask.

"It's difficult. Everything's written in ink and initialed. If someone tried to white-out the readings, you'd see it." She nods toward the register which Geoff and I study, finding no evidence of tampering.

"What did you do after you dismissed Nellie?" he asks.

"I stayed in the office and tidied up my book work."

"And how did you get back to the staff quarters?" I ask.

"I went back with Cameron."

"But how did you get back in the morning?"

"Normally, I grab a ride with one of the staff from the station, or I call here, and someone runs down and gets me. It sounds tricky, but it usually works out okay."

"And Thursday morning, how did you get to the homestead?"

"Hayley came down and got me."

I lean closer to Geoff. "She's the guide who Gillian organized to take me to Tommy George's and who was with Mimi and me at Jackaroo's Waterhole." He nods his understanding, and from the corner of my eye, I notice Amy edging forward on her chair.

"Is that all, Senior Constable?" she asks.

He gives me a look, and I shrug a reluctant yes. "Thanks, Amy."

When she stands to leave, I ask, "What did you buy in town on Wednesday?" Her face tries to frown, but her brow doesn't crease. *Botox.* That's why she's got the same unemotional, almost plastic expression all the time. Even if she tried to convey emotion, the upper part of her face remains inert.

"Um, more paper serviettes, balloons, some groceries for chef, alcohol, and I had a final meeting with the photographer for tonight."

"Did anyone go with you?" Geoff asks.

"Just me. Too much to do around here to take someone off roster." She shifts her weight from foot to foot, keen to be on her way.

I smile up at her. "Thank you, Amy."

"You can go," Geoff says. "All the best with tonight."

"Thanks. Lots to do." A quick smile, and she's gone.

Geoff reclaims his chair and cocks a brow at me. "What do you make of her?"

"Sharp. Very sharp." My gaze searches the bookcase.

"She certainly is. Quick as a whip, that one."

I angle him a serious look and shake my head. "Not sharp like that."

"What do you mean?" He runs his fingers through his buzz-cut hair.

I find the files on my PC and explain. "I think she's as ETSJ, extroverted, sensing, thinking, and judging. Hard-working, likes to take charge, logical, sets goals, and thrives on achieving them, complies with schedules and procedures."

"That sounds right. But I still don't understand what you mean by sharp?"

Then my eyes spy what I'm looking for. The desk tucked in the corner under the window. "She's like a table with sharp corners. If you run into them, you hurt yourself. They leave a nasty bruise."

Confusion traces lines on his forehead.

I walk to the desk and rub my hands on the corners. "Her corners need rounding."

His face brightens. "You mean like sandpapering the edges until they're smooth."

"Yes. Amy's edges need rounding. They need smoothing."

"Maybe you're right. But I bet she gets the job done."

That I've no doubt, but at what emotional cost to others?

★ ★ ★ ★

THE STRANGEST PART OF THE experience in a doors-off helicopter is take off. Before my brain registers that it's the chopper gradually lifting off the ground, it sends distress signals telling me that the ground is falling away. That planet earth is off-kilter. An odd sensation until my brain and body find equilibrium and recalibrate. A little like the seasickness I'd experienced on the *Silver Galapagos*, but more manageable. By the time the chopper reaches its turning height just above the African mahogany trees, I'm like a kid in a candy store. I can't wait to experience all that the Kimberley has on offer.

Dale executes a slow one-eighty turn and sets course for Amaroo Falls. I'm harnessed in the front next to him with Peter and Kristen behind us. Though Dale doesn't mind having a plus-one on the flight, when Peter discovered me waiting for the same excursion, he took him aside, his displeasure, obvious. On the other hand, Kristen welcomed my inclusion and skillfully calmed him down. With the four of us on board, it's a snug fit in the glass bubble and because there are no doors, the only handhold for me is either the frame of where a door should be or clutching onto the lower, outside of my seat.

With unrelenting force, the wind pummels us, tearing at our clothes, wanting to strip us bare. I don't dare turn my head too far left or right for fear my sunglasses are stolen by its treacherous fingers. When Dale banks the chopper to the left, a searing sweat flashes over every inch of my skin. The angle tilts me dangerously to the side, and I clamp my mouth shut so I don't scream. I know I'm safe because of my full harness seatbelt, but my heart, pounding wildly, begs to differ. The flight, fight, or freeze response is alive and well in my body this morning, literally and metaphorically. The chopper levels and I breathe easier. But every now and then, random gusts buffer the chopper harder. A constant reminder of the precariousness of life, and I cling tighter to mine.

Dale begins his well-rehearsed, though lackluster commentary, which is barely audible through our noise-reducing headsets. It doesn't matter. The landscape speaks for itself. With a wedgetail eagle's vantage point, I gaze down, fascinated by the stark, fractured layers of red earth cleft by the Chamberlain River on its way to join the Pentecost River. Like a prehistoric Lego set, the landscape is strewn with chunks of broken earth, misshapen trees, and unseen wildlife, waiting to be restored into new versions of itself. The spirit of long-ago men on horseback, droving cattle across the unending plains whispers in my ears. I imagine them, hollering and galloping in clouds of choking dust, mustering their cattle to the far north. I'm disappointed that Mimi is missing out on this spectacle, but she preferred to paint with Maria. And while Geoff, Timson, and Hamers continue the routine interviews and search for the murder site and weapon, I'm conducting my own undercover reconnoiter with Dale. All in all, I figure I got the best end of the bargain.

"We'll land here and trek into Amaroo Falls."

The chopper hovers for a few moments like an angry hornet lining up its target before he lands it on a handkerchief-sized piece of ground between towering cliffs with barely a bump.

After alighting the chopper, we throw on our backpacks, and I fetch my walking stick from under the seat. "We've got a twenty-minute hike up to the falls," Dale says. "It'll be a bit tricky at times. If you need help, let me know."

That's enough for me. I'm staying close to him while Peter and Kristen can bring up the rear. In long loping strides, he sets off and my shorter legs move faster to keep up. It's hard work, made even harder since the narrow track means we can't walk abreast. I'm trapped in single file, unable to slow down or converse. Luckily, my walking stick supports not only my balance but my confidence. Though the scenery is spectacular, there's not much time to appreciate it. Huffing out a breath, I put my head down and hike harder.

From behind me, Kristen calls out, "We're definitely seeing rock art today, aren't we, Dale?"

I glance up from under my Akubra to catch his head nodding. *A man of few words.* Based on my limited contact with him, I'm sure he's an ISTJ—introverted, sensing, thinking, and judging. His serious, practical, no-nonsense approach to his job and his utilitarian, orderly persona hints at this personality type. If I'm correct, he's dependable, systematic, and cautious, which is probably why Amy uses him for her events.

I catch my breath and ask, "I thought you were flying in special guests today for Amy?"

He turns his head and calls over his shoulder, "This afternoon, once we get back."

"Who are they? Anyone famous coming in for the event tonight?" I try to keep my enquiry casual, but I'm sure he's cringing at the busybody behind him. *Too bad.*

"Sorry. Don't know." He picks up pace, no doubt in an attempt to shut me up.

By the time I've sweated through my shirt into my backpack, drenched the headband of my Akubra, and soaked my socks, I've lost interest in finding out more about the elusive Dale Baker. Thankfully, he stops, and we shunt up the back of each other like freight train carriages.

He swings around and drops to his haunches, indicating we should do the same. Easy for Kristen and Peter, a little harder for me with my aching knees. Not to be outdone, I bend, and my joints take the flexion in measured stride.

"If you look under this outcrop, you'll see examples of the Aboriginal Period figures that followed the Clawed Hand Period."

We crane our heads further and witness big black eyes staring from expressionless white, mouthless faces. Though faded over thousands of years, the figures wear elaborate headdresses and resemble aliens from another planet.

"Mimi would've loved this."

"It's wonderful," Kristen agrees, then belly-crawls under the ledge to get a closer look.

I glance sideways at Peter whose indifference to the ancient artwork defies belief. He may say he loves his wife, but his actions don't show it.

Unconcerned, Kristen assumes the role of tour guide. "They're Wandjinas and deeply sacred to Mowanjum people." She continues with an enthusiastic dissertation about the oldest sacred painting movement on the planet and how only certain artists are permitted by law to paint Wandjinas. While she finds an avid listener in me, I notice both men seem unenthused, but remain mildly attentive.

"Can I take a photo?" I ask.

She waves a frantic hand. "Oh, no. No photos. It's sacrilegious to the spirits."

"I understand." But I'm sure other tourists wouldn't be as respectful, particularly since Dale doesn't seem to mind.

"If everyone's ready, the falls are just around the next bend." Dale rises and we scramble to our feet.

True to his word, he leads us around the next bend where in front of us, Amaroo Falls rains down into a small, protected waterhole. "It's not as big as some of the other gorge pools, but because it's harder to get here, it's usually empty."

Perfect. We have the picturesque spot to ourselves. Some peace and quiet to reconnect with my subconscious mind after this morning's early interruption is just what I need.

"Why don't you come sit over here?" Kristen cups my elbow and guides me across to the far side of the pool that's shaded from the sun by an overhanging ledge where she helps me struggle my backpack to the ground.

"Are you going for a swim?" I ask her.

"May as well make the most of it."

While she removes her boots and peels off her sweaty hiking gear, I notice Peter lingering, lost in his thoughts, on a low ledge above the waterhole edge. It's easy to imagine the awful pain he went through as a young boy when his parents were murdered. A pain that still touches every part of his life as a man. Not dissimilar to the pain the Torrens must feel over Stephanie's death. When my gaze travels further around the waterhole, I notice Dale's disappeared. Strange that our guide leaves us alone. Perhaps he's taking a toilet break.

When Kristen hits the icy water with a squeal, I decide to remove my boots, roll up my trouser legs and at least test the water to my knees. This waterhole isn't edged by the palm-sized ripple rocks of Emma Gorge, but by a jumble of man-sized boulders and fractured stone blocks. It's a dicey maneuver just to get to the waterhole, but I persist, until sliding down a sloping rock-face on my butt, my feet touch the water. *Freezing.*

"You can step in there. It's not deep," Kristen yells, pointing to my right.

"You sure?" I slide a little lower.

"Yes." She swims toward me.

As my toes find traction on the underwater rocks, the chilly water rises past my ankles to my shins. Venturing out deeper, I totter around under the ledge toward her. My gaze travels upwards to the falls zigzagging down the opposite cliff, and I marvel at the determination of the trees to make their home in the fissures. Overhead, the searing sunlight cuts sharp outlines of the cliff face against the royal blue sky. Birds shriek and . . .

"Lookout."

By the time I snap my head upwards, the rock is careening off the ledge, straight for me. Instinctively, I jump out of its way and slam backwards into the water. The large chunk of sandstone lands with a mighty splash, just missing me.

"*Argh.*" My right ankle wedges under a submerged rock and snaps a sharp quarter-turn. "My ankle." With water lapping under my chin, I lean down, grasp my ankle, and struggle it free. It shrieks in agony. Holding back the tears, I rock back and forth, praying for the pain to pass.

Kristen kneels beside me. "What is it?"

I grit my teeth. "I've twisted my ankle."

"Which one?"

"My right one."

"Can you show me?"

Clutching my leg behind the knee, I raise my foot above the water. Even though the outside of my ankle balloons, my toes still wiggle, but the effort's short-lived because of the pain.

Behind me, I hear splashing and when I swivel my head, I see Dale and Peter rushing toward me.

Kristen goes straight into medical mode. "I think she's sprained her ankle. You'll need to chair-carry her back to shore. There's no way she can put any weight on it."

Dale eyeballs Peter. "You know how to do a chair-carry?"

Peter nods. "Yeah."

Kristen stares at me. "Dale and Peter are going to cross their arms and form a chair. You'll need to shimmy back onto their lower arms and then hold them around their necks. Then, they'll lift you up and get you back to shore. Okay?"

Even though the shrillness of the pain has reduced slightly, an excruciating throbbing is beating a war dance in my joint. "Got it." I bite down and take a steadying inhale. Holding my breath, I push back onto their intertwined arms. With tears in my eyes, I encircle each man's neck and hold on tight. I give a brave nod and swallow hard.

"On three," Peter says. "One, two, three."

The two men stand in one fluid movement, and I'm aloft, wringing wet, but grateful that both men are strong and of similar height and arm lengths.

"Follow me. I'll find the best way back to shore." Kristen steps off in front of us, picking her way through the shallows of the waterhole to find an even exit point over which I can be carried.

Which leaves me to deal with my pain and stupidity while suspended between Dale and Peter. I offer them each a meek smile and receive a mute nod in return. While they focus on the task of getting me safely to shore, a whirlpool of thoughts spin in my mind. Why did I venture down to the water? Why couldn't I just sit there and enjoy the scenery like I normally do? How in god's name am I going to get down a steep, single-file track and back to the chopper? Could this be any worse?

But what upsets me most is the promise I gave Tommy George to find Nellie's killer. With an ankle fast becoming the size of a grapefruit, how am I going to keep my promise? *Stupid. Stupid. Stupid.*

CHAPTER ELEVEN

This isn't how I wanted to spend my time in the Kimberley. Propped in bed with my foot hoisted on a pillow with bags of ice tied to my ankle. On my return from Amaroo Falls, Mimi ran interference with everyone except Geoff, who now reclines on the window seat in my retreat, a smug look on his face.

"I'm impressed." He cocks a brow at my foot. "You hobbled back to the chopper with that?"

He may be impressed, but I'm not. "Thank goodness for Tommy George's walking stick. I couldn't have managed without it." Reaching out toward the old, hand-carved branch resting against my bedside table, I stroke it with as much love as I stroke Berty, my aging cocker spaniel.

Mimi fluffs the pillows behind my back. "Still, that walk didn't help."

I agree. Although Peter, Dale, and Kristen took turns shouldering my weight as best they could on our way back along the narrow track to the chopper, by the time I got there, a bushfire blazed in my ankle. At least the pain worked as a distraction on the return chopper flight, which reminded me of a scene from *Platoon* with the fast-flying Chinook helicopters. Dale certainly flew at breakneck speed to get me back to the homestead in record time. He's a fine pilot. But I much prefer to be back on solid ground, forced incapacity and all.

Mimi squeezes in beside my foot pillow and crosses her legs like a swami. Her previous concerned expression gone, instead replaced by her trademark eagerness. "So . . . do you think it was an accident or was the rock deliberately pushed?"

I'd considered this question off and on over the last couple of hours between the pangs of pain. "I don't know. Before I went into the water, I noticed Dale had disappeared. Maybe he went behind a tree for a toilet break. Who knows? I remember seeing Peter up on a ledge on the other side overlooking the waterhole. Kristen was swimming only a few meters from me when it happened. I guess Dale or Peter would've had time to sneak around to the overhanging ledge above me, find a sizeable boulder, and push it over."

"But what's the motive?" Geoff asks.

Mimi's face lights up. "Nellie's murder. Diana's getting close to finding out who did it and someone wants to silence her." She looks utterly gleeful at the thought of my demise.

"Sounds good in theory, but there are a number of questions to consider," I say.

Her face falls in disappointment, and I hold up a finger one at a time as I explain. "One. Would the killer expose themselves this early in the proceedings? Unlikely." By the twist of his mouth, I notice Geoff's not as convinced as me on this point. "Two. What if the other man saw the incident? He'd be an eye-witness." Geoff nods. "And three. Even if I had been fatally wounded, whoever did it would still have to contend with Senior Constable Mitchell here." He smiles his approval on this point.

Even though the air conditioning is on full blast, I notice beads of sweat trickle down his face. The air con can't rival the blistering sunlight slicing through the window into the alcove where he sits. He relocates to the end of the bed, tugging his damp shirt off his back. "I agree in theory. But my grandmother used to say, if it looks like a duck, walks like a duck and quacks like a duck, it's probably a duck."

Mimi blinks at him. "I don't get it."

He mimics my finger pointing. "One. Rocks don't spring off ledges in the Kimberley. Two. There were two people there who had the strength and the means to throw that rock. Three. Who else could have done it? It looks like a duck, walks like a duck, and quacks like a duck. Therefore, it's a duck. It was no accident." His face splits into a self-satisfied grin.

"So, I'm right." Mimi sounds triumphant. "Either Dale or Peter pushed the rock over the ledge hoping to injure Diana?"

"Or scare her," Geoff interjects. "But which one of them?"

I frown. "But it's very risky."

"If it wasn't either of them, who was it?" He folds his arms, pinning me in a steady stare.

I don't have an answer, but the churning in my gut suggests Geoff's theory isn't as crystal clear as he thinks. "I guess we'll find out when we interview them." But I'm not confident in finding an answer then either.

When we hear the chopper overhead, he glances upwards. "I doubt we'll see much of Dale this afternoon. Amy's got him ferrying people in for the event tonight."

A bag of ice slips off my foot, which Mimi repositions, securing it in place with the towel. When I wince, she casts me a worried look. "How are you going to go tonight?"

"Don't worry about me. As long as I've got a little help, I'll be fine." Though I wonder if my resolve isn't a tad optimistic.

Thump-thump-thump. A fist pounds on the front door. Geoff does the honors, and though Mimi and I can't see who's there, we can hear the conversation.

"Sir, we think we found the murder weapon." A note of excitement tinges Timson's words. He's obviously pleased with their progress.

"Where?"

"Down near the waterhole."

"It's a rock, sir." Hamers takes a calmer approach, her voice is cool and measured. "Looks like the killer struck the victim on the back of the head with it and then tried to throw it into the water. But it caught up in some branches and debris on the bank. It's got blood on it, sir."

"Good work. Did you find any evidence of where the murder actually happened?"

Hamers rushes on. "Not yet, sir. But we're going to comb every inch of the ground in a wider circumference from the picnic table, down to where Nellie's body was found and the surrounding bush. Since there's no sign of blood in the cars and if the rock is the murder weapon, she must have been killed nearby, carried, and then dumped."

"Good," Geoff says. "Hamers, you go back and continue the search. Timson, take the rock back to Kununurra and see if the blood matches Nellie's. Sort out a change of clothes. I want you two on duty here tonight. I'll square it with Gillian Richards. Off you go then."

"Yes, sir." The sound of marching boots fades from the front door.

He reappears. "You heard?"

We nod.

"If the blood matches, we've got ourselves a murder weapon. I suspect the murder site won't be too far away. We'll find it. The savannah bushland may be an inhospitable place and the perfect cover for a murder, but a head wound bleeds fast. Even if the killer wrapped Nellie's head to stem the flow of blood to carry her to where you found, there'll be a trail. There's always a trail."

And if we can't find it, I know someone who can. Tommy George.

★ ★ ★ ★

AFTER HE LEAVES, MIMI FILLS more bags of ice. Tentatively, I unroll the compression bandage Kristin applied and touch the taut skin on my ankle. Having sprained my other ankle in ballet classes decades ago, I know what to expect. Back then, as a pre-teen dancer, I couldn't sit my ballet exam that year because of my injury. I was devastated. But at least the experience taught me how to rehabilitate a sprain as quickly as possible. RICE. Rest, ice, compression, and elevation. Wrapping the bandage even tighter, I pin it into place by the time Mimi returns and balances fresh ice around it.

"Can you get another pillow under my foot please?" While she rummages one from the closet, I call after her. "How did your painting go with Maria this morning."

She rounds the corner, pillow scrunched in her arms, her face pulled tight. "Awful."

"Why? What happened?" After sliding the pillow into place, she stands at the end of the bed where she takes center-stage. I smile, knowing I'm in for one of her dramatic performances.

"I turned up at the Chamberlain Suite as planned. But before I knocked on the door, I heard them having an almighty row."

"About what?"

"The Hadley's Art Prize." She pauses for effect, but I've no idea what she's on about.

I wave an impatient hand at her. "Go on."

"From what I could make out, Maria said she didn't want Jo's help with her art career. She was sick of Jo telling her what to do. And that if she wins the $100,000, she won't need Jo's financial support anymore. Maria really went to town."

So, the worm turns after all. "What did Jo say?"

"Nothing. Not that I could hear. No matter what Maria said, Jo said nothing."

"Then how do you know she was even there?"

"She was there all right. I was standing outside, gob-smacked when the door flew open and Jo stormed out. She gave me a death stare worthy of Darth Vader."

"That's embarrassing." I'd been caught eavesdropping on the *Silver Galapagos*, so I know how awkward it can be.

"Anyway, when I went inside, Maria was balling her eyes out. Poor kid was a mess."

"What else did she say?"

"She took the blame totally. She confessed to being too highly strung, that Jo only ever wanted to help her, that she shouldn't have reacted like that. You know, the usual, 'it's all my fault.'"

"Did she say how it started? What made her so angry?"

"Seems that Jo is the jealous type . . ."

"I don't doubt that. She strikes me as a classic INTJ personality type."

With a roll of her eyes, Mimi begrudgingly acquiesces to my narrative.

Talking out loud as much for myself as for Mimi, I continue, "INTJs are introverted, intuitive, thinking, and judging. They're typically reserved and serious, logical, and efficient. They thrive in a structured environment and are likely to be perfectionists and high achievers, which fits Jo to a tee. They're normally devoted and supportive, so for Maria to reject her like that probably hurt Jo deeply."

"You could be right."

"But did Maria say who Jo was jealous of? Or why?"

"No."

My ankle stops throbbing long enough for me to register the nudge in my gut, but Mimi forges on. "I didn't want to pry. All I know is, Maria and I didn't end up painting. Instead, she stayed in her room, and I did some sketching."

"I wonder what Jo ended up doing?"

She shrugs. "No idea. I didn't see her."

"They're supposed to be going to Miri Miri Falls this afternoon with Dale." I glance at my watch. "Come on. Let's go." I drag my leg off the pillow and scoot to the side of the bed.

"Are you nuts? You can't go anywhere with that."

"Watch me." While my right hand grabs the walking stick, I flap the other in Mimi's direction for help. "There's work to be done, Watson," I joke, winking at her.

She groans. "God, there's no stopping you is there?"

Obviously, a rhetorical question.

★ ★ ★ ★

NAVIGATING THE SLOPE FROM THE retreat to the homestead takes longer than usual and tries my patience. Though hopping is risky, putting any weight on my ankle is still too painful. Gritting my teeth, I distribute myself between Mimi and my stick, and carefully bunny-hop on my good leg, praying I don't take another spill.

I pause, indicating to our right. "The chopper's still here, which means so are Maria and Jo."

After much effort and perspiration, we finally round the veranda corner and prop. The usual silent tranquility of the homestead is shattered by an audible buzz of activity. At least a dozen people juggle tables and chairs onto the timber dais that covers most of the lower lawn. Once the workers align one row of furniture, they wait for Amy's approval before proceeding to the next. In the trees near the pool, young men hang like monkeys as they tie paper lanterns and string fairy lights. They too wait for Amy's expert eye before scrambling to the next branches. A precision operation which the homestead manager directs with authority. She's certainly got an eye for detail. Behind her, the food and beverage staff conduct a stock-take of the piles of cutlery, crockery, and table linen on a trestle table, marking off the items on a register I suspect Gillian has implemented.

Mimi's support slackens with her surprise. "Where did all these people come from?"

I clutch harder at her arm. "I expect Amy seconded them from the station to set up. Help me to that seat out there." I flick my stick toward my chosen chair on the veranda.

When I lower into it, another pair of hands steadies me. "How are you?" Gillian asks.

"I've been better."

"Is there anything I can get for you?"

"A couple of bags of ice would be terrific. Thanks." While she tends to my request and Mimi drags over a chair to support my foot, I notice Dale smoking down at the bottom of the lawn, away from the commotion.

"Good. He's here."

"Who?"

I nod in his direction. "Can you find Geoff and see if he wants to interview him before he takes off to Miri Miri Falls?"

She pouts. "But I just sat down."

"Sorry, but . . ." I lift my leg as my excuse.

"All right. But you owe me. Big time." She stands with exaggerated effort and, with a swing of her arms, marches off to find the Senior Constable. Meanwhile, I keep my eye on Dale, as Sylvia slips into Mimi's vacant chair.

"I'm sorry to hear about your accident. How are you feeling?"

"It's only a sprain. I'm sure I'll be up and about in no time." Though I suspect that's more positive thinking on my part.

Gillian swoops in. "Here's your ice." After tucking the dripping bags around my ankle, she rushes off toward Amy.

"How are you and John holding up with all this business about Nellie?" I give her a sideways glance but return to watching Dale, for fear of losing sight of him.

She lets out a breath. "Senior Constable Mitchell just interviewed us. It brought back so many ugly memories of Stephanie's death."

"And John?"

"He's taking it really hard. More so because of what Peter Pullman called Nellie on Wednesday night. What a terrible thing to say."

I notice the sharp edge of judgment in her tone. As much as she tries to hide it, buried anger infects her heart. "About Wednesday night, after dinner, do you remember anything strange, hearing something different? Anything?"

"No. We told the Senior Constable as much," she says, disappointed.

But my gut tells me differently. Perhaps they noticed something but disregarded it as routine. I've learned that the best cover for a killer is right under the witness' nose. The hard part is for the witness to recall what they previously thought was inconsequential. Convinced of the Torrens' value, I take another direction. "Have you seen Maria or Jo today?"

Sylvia bristles. "Well . . ." Her eyes dart from side to side.

Bingo! I recall Mimi's story and reframe the question. "Perhaps you *heard* them."

She fidgets, moving her chair a little closer. "I wouldn't normally say anything because I know how gossip can destroy people, but" —she looks for my approval which I give with a nod— "every morning I go for a walk down to the lower rock ledge and along the river. Normally, it's deathly quiet, but this morning I heard yelling coming from the Chamberlain Suite. You know how the sound travels out here."

I nod again.

"I didn't mean to eavesdrop, but it was so loud." She proceeds to confirm Mimi's story about Maria's fight with Jo and that she heard only one raised voice. As she speaks, my gaze remains on Dale, who having stubbed out his cigarette and pocketed the stub, lingers by the tree. I wish Mimi would hurry up.

I spare Sylvia a quick glance. "Have you seen Maria or Jo since?"

She shakes her head. "No. To be honest, I'd rather just go back to Melbourne and be done with this place."

I tend to agree. Despite the party atmosphere for tonight's event, there's an uncomfortable energy brewing at the homestead. A hand taps my shoulder, and my gaze meets Mimi smiling above me.

"Sorry to interrupt, but the Senior Constable wants you in the library."

I follow her gaze to see Geoff escorting Dale toward the homestead and breathe a sigh of relief. "Sorry, I've been summoned." I grapple my stick and with the two ladies' help, stand, and get my balance.

Sylvia touches my forearm. "You know we'll cooperate with you and the police with whatever you need."

"Of course."

"I hope you find whoever killed Nellie. She seemed such a lovely girl." Sylvia's gaze drifts past my shoulder, and I suspect she's comparing Nellie's innocence with that of her daughter's.

"I'm sure we will. Please give my regards to John." With Mimi's help, I shuffle a shunting turn.

From over my shoulder, a cold thin voice clips my ear. "Find Nellie's killer, Diana. For all of us."

CHAPTER TWELVE

THOUGH I DISLIKE PEOPLE FUSSING over me, Mimi is a godsend. Within no time, she's got me comfortably ensconced in the library, foot elevated, and laptop in front of me. I'm sure extra flints of blue twinkle in Geoff's eyes as he watches, amused by her whirling dervish routine.

"Do you need anything else? Oh, magnificent one," she jokes with an exaggerated bow.

I giggle. "No. Thanks, Mimi. Go get yourself a stiff drink."

"As you wish. I'll be at the bar, awaiting your next command." With elaborate flourishes of her hand from the top of her head to her waist, she backs out of the library.

"She's quite the eccentric," he says, his eyes still on the door.

"Yes, she is, but she's a lot smarter than most people credit her."

"Eccentrics usually are." Wiping the smile from his face, he turns to me. "You ready to interview Dale?"

"Yes." Though I've already given Geoff a quick update on the characteristics of ISTJ's, I add a précis. "Remember, for Dale, everything is done by the book."

"Got it."

In contrast to Mimi's dynamic energy, Dale enters the room without disturbance. An old Australian expression springs to mind. He's like a long drink of water. Cool and still. When he folds his limbs into the chair, he interlaces his fingers in his lap, probably to occupy them since he can't smoke. He gives me a courteous smile through his mane of red hair and waits to be addressed. After explaining why I'm at the interview, Geoff readies himself to take notes on his tablet. "Can you tell us your movements on Wednesday night after the dessert incident with Nellie and Mr. Pullman?"

"I went to my room."

"And what time was that?"

"A little before ten."

"And which room is that?" Geoff asks while I check the timelines of the other guests' whereabouts on the giant chart on my laptop.

"Livistona."

"Is that the room in the middle of the Garden View rooms along the veranda?" I ask.

"Yes, Paperback and Acacia are to my right . . ."

I whisper to Geoff, "That's where the Torrens and the Wilsons are staying."

"And Cajeput and Ghost Gum are on the other side," Dale finishes.

Geoff leans towards me and whispers, "Timson's staying with me tonight in Ghost Gum and Hamers is in Cajeput."

While Dale tugs at his beard and waits for further questions, there's no tell-tale sign of anxiety in his body language. I wonder about his younger years and if anything happened to make him so collected, almost detached.

Geoff's fingers move easily over the keypad. "Did anyone see you go into your room that night?

Dale lifts and lowers his shoulders in slow motion. "I don't think so. I didn't see anyone."

"After you went to your room, did you come out again?"

"No. I showered and went to bed."

Having watched Dale's love affair with cigarettes, his answer didn't feel right. "Not even for a last cigarette?"

"I had my last smoke before I went to my room. Once I shower, that's it."

Geoff stops typing. "Did you hear anything during the night? People talking or the sound of cars?

"Sorry. All those years flying choppers have affected my hearing. Once I'm asleep, it's hard to wake me. If there'd been anything going on, I probably would've slept through it."

"So, what does wake you?" I ask.

"If someone tries to start my chopper." A fleeting smile lifts his mouth, and I realize his helicopter isn't just his meal-ticket, it's his pride and joy.

Desperate to get him into a real conversation, I try a more personal approach. "How long have you been working for El Kwestro?"

He casts his eyes upwards. "A few years now, off and on."

"Was it Amy who first contracted you?"

"Yes."

Getting him to open up is like trying to shuck an oyster with a hammer. I push on. "How did you and Amy meet?"

"I was flying for the mines, and she asked if I had time to do some flying for her."

"What did you do before you moved up here?" Geoff asks.

"I'm like a lot of the crew around the Kimberley. In the wet season, I go down south, grab work there, and then come back here in the dry. We're working nomads."

Geoff closes the lid of his tablet, folds his arms on the table, and nails Dale in his intense blue gaze. "Can you tell us what happened today at Amaroo Falls?"

"I heard Mrs. Daniels and Mrs. Pullman screaming, and I rushed down to the waterhole."

"But where were you?"

"I was up on the other ledge."

"Can you prove that?"

"No. I was alone, taking a piss."

"Language," Geoff scolds and inclines his head toward me.

"Sorry," Dale says, though I suspect he's not.

"No one saw you then. Did you see anyone? Perhaps Mr. Pullman?"

"Nope. The first I saw of him was back at the waterhole."

"If you were on the other ridge, and you didn't see anyone and no one saw you, who do you think pushed the rock over the ledge?" Impatience grows louder in Geoff's voice.

"Sorry. Can't tell you. All I know is what I did."

Geoff blows out a breath, and I give him a break. "Are you taking Jo and Maria to Miri Miri Falls this afternoon?"

"No. It's been canceled. Amy's got a couple of guests who need to be flown in from town." A glance at his watch. "If there's nothing else, I need to get going." He remains unemotional and shows no urgency in departing. In fact, the only time I've seen Dale behave urgently was flying me back from Amaroo Falls. Unless his chopper's involved, nothing much moves him.

With a wave of his hand, Geoff dismisses him. "That's fine, Dale. If we need anything else, we'll track you down."

After he leaves, Geoff moans, "He's hard work."

"As I said, by the book. But he's a closed book. Gives nothing away. Classic introvert. I suspect the closest thing Dale has to a best friend is his packet of cigarettes."

Geoff drags his hand across his jaw. "Interviewing him is like pulling teeth. Not only is it bloody painful, but it also takes so long to get anything out."

His dry sense of humor and use of Australian slang make me laugh.

"It's true," he says, frustrated. "What's your take on him?"

"Well, aside from his reticence to converse, there's no one who can verify his whereabouts for either Wednesday night or today at the falls."

"Bloody inconvenient in my opinion."

"Or convenient for Dale," I say. "We only have his word."

He scratches his scalp with both hands. "Let's get that Pullman fellow back in here. See what he has to say about your accident."

After he marches off to find him, my sixth sense hints that Peter's story is going to sound a lot like Dale's. Didn't see anything. Doesn't know what happened. Came running when he heard Kristen and me crying out. I shift my ankle to a new position and wince. At least, the throbbing has eased. A good sign.

The sunlight dances in through the library window, cutting its sparkling diamond patterns on the furniture. It teases me, as does the Beatles song, from three days ago when I arrived. Glimpses of words chase each other across my mind. Flowers of yellow and green, a bridge by a fountain, everyone smiles. Nothing makes sense, yet my sixth sense insists I keep my head in the clouds. To take a helicopter view of Nellie's murder. *Of course, I'm too close.* I'm focusing on one thing, the murder, while the other pieces of the puzzle lay discarded on the ground. *Literally.*

★ ★ ★ ★

I STARE GLASSY-EYED INTO the bottom of my empty wine glass. I miss Nellie's deadly kisses, and although other staff have offered to make them for me, I've refused. It'd be a betrayal on my part. No. I'll only have a deadly kiss when I find Nellie's murderer.

Outside the preparations are almost complete, and I can hear Dale's chopper taking off once more. He's done a couple of trips since Geoff and I interviewed him. Beside me, Mimi settles onto the sofa with another glass of white wine for each of us. She clings to hers, while I leave mine to drip onto the coaster on the coffee table.

She takes a quick swig. "What ended up happening with that horrible Peter Pullman?"

"As expected, he denies knowing anything about what happened at Amaroo Falls."

She grunts. "Not surprising."

"And when we asked him where he was between ten and eleven on Wednesday night, he shrugged it off. He said he forgot that he went for a walk around the grounds while Kristen took a bath."

"Bastard." Mimi hisses like a viper. "I bet he snatched poor Nellie and killed her."

I gaze at my glass, shaking my head for many reasons. Overly obvious suspects. Unsubstantiated alibis. And Mimi's waste of a good glass of wine because I just can't drink it. "My head hurts."

"But you've only had one glass of wine," she reminds me.

I snap. "Not from the alcohol. From this case."

She recoils, reminding me of Berty when I chastise him. I scold myself inwardly for being so impatient, while she retreats into silence and sips more wine.

"I'm sorry, Mimi. You've been a wonderful help. But there's something I'm missing here. I can feel it." I pause. "Have you seen Maria or Jo?"

"I haven't seen Maria, but I saw Jo outside watching the set-up for tonight."

"And?"

"I didn't speak to her if that's what you mean. Not after this morning."

"Did she speak with anyone?"

"Some of the staff went over to her." Her eyes drift upward as she recalls what she saw. "And Peter Pullman spoke to her. Not for long, but he handed her something."

"Really?"

"Yes. Whatever it was, was small. It fit into the palm of her hand. She looked at it quickly, then put it in her pocket. He left after that." Her face lifts with pride. Again, reminding me of Berty.

"There's nothing terribly strange about two guests having a chat while watching the staff set up. Maybe he gave her his business card with the offer of helping her invest in shares." Though I intuit that wasn't what happened.

"Sounds feasible," Mimi agrees, but I can tell she's being careful not to say the wrong thing.

"When you finish your wine, can we go back to our rooms and get ready for tonight? I'm afraid, it's going to take me longer than usual."

Setting down her half-full glass, she stands. "Let's go now. Come on."

As I gaze up into her ageless face, tears prick my eyes. I'm struck by her resemblance to my darling Tom. I still miss him. Still miss his guiding touch and strong arms. Being in a couple has its advantages, and now, as Mimi helps me to my feet, I appreciate how she's filled a void in my life. Not just by physically assisting me with my wretched ankle, but emotionally by her patient, quirky personality. I'd be lost without her.

Once on my feet, I hesitate. "Thank you, Watson."

She nods her love and understanding. "Think nothing of it, Holmes."

And like the quintessential pair from 221B Baker Street, we return to our rooms, resolute in our determination to find Nellie's killer.

CHAPTER THIRTEEN

STANDING IN FRONT OF MY closet like a sergeant major, Mimi holds a hanger on high. "Is this the only thing you brought aside from jeans and pants?"

I take my reprimand with fortitude. "I didn't think I'd need anything else. I only threw that in at the last moment."

She eyes the dark brown pencil skirt with disdain. "How on earth are you going to get around in this. You can barely get up and down stairs as it is."

Good point. "But it's all I've got that's suitable for tonight."

"Okay. But don't say I didn't warn you. Come on." She bends down and I step into the trim skirt with my bandaged ankle and then hobble my good leg in while clinging to her shoulder. Once in, she tucks in my cream, long-sleeved blouse, zips me up, and angles me a stern look. "Weren't you getting rid of your dreary, conservative clothes after the cruise?"

Even though she's right, my defenses go up. "I did . . . Well, most of them." I promised myself a brand-new colorful wardrobe, but I'd kept a couple of traditional pieces, just in case. In case of what, I still don't know.

"Thank goodness you have me to act as tasty eye candy." She giggles and executes a spin in her multi-colored, tie-dyed scarf dress, lifting it high to her hips. She finishes with a deep curtsey, her dress billowing over her legs like a parachute.

I mirror her cocky grin. "Yes, you're right. You're fabulous. Now, let's go."

Laughing, we assume our conjoined walking position and make our way to the Kimberley Under the Stars art event.

We reach the great room without incident and, when we step onto the veranda, we both gasp. A fairyland lies before us conjured by a magician. Long trestle tables draped in crisp, white linen, each with a dozen chairs similarly covered in white, run perpendicular to the homestead in nine neat rows.

Romantic candlelight shimmers from clusters of etched-glass candle holders strategically placed on either side of a center row of posy bowls brimming with plump white roses and delicate white orchids. *Where did they get the flowers?* Drifting elegantly in the early evening breeze, dozens of paper lanterns of all shapes and sizes dangle from the trees and pool poles. The white-on-white theme is inspired because the *pièce de résistance* of this masterpiece is nature itself. Across the vast, translucent sky, the sun strips the last blue from the day's canvas before it begins its fiery descent into its sunset palette. For those brief moments, El Kwestro is suspended on a bed of lush green and illuminated by a strange, ethereal glow from the heavens. Aside from Mimi and me, only a few other guests are hovering around sipping champagne, while Michael Bublé croons from the lawn speakers.

"My god. This is beautiful."

I agree. In addition, a colonnade of timber easels each displaying Aboriginal art curves down the lawn to our left. "There must be at least twenty paintings there."

"Let's take a look." She eases me down the stairs and across the lawn. I decline the offer of champagne as I've no free hands, but Mimi accepts. We linger in front of the first few easels, reading the plaques and admiring the art.

"Hello, Diana. How're you feeling?" The voice glides over my shoulder accompanied by a gentle touch.

"Hello, Kristen. I'm feeling better. The throbbing's eased."

"Good to hear. You're lucky you didn't break a leg." She's dressed in a floating emerald green gown, her auburn hair falling naturally to her shoulders. *Sweet girl. Competent nurse.* "Oh, look." She points to a painting to our left. "Wandjinas." She regales us with the story she told this morning at Amaroo Falls, which Mimi delights in hearing for the first time. While they chat, I scan the colonnade and spot Maria a little further along. She's by herself, studying one particular painting in earnest. Leaning forward, she stares hard at the canvas and plaque below, then steps back and frowns. Jo appears carrying two glasses of champagne and hands one to Maria with a peck to her cheek. They've obviously made up. A fond memory of Tom and I comes to mind. Not often, but when we did have a frightful argument, making up was sweet, but tough. It took willingness and forgiveness. Forgetting is harder. I wonder if Jo can forget the hurtful words Maria wielded this morning?

"Don't stay on your feet too long. And plenty of ice." Kristen gives my forearm a soft squeeze and returns to her husband. She slides her hand into the crook of his arm, drawing a smile from his face. Such a handsome young man with such a sad past. Kristen's got her work cut out for herself there.

My gaze drifts back down the colonnade, and I tug Mimi's arm. "Let's join Maria and Jo."

"Do we have to?"

"Don't be silly. Forget about this morning. Come on."

She has no other option but to comply since she's my only means of support.

"Hello, ladies. Isn't this magnificent?" I wave my walking stick in a grand gesture.

"Yes. They've done an outstanding job," Jo says.

Mimi smiles hello but says nothing.

"And the art. What's your opinion, Maria?" I glance at the painting she was scrutinizing before.

"It's really good." Yet she isn't filled with her usual elation when discussing art.

I point my stick to the plaque below the painting. "Do you know this artist?"

"I do." She purses her lips and sips champagne.

Mimi leans forward and reads out loud. "Lucy Numa's Rainbow Bush Art represents the beauty and uniqueness of Australian flora. Her simple strokes and vibrant use of color capture the essence of native art at its best."

Mimi shifts her gaze to Maria. "How does she do it?"

We all listen while Maria explains that the artist uses only one brush, which she never cleans and strokes the paint on in short, fluid movements.

"Have you seen this artist at work?" I ask.

"Yes. I've been to her studio in Victoria. She makes it look so easy. I've tried, but I can't get the hang of it."

Mimi's leans closer to the canvas, her nose almost touching. "I'm going to try when I get back home."

"Good luck. It's harder than it looks. See you later." Maria manages a weak smile and moves off to the next collection of paintings, while Jo scurries in beside her.

Mimi's face is still up close to the canvas. "Amazing."

"Sorry, but can you take to me to our table, please? I need to get my foot up for a while."

"Sure," she says, though I suspect I'm a bit of a bother already.

After I'm settled with a glass of champagne and both legs elevated because of my restrictive skirt, Mimi dashes back to the colonnade. Secure in my seat, I relax and watch the crowd mushroom. Most of the guests face the gorge, marveling at the sunset. The sky is awash in sizzling color as if some giant hand upended bottles of peppery spices from high in the heavens. When I spot Tony and Trish Wilson wandering up from the colonnade, I give them a wave. Trish makes a beeline toward me while Tony detours to the temporary beverage bar on the lawn.

"I heard about your awful accident today. So sorry." Though she looks neat in her navy-blue shift dress, cinched with a white belt which emphasizes her reed-thin waist, she slurs her 'ss' more than a couple of champagnes would account for.

"Thanks. But I'm sure I'll be up and about in no time. How were the Bungles?"

"Unbelievable. You must go before you leave. Worth every cent." She slurps down another mouthful of champagne and continues in her effusive description. While I utter the requisite sounds of interest, my gaze fluctuates between her and the milling crowd behind. Intrigued by Maria's manner in the colonnade, I search her out and spy her talking to Amy.

"Here you go." Tony's drawling voice interrupts my thoughts and his wife's commentary. "More champagne." He hands a glass to Trish, who's already finished the one she arrived with, and he places the other in front of me.

"Thank you," I say, and we salute. "What do you think of the art on display?"

"Damn fine," he says, raising his glass.

I lift a brow at Trish swilling her champagne.

"Agreed. There are several pieces we want to buy for the gallery."

"Such as?"

Before she can reply, Tony jumps in. "We usually have a few of those Rainbow Bush Art paintings in the gallery. They sell well."

"Anything else?"

"Probably, but we'll need a closer look," he says. "Come on, Trish. Let's find our seats." As he ushers her away, she tosses me a wave over her shoulder.

I wonder if I was wrong about them. Maybe he does know she's an alcoholic, and he enables her addiction. But why? Why keep your wife in a state of intoxication? Because he doesn't want her to know. But know what?

"Excuse me."

I glance up into Geoff's searing blue eyes and blink. Instead of his damp police uniform, he's in civvies and looks smart. In dark blue jeans, polished boots, and crisply ironed dark gray shirt, he's shaved and has splashed on a quality aftershave. His appearance makes me smile. During my years in business, the insight I glean about a person the moment they dress in their civvies reveals more than most people imagine. It's then that I see who they truly are. I guess that's why I still have a few conservative pieces in my wardrobe. I don't want to give anyone else that deeper insight into me. In Geoff's case, his neatness confirms my first impression of his systematic methodology before conjecture.

He grabs a nearby chair and sits close beside me. "We found it."

I lean closer so he can keep his voice at a whisper.

"Hamers found the murder site. It's about a hundred meters inland from the picnic table at Jackaroo's Waterhole."

"That means whoever killed Nellie had to have the strength to carry her to where I found her."

He nods. "Or they had an accomplice."

"True."

"Hamers dug up a cloth that smells like it was soaked in some sort of knock-out drug. We'll get that into town tomorrow for testing."

"Did Timson get a match on the blood on the rock yet?"

"We should get that tomorrow too, hopefully."

I glance around. "Are Hamers and Timson here?"

"Getting changed."

"I meant to ask you earlier, why are they here?"

"With all the extra visitors, I figured there's increased opportunity for the homestead guests to catch a ride into town and jump a flight. Hamers and Timson will check everyone when they leave to make sure there are no stowaways.

The genteel atmosphere is shattered by a woman's voice, incensed and loud enough for those of us at this end of the dais to hear. "You're being ridiculous." We swivel around to see Maria, her face flushed with irritation, tugging her hand free of Jo's, and marching off.

"What's all that about?" Geoff asks as we watch Jo chase after her.

"Maybe more of the same." I proceed to tell him about the argument between Maria and Jo that Mimi and Sylvia overheard this morning.

No sooner had I finished than three light taps on the microphone indicate that official proceedings are about to commence. Geoff hurries back to his post on the veranda and Mimi slides in next to me. "Did you see that?" She cocks her head in the direction where Maria and Jo exited.

"I did."

Everyone quietens as Gillian, composed and elegant in her simple, black cocktail dress takes to the lectern. In her welcome, she acknowledges Amy for the fine work she's done in managing the annual event and encourages the buyers and sellers to mingle through the night. "The Kimberley Under the Stars art event is designed to bring people together in the spirit and harmony of the country."

I glance backwards and glimpse Jo, alone, looking dejected and sullen. *Not much harmony there.* Obviously, whatever happened has been so upsetting that Maria is forgoing the event that brought them here in the first place. *Serious stuff.* An unpleasant sensation drops anchor in my stomach, and I recall a line from an old horror movie. *Be afraid. Be very afraid.*

CHAPTER FOURTEEN

THREE HOURS LATER, AND AFTER a delicious three-course meal, Mimi and I sip the last of a robust bottle of red. The biting chill of the outback night can't penetrate our pashminas, and like two 'bugs in a rug', we're wrapped to our chins, relaxing, and enjoying our conversation about nothing in particular. This is the holiday together we envisaged.

Liberally replenished, glasses are never empty which means tongues are loose and voices loud. People wander and mingle, just as Gillian hoped, and I can see a good many business cards and phone numbers being exchanged. A happy buzz revitalizes the homestead after the last day or two of tension, helping me forget my ankle and Nellie's murder for a short while.

Mimi tilts her head and frowns. "What's that?"

"What?" I ask.

"That noise. Can't you hear it?"

I listen, and as if on cue, everyone else quietens. A woman. Screaming. Shrieking. Calling for help.

From the corner of my eye, I see Geoff leap from the veranda and race to the bottom of the lawn. Into his arms flies Jo, hysterical and panting. Not far behind him are Hamers and Timson, guns drawn.

"She dead. She's dead," Jo screams, crumpling limp in Geoff's arms.

"Who's dead?" His voice echoes across the gorge and everything stills.

"Maria," she wails. "She's on the rock ledge under the Chamberlain Suite." As Jo collapses to the ground, Geoff hands her over to Hamers.

"Timson. With me." The two men dash to the rock staircase that leads down to the river and onto the ledge below the Chamberlain Suite.

Blood burns fire red in my veins. "Mimi. Help me up."

When I turn to her, tears well in her eyes. "Maria," she chokes.

"No time for that now." I use a cranky, unsympathetic tone, hoping to galvanize her into action. "Come on. We need to get down there. Help me up."

She shakes the shock from her head and does as instructed. Within moments, we hobble past Hamers who's trying to comfort an inconsolable Jo, and approach the steep rock staircase. "You can't get down there. Not only because of your ankle but that bloody skirt is too damn narrow."

"Take it off."

"What?" she asks, eyes wide as saucers.

"Take the bloody thing off. I've got grandmother knickers on underneath. Trust me, no one's going to be looking at me when there's a dead body to inspect."

Mimi spouts a litany of curses, unzips my skirt, and I climb out of it. My naked legs bristle at the cold snap of air, but I ignore their protest. With my skirt tucked under her arm, Mimi and I slow-step down the sharp slope of stairs. We finally reach the bottom, where she helps cover my lower body with my pashmina. I may be all-go, but I'm not all-show, despite my bravado.

"You wait here," I say. "You don't want to see this. Okay?" She agrees without protest. "Geoff, can I get some help please," I call to him.

Timson rushes over and helps me to the scene. On the cold, hard rock, Maria sprawls on her belly, limbs splayed at odd angles with her neck obviously broken. I look up at the cantilevered balcony of the Chamberlain Suite at least fifteen meters above and then back at Geoff. We hold each other's troubled gaze for a few moments.

He drags a hurried hand across his scalp and his hair stands up as if electrified. "Seems we've got another death."

Holding firm to my pashmina around my waist, I raise my chin. "I think we've got another murder."

Beside me, Timson draws a quick intake of air, while in front of me, the twinkle in Geoff's blue eyes turns dark and soulless.

"Timson, get up there with Hamers and make sure no one leaves. I want everyone in their seats, not wandering around. Keep the staff on the lawn as well. Eyes on everyone."

The young officer falters.

"Now!" Geoff yells.

Timson whips a turn and dashes up the steep steps like a wild brumby, long legs galloping. Geoff steps in beside me, and while I teeter on my one good leg and walking stick, he steadies my balance.

He eyeballs Mimi, wrapped in her pashmina, still sitting on the cold stone stair. "Is she okay?"

"She'll be fine." *But I'll need to get a stiff drink into her soon.* "First impressions?"

He cranes his head back to the Chamberlain Suite balcony above and his eyes travel perpendicular to where Maria lies. "Looks like she fell off the balcony."

"Or she was pushed."

"Possibly. But if someone pushed her, they were taking a helluva risk. What if she didn't break her neck? What if she survived?"

"True. But we both know criminals thrive on high-risk pursuits, otherwise, they wouldn't be in the game in the first place. Particularly violent criminals such as premeditated murderers. They're super optimistic. They regard their murder as a *fait accompli.*"

"Maybe she jumped?"

I slant him an incredulous look. "Like the rock jumped off the ledge at Amaroo Falls?"

"Yeah. Yeah. Right. We better get back. I'll send Hamers down with a blanket to cover the body. Dale will have to fly into town to bring out the medical examiner tonight."

I glance upwards. "We need to get up into that room and take a look before anyone goes in there."

"And we'll need to get statements from everyone."

We stare down at the talented, vibrant artist lying broken on the ledge. Another young woman cut down in her prime. A wave of fatigue washes over me.

Geoff heaves a breath. "It's going to be a bloody long night."

"Yes, but I know of at least one person who'd trade places with you.

★ ★ ★ ★

BY THE TIME GEOFF AND Mimi shuttle me up the dozen, deep stairs, I'm exhausted. My ankle throbs and the rest of my body aches. "You go ahead. Mimi can take it from here." I wave a hand at him, and he sprints off to join Hamers and Timson, mustering everyone into a manageable herd. Mimi steps me back into my skirt and clutching my waist, shoulders my weight as best she can while we shuffle toward the melee.

"Somebody pushed her off the balcony, didn't they?" she says in a brittle whisper.

"I think so. Yes."

"First Nellie and now Maria. Why?"

Slowing to a halt, I gaze skywards, and she follows my lead. Above us, cloudy galaxies of stars swirl on the inky canvas of night. "It's impossible to see every individual star or planet. They're just dots in the sky."

"So?"

"They're connected. Every one of them. A bit like painting by numbers. It's only when it's finished that the real painting is revealed. It's the same here." I meet her gaze. "Nellie and Maria's murders are connected. I'm sure of it. Currently, all we can see is a mass of random, unconnected dots. But like the stars in the sky, there's order at work."

"But how the hell does that help us?"

"Because behind every murder there's order. Our job is to find the clues and arrange them in the correct order. Once we get the right order, we'll find who's orchestrated these deaths."

Her body sags. "But how?"

I try to rally her spirits with a touch of gallows humor. "Don't despair, Watson. We'll find the killer."

"Really?"

"Fear not . . ." I say in an exaggerated English accent. "We'll get to the bottom of it. Come, Watson."

I lean into my walking stick, and in tandem, we hobble up to join the hundred or so disgruntled suspects. Overhead, Dale banks the helicopter into a sharp right-hand turn and heads for town. And though the sound of the chopper rents the still, black night, the incessant voices of Tommy George's ancestors whisper in my head. Nellie's in the sky with diamonds. I can't make sense of it now, but I know somehow, it's a clue.

Hamers races to meet us, her face flushed. "Senior Constable wants you in the library as quickly as you can." Not waiting for a response, she snaps a turn and rushes back to join Timson, who's seated behind a table taking statements. Though overwhelmed, he's taking the guests' abuse in his stride. Hamers slides in next to him, manages a professional smile, and motions the next person forward.

"It'll take them all night to get through that lot," Mimi says.

"The joys of working in a small rural police force. Let's get a move on."

But before we make much distance, Gillian sprints up beside us. "I just heard. My god, what's happening here?"

"Sorry. Can't stop. I have to join the Senior Constable in the library."

"Here let me help." Gillian shoulders my weight on the other side and like a three-legged race, with me unable to help at all, we make better time up the lawn. "First Nellie and now Maria. Who's behind this?"

"That we don't know yet. But we'll find out."

"But why would anyone want to kill Nellie and Maria. It doesn't make sense. The owners are going to have a fit." When we reach the stairs of the veranda, we're all huffing.

Gillian turns to me, and the distress I noticed earlier on her face has multiplied.

"You go back and look after the guests," I say. "Help keep them in line for Hamers and Timson. Leave the rest to us." I flip her a quick smile and Mimi helps me climb the stairs into the great room.

A serrated edge knife of pain stabs my ankle. "I'm going to need more ice."

"I don't doubt that."

Though I'm sure she's as strung out as me, Mimi does her best to support my weight as we cover the last fifty or so meters to the library. We stumble into the room, and Geoff leaps to our aid. Sitting on the sofa, Jo stares into space, dazed and shocked. She's such a tiny thing and with her elfin face, she reminds me of a fragile fairy, not the strong confident woman of only a few hours earlier. While I settle onto my chair with Geoff's assistance, Mimi rushes off and returns soon after with two bags of ice and some towels. Once she snugs them in tight to my ankle, I breathe a sigh of relief. She palms me a couple of pain killers which I gulp down gratefully with a glass of water.

"Do you need anything else?" she whispers before leaving.

"No. Go get yourself a drink and try to relax."

She mocks me with a bitter laugh. "Yeah. Right. Relax." Crinkling her nose in obvious sarcasm, she wheels a turn and leaves. It's the first time I've ever seen Mimi really annoyed. But who could blame her? This isn't the holiday we planned, and I had to get myself enmeshed in this drama. *I've got some serious making up to do there when this is all over.*

Geoff leans into my other side and whispers, "You ready?"

I meet his electrifying gaze. "Yes." My hands reach to open my laptop, and they tremble. I wring them together, try again, and ready myself for a tough interview.

Straightening, he faces Jo and motions to the chair in front of us. "Ms. Arnold, would you come and sit over here please."

Gone is the self-assured demeanor of a successful lawyer. Instead, she appears disoriented with a mantle of shocked disbelief weighing heavily on her shoulders. She takes her seat and draws a deep breath.

"Is there anything we can get for you?" he asks.

"No. I'm fine. Thanks." But she looks anything but fine.

"Can you tell us what happened?"

Her eyes study her hands. "I went to our room to find Maria."

"What time was that?"

"Ten-thirty."

"What time did Maria go to your room?" His question hangs like a broken kite in a tree.

"Earlier. Around seven, seven-fifteen." Her voice is but a whisper.

"Did she come back after then and have dinner?"

Jo shakes her head.

"Why not?"

She finally lifts her gaze, tears welling in her eyes. "Maria got upset at the beginning of the night. She went to the room and never came back."

I glance at Geoff who nods his understanding. This is what we'd heard earlier in the evening when Maria had shouted and stormed off.

Aware that guilt is staking a claim on her, I ask Jo as gently as I can. "What was she upset about?"

"It's all my fault." She crumbles into a ball of distraught emotion and stilted sobbing. Geoff hands her the box of tissues which she accepts, renting them out in clumps. We wait a few moments until she gathers herself.

"How is it your fault?" I ask.

"I said something that upset Maria at the beginning of the night, and she stormed back to the room. I followed her, but no matter how I tried, she wouldn't come out for dinner. I left her there to calm down. When I went back later to see if she'd forgiven me, I couldn't find her anywhere. I walked out onto the back balcony and that's when I saw her, on the ground." More sobbing.

Geoff stops typing. "Did you go down to her?"

"No, I came straight out and cut across the lawn. That's when I ran into you."

I lean forward on the table. "What was it you said that upset her so much?"

She lowers her eyes again. This time in shame. "I loved Maria more than anything. I'd never do anything to hurt her."

"Go on," I press.

She stares at us pitifully. "But I'm terribly jealous. It drives . . . drove Maria mad. We'd have huge rows about it, but I couldn't help myself. Whenever I saw her talking to another woman in private, I'd run stories in my head that Maria was going to leave me for someone else."

"Did Maria ever give you cause to think these things?" I ask.

Her chest heaves a deep sigh. "No. It was my own craziness. And now look what's happened? Because I upset her again, she was alone in her room and someone's come in and pushed her off the balcony."

Geoff jumps in. "You don't think it was an accident then?"

"Of course not. How do you accidentally fall off a balcony that's got a waist-high railing?"

"Perhaps she jumped?"

I watch Jo's grief turn to anger. "Jump? Why on earth would she kill herself? She was on the cusp of a great career."

He goes for broke. "Maybe it was the only way to be free of your jealousy?"

"What? How dare you." She springs from the chair, hands clenched by her side. Not only has she got a short fuse when it comes to jealousy, but also on being asked uncomfortable questions.

I wave my hand up and down. "Please, Jo, sit." She does, but not without a final withering glare at Geoff. "So, if Maria was killed, who do you think did it?"

She shrugs. "I don't know. Everyone here is a stranger. We hadn't met them before we arrived."

"If that's the case, that means you're our prime suspect." Before she has a chance to explode again, Geoff hurries on. "From the perspective of motive, means, and opportunity, you have all three. You went back to the room, had another fight, and pushed her off the balcony in a fit of jealous rage."

"No. No. I didn't do it. I swear. I loved her. Please you have to believe me."

Geoff nails her in a frosty stare. "Well if it wasn't you, who?"

She folds into a quivering mass of tears. If she did murder her lover, she's doing a good job of covering it up. Geoff and I exchange a resigned look and call it quits.

"Please wait here for a few minutes, Miss Arnold. I'll get Constable Hamers to look after you."

When he shuts the door behind him, Jo stares at me, a desperate plea in her eyes. "I didn't kill Maria. You have to believe me."

But there's more to Jo's story than she's letting on, but it'll have to wait until tomorrow. My ankle's killing me.

CHAPTER FIFTEEN

ONCE AGAIN, I FIND MYSELF propped up in bed, ankle iced, and with Mimi performing the role of dutiful nurse. Fortunately, she appears more amenable. No doubt because of the drinks she's imbibed while I was in the library with Geoff interviewing Jo. Overhead, Dale's chopper signals his return with the medical examiner.

"I grabbed us a bottle of vodka and some tonic. Here." She hands me a glass, sans ice or lemon.

"You're an angel." I sip and wince. More vodka than tonic.

"Go on. It'll do you good. Get rid of the pain." She slugs a hefty mouthful and smiles.

I lift my glass and do the same. After the initial shock, my taste buds adjust, and I lean my head back on the pillows. I could sleep for a week. "What a mess."

"Yeah. Some bloody holiday." She swills again.

I glance an apology at her. "I'm sorry. I had no idea any of this would happen. I should've taken your advice and just let the police handle it."

"I'm not mad at you."

I meet her compassionate gaze with a smile. Dear Mimi, she's one of those rare human beings you can count on, no matter the circumstance. Like the younger sister I never had, she inspires me with her bubbly boldness while I try to protect her from the unsavory world lurking on the other side of her rose-colored glasses. A world she's had little experience in.

"To be honest, I'm pleased you're helping them," she says. "The Senior Constable and his side-kicks seem okay, but I think you're the one to piece this together."

I sigh a breath of relief. "Thanks for understanding. Spraining my bloody ankle hasn't helped though. Geoff and the doctor are down there now examining Maria's body, and I'm stuck up here like a recalcitrant child."

She laughs. "That's a pretty good description of you."

"Very funny." I pout, gulp another large mouthful and shudder.

She slides onto the bed beside me propping herself on the spare pillows. "Okay, Sherlock. Where are we up to?"

Pleased that she's forgiven me and has returned to her playful self, I proceed with the business at hand. "We have two murders. Nellie was killed on Wednesday night by what looks like a blow to the back of the head with a rock. Seems she was drugged, killed nearby, and then dumped at Jackaroo's Waterhole where we found her."

Beside me, Mimi finishes her drink in one long swallow. "Go on."

"Then there's Maria who it appears was pushed off the balcony of the Chamberlain Suite tonight. A risky move by the murderer because she could've survived."

"But she didn't."

I pat Mimi's hand. "No, she didn't."

"Do you think it's the same person?"

"It has to be. I can't see how two seemingly unconnected murders that happen in the same location, two days apart, can be committed by two different people."

She nudges me to finish my drink which I follow with a breathy, boozy exhale. Then with empty glasses, she springs off the bed. "Say you're right, and both murders have been committed by the same person. What's the motive?" she shouts over her shoulder.

"I don't know. But whatever it is, it's big." My mind lines up the usual motives for any murder: greed, power, love, sex, jealousy, psychosis, a crime of passion. Like a puzzle, the pieces are scrambled, none of them slotting neatly together. *There's a piece missing.*

Mimi nudges me with another drink and slides back onto the bed. "Well, whatever it is, two people are dead because of it."

I take a tentative sip and am grateful she's made this one weaker. "I've got a hunch there's more than just one motive behind this."

"Maybe your little red book of Tennyson poems will help?"

I catch her mouth curve into a cheeky grin. "You're full of clever ideas, aren't you?"

"Just checking," she replies with a giggle.

"Checking what?"

"That your steel-trap mind is on task because you've only got a couple of days to find a killer before we leave." She raises her glass in a toast and sculls.

I follow her salute and throw back my drink. "Never fear, my dear Watson," I joke. "Motive is easy, execution takes nerve."

At that, we both become silent and stare out through the glass sliding doors into the black void of night. Like me, Mimi probably mulls over the same, obvious question. *Who has the nerve to execute two murders in two days?* Once we work that out, the motive will reveal itself like a card in a magic trick.

★ ★ ★ ★

"HOW DID YOU GET ON with the medical examiner?" I ask Geoff after settling down for breakfast at the private table for five that Amy's set for us away from the other guests. By their ragged expressions and blurry, red eyes, I suspect Hamers and Timson haven't had any sleep. The Senior Constable doesn't look much better. Though his blue eyes still startle, there's a heaviness to his lids, and his clean-shaven face from last night now sports its trademark stubble. I suspect they're envious of the sleep Mimi and I have had, though mine was broken and unrewarding.

"Dr. Morrison reckons Maria broke her neck, probably from the fall. Once he conducts the autopsy, he'll confirm," Geoff says.

"Time of death?"

"Roughly around ten."

I turn to Hamers and Timson. "Can anyone you interviewed confirm seeing Jo between nine-thirty and ten-thirty before she supposedly went to find Maria?"

Before they can answer, Geoff says, "I've already asked them to go through the statements after breakfast and see if they can find anything regarding Ms. Arnold's movements during that time. Generally, the interviews were pretty standard stuff."

Amy and another staff member arrive laden with breakfast for each of us. After they leave, we focus on the mountains of food for a few minutes. Lashings of eggs, bacon, hash browns, and toast ease the tension and quiet the appetites.

I scrape butter on a piece of multi-grain toast, ready to pile my fluffy scrambled eggs on top. "Did you find anything in the Chamberlain Suite last night?"

Geoff answers through a mouthful of eggs and bacon. "Not much. We'll have to wait for the forensics team to turn up."

Hamers glances at her watch. "They should be here soon."

"Whoever was in there with Maria before they killed her, was someone she felt comfortable enough with to let into the room," I say, glancing at each of the police officers, who defer to their boss.

"Seems so." He bites down on a piece of toast.

"And that could be anyone," Timson says. "Homestead staff or any one of the guests. There's no evidence of forced entry. Whoever it was, Ms. Loukas let them in of her own free will." He reaches for another piece of toast and lathers butter on it. For a skinny fellow, he eats like a sumo wrestler.

"And once they got her out onto the balcony, even if she cried out for help, no one would hear her over the music playing," Mimi says.

We nod in agreement. "What happened to Jo?" I ask.

"She stayed with me in Cajeput." Hamers wipes up the last of her eggs and bacon with a half slice of toast before taking a fierce bite.

"That's where she'll stay until we get this business sorted out," Geoff adds, likewise tearing at his toast.

"God, these scrambled eggs are the best." Mimi's face glows as she forks the last fluffy yellow morsel into her mouth.

I agree. Within no time, we finish our meal and the plates are cleared. "What's on the agenda today?" I ask Geoff.

"After Hamers and Timson reference the statements, they'll go back to town, sort out some things and return here this afternoon. I need to follow up on a couple of things and then I thought you and I would continue the interviews."

"Would you mind if I spoke to Jo alone this morning?"

"No. Knock yourself out."

"Please don't say that, even as a joke," Mimi pleads. "It's bad enough her ankle's busted, without wishing a head injury onto her."

Laughter lifts from our table and for an instant, I feel in a holiday mood. "I need to get something from the Chamberlain Suite, if that's okay with you," I ask Geoff. "I'll explain on the way."

"All right then. Let me help." With him on one side and Mimi the other, they foist me to my feet. "How is it?"

"Not nearly as painful." I lean into my walking stick and the three of us make our way to the Chamberlain Suite.

★ ★ ★ ★

BY THE TIME I SETTLE on a sun lounge at the pool to wait for Jo, the decorations and set dressing from the night before have vanished at the hands of busy staff. Nothing remains of the Kimberley Under the Stars event except Maria's dead body, limited clues, and a murderer whose identity I'm no closer to exposing. I close my eyes and breathe in the glorious morning hoping to calm my mind. The serene stillness is punctuated only by nature and for an instant, all seems right with the world. The healing energy of the Kimberley wraps me in its embrace until my eyelids spring open, and I spy Andrew working on the lower pool level. *No time to relax yet.*

I beat my stick on the timber table beside me to get his attention. "Andrew. Up here. Andrew."

He raises his hat, and on recognizing me, saunters up the lawn. "Good morning, Diana. How're you doing?" He glances at my iced ankle.

"Much better thank you. Please sit for a moment." I tap the nearby chair with my stick, thinking how much I remind myself of an insufferable old woman who commands everyone to do her bidding. "How are you coping?"

He rolls his Akubra hat around in his hands. "Not real good. I still can't believe Nellie's dead."

I murmur my sympathy. "Have you heard when the funeral's going to be?"

"No. Until Nellie's grandfather is allowed to claim her body, nothing can be arranged." He lapses into silence.

"Have you seen Tommy George?"

"Nope. No one has. You?" He angles me a hopeful stare.

"No. And this bloody ankle means I can't walk out to see him."

He mutters something and drops his gaze once more to his hat.

"Andrew . . ." —I wait for him to look at me and for his fidgeting to stop— "Senior Constable Mitchell will be speaking with you today about Nellie's death and Maria's."

He blinks. "But I don't know anything, about either of them."

"Perhaps you don't." I pause for effect. "But a word of advice, I suggest you tell him everything you do know." I lift a brow at him and notice a thin sweat gloss his temples.

"I don't know what you mean." His voice tightens.

"You need to tell the truth, Andrew. All the truth. Understand?"

Rising to his feet, he shoves his hat on his head. "I've got to get back to work, Mrs. Daniels. I'll see you later." Without missing a beat, he pivots and marches back to the lower level lawn.

That young man is going to do himself more harm than good if he's not careful. I watch him bundle up his tools and head for the grounds and maintenance area. He disappears around the corner but not before I see him hail someone. By the time I struggle to my feet, he's gone and whoever he waved to has also disappeared. I wonder if it was Andrew who Tony was arguing with on Thursday afternoon in the grounds and maintenance area.

"Good morning, Diana. Mimi said you wanted to see me." Jo startles me, but not nearly as much as the wretched expression on her face. Another person who's aged ten years in a day. Yet behind the sadness in her eyes, there lies a steely focus.

"Good morning, Jo. Won't you sit with me?" She nods and slips onto the lounge opposite. "How are you holding up," I ask.

She stiffens and squares her shoulders. "Actually, I'm good."

Her response surprises me. "Really?"

"Whoever killed Maria has got to be here." She lifts her arm towards the homestead. "Which means the murderer is sitting right under our noses."

I nod.

"I'm a bloody good forensic lawyer, so I should be able to ferret out whoever did it and expose them." Her jaw tenses, matching the wiry muscles twitching in her arms. She means business, which means she's in danger.

I decide not to pursue the topic. "Look what I was able to get from your room." I reach beside me and place a lacquered black box on the table between us.

Her demeanor softens. "My chess set."

"I hope you don't mind my getting it from your room. I thought we might have a game together. Take our mind off things for a while." I open and empty the box while Jo murmurs her willingness to play.

She chooses black, and while we arrange our pieces on the board, cheeky white-feathered corellas chatter overhead, swinging upside down from the branches. Like an excited audience, they squawk their impatience for us to start. Their noisy interruption lightens the mood, steering our conversation from murder to the world's most strategic game. We ease into the contest with each of us assessing the other's skill. Chess was Tom's favorite game, and he was quite the champion at it. So, I had a good teacher. Within a few moves, I realize Jo's also a proficient player, which doesn't surprise me. As an INTJ personality type, she's a mastermind at strategic, logical thinking. But my intention isn't to win, it's to find out information.

I move one of my pawns forward. "Did you get much sleep last night?"

"Not really. What with everything that happened and then having to share with Officer Hamers, I doubt I got more than a couple of hours sleep." She swipes my pawn with one of hers.

"Maybe tonight will be better. At least, you'll have the room to yourself." My hand hovers over my knight before I move it forward and across. We fall into focused silence while I watch her concentration zero in on the game. Her ability to block out all distractions is advantageous in chess, but that level of perfectionism would be hard to live with, I suspect. No wonder Maria argued with her. I purposely make a couple of simple, but not too obvious, wrong moves, and watch Jo's expression brighten with the expectation of winning. When I think she's sufficiently absorbed in the game, I make my real move. "Who were you jealous of here at the homestead?"

Jo's hand freezes over her bishop. Our eyes meet and for an instant, I see them flicker with irritation before she remembers I'm working with the police. Her shoulders slump. "The manager."

"Gillian?"

"No. Amy." She pushes back from the board game, her focus broken.

"Why were you jealous of Amy?" From my perspective, even if Amy were gay, she wouldn't pose a threat to an attractive woman like Jo.

She curls her lip. "I know. I'm an idiot. That's what Maria said when I confronted her." The flash of anger passes as quickly as it came.

"But there must have been something that happened between Maria and Amy that brought up your jealousy. What was it?"

She shrugs. "Little things. I'd catch Maria watching Amy whenever she was around. Sometimes she was so fascinated, she didn't even hear me if I spoke to her. But Maria denied being attracted to her. Said there was nothing to be jealous about."

"And last night?"

"I saw the two of them, having a private conversation down on the lawn, not far from the colonnade."

I saw them too.

"When I asked Maria about it, she said she'd tell me later. But I couldn't leave it alone, could I." She snorted. "No. I harped on about it until Maria yelled at me and stormed back to the room and wouldn't come out no matter how much I apologized. So, I left. I left her there all by herself until some bastard came in and killed her." The emotional dam broke. Jo cried tears of grief and guilt, while I did my best to comfort her. She didn't kill Maria, I was sure of it, but her possessive nature gave the murderer the opportunity to find Maria alone. If their argument hadn't been so public and if Jo hadn't returned to the function by herself, Maria might still be alive. Though my hunches told me both murders were connected, both circumstances indicated that our killer was opportunistic. That they watched everything and took advantage of the situation at hand.

Jo drags her hand across her nose. "I'm sorry Diana, but if I hadn't been so bloody jealous, Maria would still be alive."

More than likely. "Don't blame yourself. Whoever killed her may have found another opportunity."

"But I still don't understand why?"

"I'm not sure either." I glance at the chessboard. "But if I'm not mistaken, there's a strategy at play here that links Maria and Nellie."

She digs into her jeans pocket, then hands me a small, red velvet box. "I was going to ask Maria to marry me."

I open the box and spy a dainty pink diamond ring tucked in its plush interior. "Oh, I'm so sorry, Jo."

She gives a sad nod. "Me too."

"It's such a pretty ring. Did you bring it all the way from Melbourne with you?"

"No. It was spur of the moment actually. I bought it from Peter Pullman, here, at the homestead."

My brows shoot upward involuntarily; my poker-face gone. "Go on."

"Wednesday night, before dinner, when we were gathered in the great room, I got talking to Peter about the Argyle diamond mine not far from here. I told him how I've always wanted to give Maria a pink Argyle diamond ring, and he said he had one." She nodded toward the box, which I handed back to her.

"Really?"

"Peter said he buys the raw diamonds from the mine manager and then gets them set into different pieces for his Perth stockbroking clients at one of the jewelers in Darwin."

"But how did he happen to have this ring with him on his honeymoon?"

"He picked it up in Darwin before they drove here. When he called his client to say he'd bring it back with him, the client said his girlfriend just broke up with him, and he didn't need the ring anymore."

"So, he offered it to you?"

She nods sadly. "A lot of good it's done me."

My intuition somersaults in my stomach. "If you'll forgive me, but that seems impetuous of you, especially since you're a lawyer, to buy a diamond ring from someone you've only just met."

"You're right. I don't know what came over me. But when I saw it, I knew I had to have it for Maria." A breathy sigh shudders from her mouth. "Love makes you do strange things." She gazes at the glittering gem, a wistful tone in her voice.

"But how do you know it's an Argyle diamond?"

"Pete gave me the valuation certificate from his Darwin jeweler. It's a pink Argyle all right."

It's my turn to nod, not so much in agreement but in consideration. "Do you mind if I take a look at the certificate?"

"Not at all. It's in the Chamberlain Suite, but I can't go in there."

"That's okay. The Senior Constable and I will get it. Do you mind if the police hold onto the ring as well? Just for a few days."

She hesitates, her expression grim. "Okay." She pushes the box toward me with a reluctant hand, eyes glinting with fresh tears.

I suspect it'll take Jo some time to come to terms with Maria's death. More so because of her underlying guilt in needling Maria and leaving her alone as unsuspecting prey for a killer.

When her gaze catches mine, I glance at the chessboard. "Would you like to finish the game?"

She shrugs. "Sure. Why not."

We revert to our pieces on the checkered board. Unlike other games, chess has no hidden information. Each player can see the other's pieces. It's a game about engineering opportunities to take advantage of your opponent by placing their king under the inescapable threat of checkmate. In many ways, I feel like the king, trying to calculate other people's moves before I'm caught in checkmate. But Peter Pullman's connection to the Argyle diamond mine and the coincidence of the diamond ring scuttles me. *Murder and jewelry.* I recall the mayhem onboard the *Silver Galapagos* a year ago with a quiet moan. *Not again.*

CHAPTER SIXTEEN

G EOFF LIFTS THE CRIME SCENE tape stretched across the front of the Chamberlain Suite, and Mimi helps me hobble under. We wait while he rummages in the closet and returns waving a laminated piece of paper in the air. "Here it is."

He gives a long whistle while we read the diamond ring evaluation. "Bloody expensive."

"Pink Argyle diamonds are," I say. "They're the rarest in the world and with the mine shutting down shortly, it makes them even more valuable."

"Still . . ." He stares bug-eyed at the figure.

He's right though. Jo ended up with very little change from her fifty-thousand-dollar investment.

"Big money to pay a stranger for an engagement ring."

"I agree. But with Jo's jealousy alienating Maria, she needed a grand gesture to win her back. INTJs can be deliberate and calculated in their approach."

"Hell. If I was Maria, I would've said yes." He snorts a small laugh.

"Spoken like a true mercenary," I tease, tutting loudly.

I glance around for Mimi, but she's out onto the balcony, looking over the railing at the spot where we found Maria's body.

I limp in beside her.

"I still can't believe it." Her voice has a sad lilt to it. "I was sketching with her only a couple of days ago. Such a waste."

"Murder usually is."

She leans over a little more. "It's a long way down."

Geoff moves in on her other side. "Over fifteen meters."

"How do you think it happened?" I ask him.

"The murderer got her out here on some pretext and then when she was off-guard, he pushed her over the railing."

"You said, he."

"It'd take some strength to push someone over the railing, even someone as light as Maria. I reckon it was a man."

"But if the woman was strong enough, and she lulled Maria into an undefended state, a woman could do it," I press my point.

Geoff scratches his stubbled chin and nods. "I guess so."

"Either way, it takes some guts to make that sort of move, surely?" Mimi looks at us in turn, and we both agree.

Snippets of Tommy George's story of Brolga and the evil spirit, Waiwera filter from my memory while the rock-art Wandjinas white faces merge with Nellie's in the distant sky across the gorge. *In the sky with diamonds.* I squeeze the handhold of my walking stick, hard. Not so much for balance but out of surprise. Above the ancient landscape, I sense past and present collide in a kaleidoscope of color, endlessly swirling around one central point. As I concentrate on the images that only I can see, my gaze keeps being drawn to the center. The center of the web, the center of the matrix, the center of . . .

"Diana, are you all right?" Mimi's concern shatters my focus.

I shake the images from my mind. "Never better. Come on. We've got interviews yet to do." Pivoting on my left foot, I step off at a solid limp, pleased my ankle is improving. "Geoff, I've got an idea, but I'm going to need your police resources."

"Sure. Whatever you need." He steps in next to me and the three of us make for the door. When he lifts the tape once more, I glance back, my gaze fixed on the trees on the far ridge. A line from Tennyson's *Charge of the Light Brigade* urges me to follow my hunch, no matter how obscure it seems. And I realize, *mine is not to question why, mine is to do or die.*

★ ★ ★ ★

"WHAT WAS ALL THAT ABOUT?" Mimi asks while we sit on one of the sofas in the great room, waiting for our coffees.

Though the room's deserted except for us, I keep my voice low. "Don't worry about that. I need you to be careful."

Her brows pucker. "What do you mean?"

"Think about it . . ."

I break off until the waiter delivers our coffee and leaves. "Whoever killed Nellie and Maria thought they knew something, had said something, or were about to expose some secret that would implicate them in some way."

She spoons a dollop of foam into her mouth. "I guess so."

"Of course, it's so." Unlike Mimi, I stir my coffee, swirling the foam into a whirlpool.

"But how do you know?" Another dollop goes in.

"I don't know how I know. I just do."

"Your hunches." Though she nods sagely, reminding me of an ancient, wise man, her tone mocks me. She finally lowers her spoon and sips.

My patience wears thin. "Call it what you want." I hit the spoon to my saucer a little too hard, and she jumps. "Mimi, listen to me. You're probably the only person, aside from Jo, who's spent time alone with Maria when you were sketching. The murderer might think she told you something."

"Like what?"

"I don't know. Did Maria talk to you about anyone here at the homestead?"

"Not that I remember."

"Are you sure?" I sip my coffee while Mimi searches her memories.

She huffs out a breath. "Nothing. All we talked about was the light, the sketching, our painting. That sort of thing. We didn't talk about anyone."

"But the murderer doesn't know that," I remind her.

Mimi's cup hovers near her lips. "You mean . . ."

"I mean you might be the next target."

The color drains from her face as she lowers her cup and saucer onto the coffee table. The truth of how dangerous this situation has become especially for her since Maria's death has finally sunk in. I didn't want to frighten Mimi, but she needs to keep alert from now on. From over her shoulder, I notice Trish marching down the veranda in our direction. Her jaw is set tight to match her pursed lips, and her arms swing by her sides. Eyes lowered, she sweeps into the great room and heads straight for the fridges. Grabbing a bottle of white wine, she upturns half of it into a large wine glass and slurps down a solid mouthful. I glance at my watch. Ten-thirty. At this rate, she'll be smashed before lunch. Following my stare, Mimi casts a quick glance over her shoulder.

There's only one thing to do. Be proactive. "Good morning, Trish. Beautiful day isn't it." I nudge Mimi to match my sunny smile, and I suspect we look like a pair of grinning cats who've cornered the mouse eating the cheese.

Poor Trish nearly chokes on her second gulp of wine. "Morning," she splutters and walks over, more subdued than her frosty entrance.

"Please join us."

Still with the wine bottle in one hand and glass in the other, she slips onto the opposite sofa, depositing her liquid friends on the table. "You'll have to excuse me," she says, glancing at the alcohol. "I've had a bitch of a morning."

Haven't we all.

Beside me, Mimi takes the lead. "Would you like to talk about it?"

Obviously delighted to download, Trish leans forward. "Seriously, men can be such idiots."

We nod in sympathetic silence while Trish swallows another hefty swig.

"I mean, I tried to tell Tony to go steady on buying all this Aboriginal art. But no . . ." she says, waving her glass around. "He's in there now with Amy" —she cocks her head towards the office— "haggling over some of the pieces from last night." Another swallow and the glass is empty. Without missing a beat, she upends the bottle into her glass and starts over again.

Her alcoholic fog is thickening, so I tread carefully. "But why's he negotiating with Amy?"

"She acts as an intermediary with the sellers and the buyers of some of the art." More wine.

"Really?"

"Yes. We buy all our Aboriginal art through her. Tony says it's easier than going directly to the artists. I don't know why though." She mutters a curse and slurps.

"Does Gillian know about this side business?"

"I think so. You'll have to ask her." Another gulp.

I intend to. "I thought Tony said your gallery did well selling the Aboriginal art?"

She blinks at me as if startled. "We do. But . . ."

"But what?" I press gently.

"Nothing really. It's just that every time I bring it up, he gets so goddamn angry. Tells me to let him do the business with Amy. If I didn't know better, I'd say he was having an affair with her." She uplifts the glass, and we watch her swallow the last of it.

How much abuse can a human liver take? "I'm sure Tony isn't having an affair with Amy. Don't go worrying yourself over it. Tony strikes me as a man who likes to do things his way."

She barks a bitter laugh and salutes her empty glass. "You're right there."

"What's his previous track record with his art purchases? Have they sold well in the gallery?"

Trish lowers her glass to the table. "I guess. He's usually pretty good. Sorry. I shouldn't have said all those things. I don't know what came over me." She glances up at us, shamefaced.

"No need to apologize. The green-eyed monster bites everyone from time to time."

She reclines on the sofa, obviously no longer interested in drowning her emotions. "I just wish he knew I was alive. That's all."

"Every woman needs a little tenderness. We understand."

My heart goes out to her. She's probably an ISFP. A gentle, cheerful soul with a strong sense of creating aesthetically pleasing surroundings. Hence her love of art and dependence on alcohol to cope with her unfulfilling life. Being married to Tony, who's on the bombastic end of the ENTJ personality, would be difficult, to say the least. That he's in the office with Amy, another ENTJ, hammering out a sales deal is ironic. It's not a negotiation Trish could handle, and I suspect Tony's met his match in the efficacious homestead manager.

★ ★ ★ ★

"HOW DID THE INTERVIEW WITH Andrew go?" I ask Geoff as we review our notes-to-date in the library before lunch.

"Seems a personable young man. Pretty cut up about his girlfriend's death. I doubt he had anything to do with it. What do you think?"

"I tend to agree." I shift in the chair, trying to find a comfortable position for my ankle. "Did he say anything about coming back to the homestead on Thursday after Gillian drove him to the staff quarters?"

"No. Why? What happened?"

I recount the story of Mimi and I seeing Andrew fossicking around in the bower bird's nest, pocketing something, and then running off. "Before his interview with you today, I suggested he tell you everything. I was hoping he would."

Geoff gives a slow shake of his head. "Nope. He didn't mention anything about it. Do you think it's related to the murders or your accident?" He gestures air-quotes on the last word.

"At the moment, I think everything's related to everything." I rake my fingers through my hair and massage my scalp hard, wishing it would stimulate my little gray cells.

Geoff glances at his watch. "We've got time to interview Tony and Trish Wilson if you're up to it?"

"Sure. There are a few questions I'd like to ask Tony. Let's start with him. I think Trish needs a little time to sober up."

After Geoff sends Hamers off to find Tony, I explain our recent encounter this morning with Trish. "The poor woman is married to a boor."

He shrugs. "There's always divorce."

"Out of the question for Trish. She's the ultimate peacekeeper. Peace at any price, including sacrificing her mental, emotional, and physical health."

"Do these types ever turn? You know, go off the edge, so to speak."

"It's rare, but anything's possible if the motivation is strong enough." My mind wanders to Trish's jealous outburst and Tony's straying eye. I noticed on more than one occasion his furtive glances at Sylvia, Maria, and Nellie. And even Amy when she strutted past him in her tight skirt and flirty ponytail. He mistakenly believes himself to be a bit of a lady killer. I wonder if Trish's jealously is misplaced or has he betrayed her before? Women have been known to remove their competition with vicious gossip and character assassination. What's to say Trish isn't capable of taking it one step further.

Hamers pokes her head around the door. "Excuse me, sir, I've got Mr. Wilson here for you?"

Tony steamrolls through the door, his face flushed and creased with a ferocious frown. "Listen here. I know two women have been killed and you're just doing your job" — he sneers— "but couldn't your officer have waited until I finished my business meeting. We were right in the middle of a delicate negotiation." He drags the chair further back from us and drops into it like a sack of cement.

"A police investigation outranks your meeting, Mr. Wilson. You can return to what you were doing whereas our victims can't." Geoff lands the last word with a full stop, and Tony backs off. "Now, firstly, tell us what you did after the incident on Wednesday night when Nellie dropped the dessert on Mr. Pullman's lap."

"My wife and I went into the great room and had a nightcap."

"Was anyone else there with you?" Geoff asks.

"No. Just us. I guess everyone else was too upset."

"Peter's racist outburst didn't upset you?" I ask.

"Listen. The guy's a jerk in my opinion, but I wasn't going to let a silly incident like that spoil my night." He crosses his leg and folds his arms.

"Do you know what time you and your wife went to your room?" Geoff glances at his notes. "You're in Paperback, I see. The one next to the Chamberlain Suite where Maria and Jo were."

"Yeah. The Torrens are on the other side of us. I think Trish and I went back just after ten. Maybe ten-fifteen."

I lean forward. "Did you see anyone or hear anything unusual."

Tony glances up to his left, searching for the memory, and then shakes his head. "No. No one. Nobody around at all."

"But did you hear anything? Geoff presses.

Tony's hackles rise. "Listen, a lot's happened since then. I can't remember."

"Who were you arguing with on Thursday afternoon?" I pause for effect, but he doesn't know where I'm heading. "In the grounds and maintenance area."

His eyes widen. "How did you see that? Were you spying on me?"

"Answer Diana's question please, Mr. Wilson," Geoff says with a direct look.

Tony huffs out an impatient breath. "If you must know it was Amy."

"And what was the argument over?" Geoff asks.

"Aboriginal art."

Geoff and I exchange a puzzled glance, but Tony needs no encouragement to explain. "The last shipment Amy sent me was missing a couple of pieces I'd bought. By substituting a couple of other canvasses, she thought she could swindle me.

When I told her that wasn't on, she refused to refund my money. That's not the way we do business, and I told her so." His nod is accompanied by a growl.

"But why in the grounds and maintenance area," I ask.

"Because she marched off when I was trying to get my money back."

Geoff leans forward. "And you followed her?"

"Of course, I followed her. She stole my money."

"And what were you going to do if she kept refusing?"

"Moot point. She finally agreed to make it right and refund my money on this purchase and shipment. That's what we were discussing just now when your officer interrupted." He scowls at Geoff.

"I'm sure you'll get what you deserve when you return to your negotiation." Geoff smirks his sarcasm, and neither Tony nor I miss his inference.

"Listen here . . ."

Not wanting another escalation, I flap my hands in the air. "Just to recap, you didn't hear or see anything on Wednesday night. But what about last night? Did you go to your room during dinner?

"Yeah. I used the toilet a couple of times."

"Can you tell us what times?" Geoff asks.

More huffing. "For god's sake man. I don't keep a timesheet every time I take a piss." He glances at me to see if I'm offended.

I'm not. "Was it before or after you and Trish spoke with me at the table?"

With less bluster, he replies, "After, but before dinner."

"And the other time?"

"After dessert, I think."

I calculate the sequence of events in my head. The argument between Maria and Jo was around seven-fifteen. Gillian did her speech at seven-thirty and the three-course dinner finished at about ten. And Jo came screaming up the lawn at ten-thirty. "Was anyone on the veranda or hanging around your room or the Chamberlain Suite when you were there?"

Tony scratches his neck. "To be honest, there were people milling about everywhere."

"But anyone you particularly noticed or knew?"

He purses his lips and shakes his head. "Sorry, can't help you."

"Very well, Mr. Wilson. If you do think of anything please let us know. You can return to your meeting." Geoff nods towards the door.

"Hang on. We're booked on a flight out of here on Monday—"

"I'm sorry, Mr. Wilson, but no one will be leaving the homestead until I say so."

Tony launches from the chair, his face red with rage. "Are you kidding me?"

"No, I'm not. At this stage, we have two suspected murders and the likely killer is here at the homestead. And until we find that person, everyone will be staying put."

Tony opens his mouth to object again, but thinks better of it, turns on his heel, and marches from the library without another word.

"He's bloody full of himself," Geoff says. "No wonder his wife drinks."

"Yes. He'd be a nightmare to live with. Still, the thing with Amy and the artwork is strange."

Geoff returns his focus to his tablet. "We'll have to get her in again and dig deeper."

"When are you telling everyone about having to stay?" Though Mimi and I aren't booked to depart until Wednesday morning, the uneasy sensation in my stomach tells me it might be wishful thinking. *She's going to be furious if we have to stay.*

"Hamers and Timson are rounding up the guests now." He glances at his watch. "They should all be in the great room."

"And Gillian?"

"She's got everything under control."

Of course, she has. Nine angry guests' faces flash before my mind's eye. Each one of them horrified at being forced to stay at the homestead until the killer is found. And none more so, than Mimi. Like a dormant volcano, long overdue to erupt, El Kwestro is on the brink of explosion.

CHAPTER SEVENTEEN

SQUEEZING IN NEXT TO MIMI, I rest my stick on the side of the sofa while keeping my eyes fixed on Geoff at the front of the group. Across from us, John and Sylvia Torrens wear the unmistakable expression of a couple trapped in their worst nightmare. They came away to escape the residual horror of their daughter's suicide only to end up in another tragedy, times two. Peter and Kristen Pullman stand at the far end of the fireplace mantle, where he cuts a dashing, disinterested figure and she casts sympathetic glances at the other guests. Tony simmers in the corner, ready to boil over, while Trish struggles to keep her eyes open from the lingering effect of her mid-morning wine-fest. At the bar, Dale stands rigid and tall, the fingers of his right hand wrapped around his trusty packet of cigarettes. He's edgy as if he can't wait to flee outside for a rendezvous with his cancerous mistress. Professional, yet exceedingly tired-looking, Hamers and Timson stand close to Geoff, awaiting his next command. While on his other side, Amy and Gillian line-up shoulder to shoulder like soldiers, ready for the onslaught of verbal attacks which will be fired once Geoff delivers his bad news.

"What's going on?" Mimi whispers in my ear.

I don't dare look at her. "The Senior Constable's got some news." I purposely use Geoff's official title to divorce myself from the message. Beside me, I sense Mimi frown, but I offer no more.

"Thank you, everyone. I wanted to give you all an update on where we are with the unfortunate events that have transpired here at the homestead since Wednesday." He pauses, but no one speaks. "The evidence we've collected regarding Miss Nellie Walker's death indicates she died under suspicious circumstances. As such we're treating her case as a possible homicide."

An audible gasp rises in the room, matching the rising temperature outside. It's close to noon, and as I glance at everyone's faces to gauge their response to Geoff's homicide announcement, they're dotted with perspiration. Mimi squeezes my leg, and I shoot her a conciliatory glance.

"In the matter of Maria Loukas's death last night, we're still waiting on the medical examiner's findings. However, until we receive his report, we're treating her fall as suspicious."

This time, a palpable murmur goes up, and Mimi whispers, "My god. This is really happening."

I meet her troubled gaze. "Wait for it."

"Therefore, based on the current circumstances, no one will leave the homestead without my express permission."

Alarmed voices rise in a groundswell of panic.

"And when will that be?" Peter's petulance stokes the unrest.

"Not any time soon," Tony says, loud and clear.

Geoff slants him a withering stare before shooting one at Peter. "At this stage, no one will leave the homestead until further notice."

Pandemonium breaks out. Hamers, Timson, Amy, and Gillian flex and strain taller as the barrage begins.

"What do you mean?" Sylvia almost shrieks. "John is sick. We need to go home." She clings to her ashen-faced husband's arm.

"Poor man looks like he's going to faint," I murmur.

"Forget about him," Mimi hisses through gritted teeth. "How long are we going to be stuck here?"

Time for serious damage control. "I'm sure we'll find whoever is behind this really soon." With a lame smile, I pat Mimi's thigh trying to reassure her, even though my own confidence lags.

Gillian saves me. "Everyone, please. I know this is terribly inconvenient—"

"That's an understatement," Tony barks.

She ignores him and rushes on. "You won't be charged for any further nights other than your original booking. However, you may need to rebook your outward flights. If there is anything we can do to make this situation more comfortable, Amy and I are here to help."

The disgruntled chorus escalates.

"And what about my Nellie?" The lone voice slices the commotion like a hot knife through butter. Claiming the great room with Andrew a step behind him, Tommy George strides forward, his presence of authority at odds with his rag-a-muffin clothes.

Everyone falls into a tense hush, their eyes on the old man who comes to a stop in front of the Senior Constable.

"I'm sorry for your loss." Geoff bows his head in respect.

Tommy George casts him an accusatory stare. "Perhaps you are. Perhaps you're not. But what are you doing about finding the evil spirit that killed my Nellie?"

Reaching for my stick, I whisper in Mimi's ear. "Come on. Tommy George needs to get his questions answered in private. Help me up."

While Gillian and Amy fend off the remonstrations of Tony and Peter, we sidle in next to Geoff, who I notice breathes a sigh of relief.

When Tommy George spies the walking stick in my hand, he smiles. "See. I knew you would need it. How is your ankle?"

I frown and glance at Andrew who shrugs at my unasked question of how Tommy George knew about my ankle. "Much better. Thank you."

Geoff steps aside. "Why don't we go where we can talk in private."

Tommy George motions for me to go first and after Geoff whispers some instructions to his officers, the five of us head to the library in silence.

After we're seated, Geoff straddles the table corner and eyeballs Tommy George. "How can I help?" If he hopes to nail the old man under his super-blue scrutiny, Geoff has met his match in Nellie's grandfather.

He returns Geoff's stare with such ferocity that the Senior Constable blinks first. Obviously pleased with the win,

Tommy George smirks briefly before turning serious again. "Do you know who killed my Nellie?"

"Not as of yet, sir."

"What *do* you know then?" The old man doesn't hide his frustration.

Recalling Tommy George's dislike for the outback police force, I step in. "Currently we know the following. After the dessert incident on Wednesday night at about nine-thirty, Nellie finished thirty minutes before her rostered shift normally ended. No one saw her after that. I discovered her body the next day down at Jackaroo's Waterhole, where a cloth doused in a strong anesthetic was found nearby. It seems she was drugged before being struck by a rock on the head. The rock was discovered in some branches on the bank of the waterhole and the blood was a match to Nellie's. Her time of death has been estimated between ten-thirty and eleven-thirty Wednesday night."

Geoff takes over. "We believe someone in a car either drugged and kidnapped Nellie or gave her a lift and then drugged her. He then carried her down to the waterhole where she was subsequently killed, and her body dumped."

"You said 'he'?"

"Based on the distance, we believe only a man would've had the strength."

"Unless of course, she walked down there with someone she knew and trusted." I turn a frosty gaze on Andrew, pinning him to the chair. His panic is immediate. His eyes dart around the room while everyone waits for him to speak.

"I wasn't there. Honest, I wasn't." He faces Tommy George, entreaty in his eyes. "I'd never hurt Nellie. You know that. You've got to believe me."

"Then what were you doing on Thursday afternoon?" I ask.

Andrew snaps his attention back to me. "What do you mean?"

"After the Senior Constable made his announcement about Nellie being found dead, and Gillian drove you back to the staff quarters, you returned to the homestead." I flick a glance at Mimi who smiles shrewdly.

Even more nervous, Andrew glances at Mimi who says, "Well?"

"I, eh . . . I um . . ."

"Andrew. What were you doing outside my retreat?"

Still wide-eyed, he says, "You saw me?"

"We both did," Mimi adds.

He deflates with a sigh, like a pricked balloon. "I was looking for something."

"We know that because we watched you pocket it and run back to the homestead. What was it?"

"Come on, lad. This is a murder investigation. You need to tell us." It's obvious Geoff's patience has reached its limits.

Andrew drops his head. "A ring."

"What ring?" I ask.

"I was going to ask Nellie to marry me." He turns to Tommy George who meets his distress with a frown. "Sorry. I know I should've asked you first, but I wanted to surprise her."

"Go on." Geoff slips behind the table and begins taking notes.

"I could only afford something small. Not a diamond or anything. Just a little blue sapphire. I left it on the bar in the great room on Wednesday afternoon just before Nellie was due to set up for a shift. I was hiding around the corner so that when she picked it up, I was going to spring out and ask her to marry me. But she didn't show up. She's usually regular as clockwork when she's on shift. I don't know where she was?"

"She was up talking to me in my retreat," I say, saddened to think that his grand gesture had been thwarted. If it had gone to plan, perhaps Nellie might still be alive. But my gut tells me the die had been cast before then.

"Anyway, while I was waiting for Nellie that damn bower bird flew in and grabbed it."

"No!" Mimi says.

"Yes. It often steals empty tea light candles or pieces of foil from chocolate wrappers. Bloody thing pinched Nellie's ring from right under my nose. I scoured around its nest and up in the trees to see if I could find it on Wednesday before I went home, but I had no luck. Then on Thursday, when Nellie's body was found and Gillian took me home, I couldn't just sit there. I had to find Nellie's ring. I came back to look for it again. And there it was. In the bower. That's what you saw me searching for and pocket. The engagement ring I wanted to give Nellie."

Tears well in his eyes matching those in Mimi's. "That's so sad and so romantic," she whispers.

"A good story, but I'll need to see this ring," Geoff says.

"Of course. We can go down now to the staff quarters. It's in my drawer."

"Yes. Let's do that," Geoff says before addressing Tommy George. "Is that okay if I leave you here for a while? When I come back, I can drive you to the Durack tree or I'll get one of my officers to take you into town if you prefer."

Tommy George flaps his hand. "Go. Get the ring." He clamps Andrew's wrist as he stands to leave. "I would've given you my blessing. Nellie loved you."

"Thank you, sir." Grief etches fresh lines on Andrew's young face. Lines that will deepen to match those on the old man's over time. Though the two men may be black and white, they're united in their love for and loss of Nellie Walker. I stare past them, praying for some sort of omen to point me in the right direction. There's a link here. I know there is.

After Geoff and Andrew leave, Mimi slides in beside Tommy George on the sofa. "Will bower birds actually do that?"

"Yes. The male bird is always on the look-out for more trinkets to attract a mate. It doesn't matter what they are, as long as they catch her eye. A bower bird doesn't care about its value, real or fake. It just has to sparkle."

"Is there a Dreaming story like Brolga?" Mimi's eagerness is admirable, and I'm sure, flattering to Tommy George.

He lowers his voice in story-telling style. "In the Dreaming, the bowerbird was a man who took pleasure in killing people, by enticing them closer with sounds of prey. He is finally caught and as punishment, changed into the bowerbird with a short beak, instead of a long one like the spear with which he originally killed. In effect, his power for destruction has been removed." He pauses and smiles at Mimi. "We call bower birds 'ghost birds' because it also collects bones for its bower. If you see ghost birds with bones, do you hang onto the old bones of your past—or are you able to release the past, especially past romantic liaisons?"

"Poor Andrew will have to let go of Nellie."

Tommy George nods. While he entertains Mimi with his Dreamtime stories, I hobble to the window. Outside, the world stands still, but inside, my mind swirls like a willy-willy wind. Kicking up dust, kicking up clues. Sending them spiraling. Whoever lured Nellie was like a bower bird. A collector of bones from the past.

"That's it!" In my excitement, I swivel too fast and the corner of the desk corks me in the thigh. "Ouch!"

Mimi dashes to my side. "Are you all right?"

"Yes. Yes." I rub furiously at the spot. "Tommy George, are you okay to stay here until the Senior Constable returns? There are a few things I must do?"

He affirms with a silent nod.

"Come on Mimi. Get my laptop and let's go." I grab my walking stick and with Mimi's help, we make for the door.

"You are close," Tommy George calls from behind.

It's not a question. He states it as a fact, and I hope he's right.

★ ★ ★ ★

I'M PROPPED IN GILLIAN AND Christopher's small management apartment while waiting for Mimi to return with more ice for my ankle. In front of me rests a cup of tea that Gillian has just brewed, while she sits opposite, brave-face, and exhausted.

"How can I help?" she asks.

"It's about the art." I watch her hands tremble as she lifts her cup to her mouth. "I understand that the artists and buyers do their transactions through El Kwestro."

"Yes. The artists display their work here during the event, buyers come, and we broker any purchases and arrange shipment and subsequent payment to the artists."

"And you get a commission?"

Yes. We take fifteen percent of every sale."

"And who manages this?"

"It's Amy's responsibility. But I do the final sign-off."

"I'm sure you have another system in place ensuring no commission goes astray?" I flash her a complimentary smile.

"Yes, I do." She relaxes and matches my smile. "I can show you the paperwork if you like."

"Thanks. Can you deliver it to my room?"

"Of course."

A knock at the door is followed by Mimi's head peering around the corner. "I've got your ice."

I rise. "No need, Mimi. I've finished. Thanks for the tea, Gillian."

She glances at my untouched cup. Both she and Mimi shoot me puzzled frowns that I ignore. "Come on, Mimi. Let's go."

Mimi steps in beside me, gripping the bag of melting ice and my laptop.

"Why did you send me off for ice if you didn't need it," she asks outside.

"I needed to be alone with Gillian."

"And?"

"Now I have to send an email."

We make for the great room, and for the first time in this terrible situation, I sense order emerging.

CHAPTER EIGHTEEN

GEOFF DROPS ONTO THE STOOL beside me at the bar with a huff. "Seems Andrew's ring story checks out." Appearing more hot-and-bothered than usual, he swipes a hand across his forehead. "Poor kid. He's pretty cut up." He eyeballs my iced ankle. "How are you doing?"

"Pretty good." I smile a cheeky grin.

He catches it. "What have you found out?"

"Nothing yet" —which is true— "but I have a couple of hunches I'm working on."

"Well, let me know if they come to fruition."

Amy's raised voice drifts in from outside. "Lunch is served."

"Great," Mimi says. "I'm starved." She removes the ice from my ankle and retreats to the sink to discard it.

"You joining us for lunch?" I ask him.

He shakes his head. "No. I think it's better if I keep a low profile. You go through."

"I'll keep you posted." With my laptop under my arm, I hobble over to meet Mimi and we make our way onto the verandah.

Not surprisingly, lunch is a stilted affair. After Geoff's bombshell announcement this morning of not being able to leave El Kwestro until further notice, no one's in a convivial mood. Jo hasn't bothered to join us which is understandable considering the circumstances.

When our main meal of roast chicken is delivered, I catch Kristen's attention across the table. "Peter not joining us?"

"No. He wasn't hungry." She offers a polite smile and returns to her food.

Mimi tries her luck at eliciting conversation. "Anyone doing any excursions this afternoon?" Her cheery tone seems incongruous with the tension.

The Torrens and Kristen murmur a no.

"We're doing the helicopter flight to Miri Miri Falls," Trish says, slurring the 's'. By the way she clutches her glass and not the cutlery, I expect her meal will go back untouched, which may be a blessing since she's going up in the chopper.

"Yes. That's where Dale is now. Doing his checks. I hear the falls there are spectacular." Delight has replaced Tony's previously sour expression. Whether it's because of their impending excursion or the chicken leg he's gnawing, I'm not sure.

While he sprouts on, I whisper to Sylvia beside me, "How are you both holding up?"

"I'm doing fine. But I'm worried about John."

I lean forward and smile at her husband. He's strung tight like a wire. "Would you like me to see if the Senior Constable can arrange a doctor to visit? Perhaps prescribe something," I say to her.

"Would you?"

"Of course."

"The last time I saw him this much on edge, he went on a rampage and punched a hole in the wall."

"Really?"

"John's not normally like that, but he was a boxer in his younger years and when his temper gets the better of him, the old way of handling things comes out. He uses his fists."

I murmur in sympathy while storing that piece of information. John Torrens. A man who reverts to violence when things get tough. That's not a trait I would have attributed to him. *Still waters run deep.*

Before dessert, I say my goodbye to everyone and amble up to my retreat, testing my ankle. I still need the walking stick, but the joint is making fine progress and the pain has mostly subsided. Full of confidence, I continue to the top of the pathway where the inclined curve proves a little trickier and slows me down. Through a copse of eucalypt trees to my right, I glimpse two figures standing near Pandanus. They're tucked in near the back verandah, hardly visible to anyone striding up the path at normal speed. But because I'm moving at a snail's pace, I notice the tête-à-tête. I shimmy in behind a large tree trunk and sneak a closer look. One of them is Dale. His shock of red hair and beard are unmistakable. He stands motionless, languidly puffing a cigarette. All I can see of the other person is half a body protruding around the corner. An arm waves animatedly. Into Dale's space, steps Peter Pullman. They face off for a moment, neither flinching. Then Peter pivots and disappears back around the corner. Dale drops his cigarette and grinds it into the ground. I slip back behind the tree praying he won't return to the path. To my right, I hear dry leaves crackle under his footsteps on his way down the slope toward his helicopter. Exhaling gratefully, I round the trunk on the other side.

"Can I help you?" Peter stands in front of me, nailing me in a cold stare.

I clutch my laptop to my chest in self-defense. "I . . . oh . . . No thank you. I just needed to rest on the way back to my room." It's the best excuse I could come up with, lame though it sounds.

He pauses for what seems an eternity. "Would you like me to help you the rest of the way?"

I'm so shocked I can't tell whether the offer is genuine or not. "No thanks. That's very kind of you, Peter. But I'm sure I can make it from here." I lean hard into my walking stick and scurry up the pathway like a demented invalid. By the time I round the corner to my retreat, my heart pounds, and my breathing is labored. I glance back but he's gone. Maybe he believed me. Maybe he didn't. But from now on, no more going solo for me.

★ ★ ★ ★

"THANKS FOR COMING IN TO see us again, Mr. Pullman." Geoff points to the chair.

"Happy to help." He directs the smile at me which troubles me. Dealing with an ENTJ can be awkward without them behaving in unpredictable ways. Either his meds are working and he's in one of his amicable moods, or he's deliberately baiting me.

Geoff dives right in. "We understand that you have a side business in diamond jewelry."

"Yes. I buy the raw diamonds directly from the mine and then get them set into different pieces for my Perth stockbroking clients."

"And who does the work for you?"

"Stuart at Top End Jewelers in Darwin."

"You sold a ring to Jo Arnold . . ." I place the ring box on the table . . . "This ring."

Peter leans forward to inspect it. "Yes. Jo and I got talking on Wednesday night about the Argyle mine. She said she wanted to give Maria a pink diamond engagement ring and as fate would have it, I had one that a client in Perth stopped the order on."

"Very fortunate." Sarcasm laces Geoff's comment, but Peter remains unfazed.

"Actually, it was. Jo got the ring she always wanted, and I got a sale."

"Pity Maria was killed before Jo had a chance to propose." I arch a stern brow in his direction.

He shrugs. "I can't do anything about that."

"Fifty-thousand dollars is a lot of money for a diamond ring," Geoff says.

"Not for an Argyle pink diamond. They are as rare as hen's teeth now. She made a good investment."

"Can you tell us what you were discussing with Dale Baker today at your retreat?" Geoff's manner is nonchalant yet direct.

Peter's eyes flash at me and the extreme side of ENTJ that dislikes being challenged appears. In an instant, it's gone and his composure regained.

"I asked Dale about Wednesday night."

"What about Wednesday night?"

"I saw Dale when I went for a walk after the dessert incident."

"But you said you didn't see anyone or hear anything during your walk around the grounds on Wednesday night. A walk you conveniently forgot to tell us about in your first interview. Now you tell us you saw Dale Baker?" Geoff controls his frustration, but I can sense its undercurrent.

"To be honest, the meds I take cause memory lapses at times, so things get a little blurry."

I huff my disgust at his weak excuse.

Geoff hides his disbelief better than me. "Go on."

"Anyway, I remembered that I saw Dale at that time, so I asked him this afternoon if he saw anything. He reckons he didn't."

"But why didn't you bring this information to us?"

"I was going to." He pauses for a moment and then adds, "Why? Didn't Dale tell you?" By the way he smirks, he suspects that Dale didn't.

We disregard the question.

Geoff stands. "Thank you for your time, Mr. Pullman."

Peter takes the hint and leaves with a self-satisfied smile, reminding me of a cat who artfully sets a trap for an unsuspecting mouse.

Geoff closes the door behind him, an exasperated expression on his face. "What do you think?"

"He's lying about something, but I don't know what it is."

"Agreed. We'll need to talk to Dale once he returns from Miri Miri Falls later and see what he has to say about Pullman's story for Wednesday night."

★ ★ ★ ★

"MORE TENNYSON, I SEE." MIMI sets a cappuccino on the balcony table beside me before sitting cross-legged in the other chair. "I should have brought you a stiff drink, but I figured you'd prefer this."

I flash her a thankful smile. "Genius. The coffee is perfect." We sip in silence for a while, enjoying the view which never loses its magic.

She cocks a brow at my little red book. "Any more omens from the great poet?"

"No, unfortunately. The first poem still seems to fit what's going on around here. Too many lies and not enough truth." Just as I'm about to elaborate further a woman calls from the front door.

"Hello, Diana, are you there?"

"Come in. I'm out the back."

Jo Arnold walks out, greets us with a nod, and steps to the edge of the deck. "Your view is different to ours." She falters but doesn't correct the plural. "You're much higher over the gorge here."

I wince at the memory of Maria lying dead on the rocks below the Chamberlain Suite. That there aren't any railings on the retreat decks or guardrails on the escarpment edge only a few meters away still worry me. It's just too easy for someone to step off or be pushed off. But then even with a railing, Maria fell to her death. If someone wants you dead, not much can save you.

Jo points down to the river. "Look, the crocodiles are baking in the afternoon sun."

Mimi and I join her, all eyes on the crocs for a few minutes, lost in our thoughts. A primitive land with pre-historic creatures and ancient Dreamtime stories of evil spirits. A place where past and present collide . . .

When Jo faces me, it's with determined focus and not distraught grief. "I got your message about needing my help. What can I do?"

"You said you're a good forensic lawyer . . ."

"One of the best."

"Then I have a job for you."

I lead her inside where I explain what I require before handing over a folder full of papers. After she leaves, I return to the deck, my coffee now cold.

"She looks remarkably good for someone who's lover was murdered last night." Mimi can't or won't hide her suspicions.

I pat her arm. "I'm sure she had nothing to do with Maria's death. Jo's an INTJ. Give her a problem, and she'll solve it. That's what I just did."

"What's the problem?"

"I think I know the motive for Maria's murder, and I need Jo's help to find the evidence to prove it."

★ ★ ★ ★

LATE AFTERNOON AND THE DAYS have rolled into one. It's not been three days since Nellie's death and not twenty-four hours since Maria fell to hers. Yet I have the strange sensation that time is at both a standstill and at light speed. Maybe I'm losing track of time because of the Dreamtime magic. Or maybe I'm just exhausted. In the background, Geoff's voice drones in and out, but in my head, ancient voices whisper about Brolgas, bower birds, Waiwera, and evil that hungers for beauty. The imagined drone of a helicopter draws my attention to the present moment where in front of us sits Dale Baker, newly returned from Miri Miri Falls.

Geoff moves to the front of the table and leans against it, arms folded. "Mr. Baker, it seems you lied to us about your whereabouts on Wednesday night."

"Excuse me?"

"You lied to us about your whereabouts after you went to bed on Wednesday night."

Dale blinks at Geoff and then at me. "No. I had my last cigarette and went to bed by ten. As I told you."

"Are you sure?"

"Of course."

"Can you explain why Mr. Pullman says he saw you on Wednesday night after that in the grounds?"

Dale frowns and shakes his head. "I have no idea."

"What were you both talking about this afternoon near his retreat?" I hope to ruffle his ISTJ personality type.

"We were discussing my flight schedule over the next few days to see when I'm free to take Kristen to see more Aboriginal art."

"Peter seemed quite heated, waving his arms around."

"He gets overbearing if things don't go his way."

Geoff interjects, "Did you agree on a day?"

"Yes. We're going Monday morning."

"And you weren't in the grounds on Wednesday night after ten?"

"No. I was in bed."

Geoff and I exchange a defeated glance, and Dale is excused.

"There we have it." The Senior Constable drops onto the sofa and dumps his feet atop the coffee table. "He's a cool customer that one."

"As I said, ISTJ's are logical, ordered, and systematic. You're not going to get more than necessary out of him."

"One of these guys is out-and-out lying. The question is who . . ."

"I tend to disagree. The question is why . . ." Like the proverbial bolt of lightning, an idea comes to me, almost launching me to my feet. "I think I might know."

"Do tell."

"I need you to do some police work first to see if my hunch is correct."

"No problem. What do you need?" He climbs to his feet, slides in behind the table, and flips open his tablet.

CHAPTER NINETEEN

Having just returned from town, Timson and Hamers stand at attention waiting to deliver their news. They furtively eye each other off to see who'll go first. Hamers wins. She usually does.

"The M.E. confirms that the time of Ms. Loukas' death was ten last night, Friday."

Timson grabs his chance. "He confirms cause of death was a broken neck from the fall."

Hamers parries again. "He found bruises to her arms consistent with hand marks and a struggle."

"So, it looks like someone did push her." Geoff rubs his forehead and exhales on a groan. "Go on."

Hamers. "That's what the M.E. reckons, sir. He'll email his report shortly. And the doctor will be out tomorrow for Mr. Torrens."

"Thank you." I hope he'll last until then without punching a wall, or worse.

"Righto. You and Timson will be on foot duty tonight. I want a police presence on the homestead all night. You work out your shifts between you."

"Yes, sir." Timson almost clicks his heels together, and I try not to smile.

"Sir, it's a big place," Hamers reminds respectfully.

"Understood. But do the best you can. Keep your eyes and ears open. Management knows you'll be out and about, but the guests won't be told. We don't need to upset them more than they already are."

"Yes, sir," they say in unison.

"Now off you go. Keep me posted."

Another ", sir", before they pivot and leave.

"She's right. If the murderer intends on taking another victim, we'll have a hard time stopping them with just Hamers and Timson," I say.

"I'm not trying to stop them. I'm trying to catch them."

"You mean, you're hoping the murderer will try again."

"Don't worry, I'll be out there as well. Between the three of us, everyone should be safe as long as no one goes wandering off on their own." He nails me a stern look for my afternoon escapade.

"It won't be me," I assure him.

"Good." He glances at the time. "It's sundowners. Let's check out how the guests are holding up." He tags on a disarming, though sarcastic smile to match his eyes.

In the great room, Amy tends bar in her usual efficient manner. "Can I get you both a drink?"

Geoff shakes his head.

"I'll just have a white wine spritzer, please."

She strides to the fridges, calling over her shoulder, "How are you going with the investigation, Senior Constable?"

"Coming along nicely."

After adding a splash of soda water to my white wine, she slides the oversized glass toward me. Not much spritz in there. I won't be able to drink all that. I'll topple like a freshly sawn tree. "Thanks, Amy. How's everyone coping?"

"They're still reeling. We can't believe it. Two people dead in three days."

I'm sure Amy has Botox injections. Her face lacks the emotional expressions expected when discussing a possible double murder of her guests. On the other hand, she does sound genuinely upset. Or perhaps as an ESTJ, she's more inconvenienced by the disruption to her neatly ordered schedule. At this stage, it's anyone's guess.

She leans forward in a conspiratorial manner. "Gillian told me your officers will be on duty in the grounds tonight."

"Yes. All night," Geoff confirms.

"Well, I feel safer just knowing that."

"Good to hear. Now if you'll excuse us." Geoff guides me outside where the guests mingle on the lawn admiring the sunset. He veers off to one side while I move toward the Torrens, not far from where Mimi chats with the Wilsons.

John and Sylvia stand in silence, sipping martinis, their gaze on the sky but I'm sure their thoughts are elsewhere.

"Good evening. Do you mind if I join you?"

"Not at all," Sylvia says.

"How are you holding up, John?"

"To be honest. I'm not sure how much more of this I can take. Everything reminds me of Stephanie. She was killed as surely as Nellie was. I don't care if it was a suicide. The bastard that dumped her, killed her. If I ever get my hands on him . . ."

"John, please."

He ignores his wife's plea. "She was such a happy, pretty girl, just like Nellie. I . . ." His voice breaks, and he dissolves into tears.

Sylvia wraps her arm around her husband's shuddering shoulders, her concerned stare meeting mine. "I'm sorry, Diana. I think we'll skip dinner."

"Of course. I'll organize for someone to bring something up to you."

"Thank you."

"The doctor will be here tomorrow."

"Thank you. Thank you." She bundles John away from the other guests, across the lawn and into the great room.

"Poor guy's a mess," Mimi whispers in my ear.

I nod while watching the Torrens disappear. "Certainly is. Let's grab a seat, and I'll catch you up on the news."

"Good idea. Here, let me help. This spongy lawn isn't good for a walking stick."

★ ★ ★ ★

NOT THAT I EVER THOUGHT I'd say it but thank goodness for Tony Wilson. During dinner, he regales us with an animated recital of the pristine beauty of Miri Miri Falls—the crystal-clear rock pools, the torrential waterfall that plunges into the massive swimming hole at the bottom enclosed by one-hundred-and-fifty-meter high cliffs, and Dale's artful piloting in and out of the secluded spot. Beside me, Mimi sighs a disappointed sound. She came on this vacation to see a part of Australia she'd always longed to visit. These deaths and my bloody ankle have certainly upended our holiday. I'm going to have to make it up to her, somehow.

I return my attention to the table and notice Trish is unimpressed with her husband's performance, but I'm delighted that my participation isn't needed. Kristen's frequent enquiries about rock art ensures Tony remains center stage while Mimi and Geoff nod their interest where needed. Jo's continued absence seems to be of no consequence to anyone while Peter and Dale ignore each other completely. I recall when my stepbrother and I were younger, rather than having an all-out fight, we just pretended the other didn't exist. Obviously, the same game is at play between the two men.

By the time desserts are cleared, everyone's fallen under the soothing spell of the outback night. A crisp chill descends which gives rise to more requests for alcohol to warm the spirits. Glasses of cognac, scotch, and vodka arrive, and Mimi's onto her third glass of wine. I have the distinct impression I'll need my wits about me tonight, so I opt for a coffee as does Geoff.

Tony swirls the cognac in his glass. "Now, Senior Constable, how's the case progressing?" His tone borders on patronizing and grates on my ears, as it probably does on Geoff's.

"We're progressing. Thank you." His answer is pleasant but clipped.

"But when will we be able to leave?" Trish tries to focus on the Senior Constable but her repeated blinking indicates she's finding it difficult.

"As I said earlier, not until we find the killer."

"Do you *really* think that one of us is responsible for these deaths?" Tony asks.

"*Everyone* is a suspect at this time, Mr. Wilson." Geoff's direct manner silences the enquiries but does little to squash the shock. "I'm sorry, but until our investigations are complete, you will have to remain at El Kwestro."

"But are we safe?" Kristen sounds worried.

"Of course, we are." Peter squeezes her hand. "There's no reason for anyone to harm us."

"To be honest, Mr. Pullman, everyone needs to be more aware of what's going on around them. Personal safety is everyone's responsibility."

"The Kimberley is a dangerous place. You can never tell whether you're the hunter or the hunted."

All eyes turn to Dale. His remark is delivered not so much as a threat but as a statement of fact. But the sideways glance he gives Peter causes the hairs on my arms to stand on end. It's not just Tony's cognac that swirls. My stomach is going around and around. A portent of something about to happen.

"I suggest that once you return to your rooms this evening, you don't venture out again until daybreak. I bid you all good night." Geoff stands, and Mimi and I accompany him to the great room.

"And that goes for you two." He eyeballs us like a strict schoolteacher. "I don't want you leaving your retreats for any reason. Got it."

I roll my eyes. "Yes, yes. We'll stay indoors."

"Good. I can escort you to your rooms if you like?"

"No, thank you. We'll be fine."

"Good night then. I'll see you both in the morning." He heads towards the front doors and out into the blackest of nights. I half expect to see Tommy George standing there and wonder how he's faring. His loss strengthens my resolve.

"Come on, Mimi, let's go."

We make our way onto the veranda that leads to the garden rooms when to our left, Amy steps out from her office. "Good evening, ladies. Did you enjoy dinner?"

"Yes. Delicious as always," Mimi says.

I glance at my watch. 9.30 P.M. "Don't you ever go home?"

"Actually, I'm hoping Cameron and I can take an early mark tonight. I'm off to see if any of the other guests need anything else. If not, we'll head off. Are you ladies fine?"

I wave a hand at her. "We're good thanks. We're on our way back to our retreats."

"Well then, I'll see you tomorrow. Have a good night's sleep." She snaps a turn and with a swish of her ponytail, marches off to the kitchen.

Mimi and I resume our leisurely stroll.

"Well, another day at El Kwestro comes to an end, but at least no one's been murdered." Mimi's dramatic irony isn't lost on me. "If I'd known that you'd get yourself into the same trouble as you did on your Galapagos cruise, I would've thought twice about coming on holidays with you."

"I'm sorry, Mimi. I'm sure this will all be over soon, and we can get back to enjoying ourselves."

She shrugs and adds a soft laugh. "That's all right. Nothing like a little excitement and chaos to liven up one's vacation. How's your ankle?"

"Actually, it's much better. I can nearly put my full weight on it, but I'm keeping the walking stick, just in case."

"Good idea."

We continue in silence accompanied by the cheery tinkling of the bells jingling on Mimi's skirt, the same one she wore on Wednesday night. The sound reminds me of the bell on a cat collar that warns birds of another approaching predator. Not that Mimi would make much of a predator. The thought makes me smile. *She's a 'good egg', my sister-in-law.*

Where the pathway begins to curve upwards, we spy Hamers patrolling the lawn, torch in hand.

"I wouldn't like to meet her in a dark alley," Mimi quips.

"Me neither if I was going to break the law. Much better to be with her than against." We wave in Hamers' direction but doubt she sees us on the darkened pathway. Again, we lapse into silence until we reach where the paths fork to Kurrajong retreat.

"Do you want me to come in?" Mimi asks.

"No. I need to go through my notes and see if I can get some of these pieces floating around in my head to fit together."

"Okay. I'll see you in the morning." She leans in with a peck to my cheek. "I have no doubt you'll get to the bottom of all this."

"I have to. I promised Tommy George. Make sure you lock up."

"I will."

I watch and hear her scamper the last fifty meters to Woolybutt where she disappears around the corner and into her retreat. Within fifteen steps, I'm inside mine, locking the door behind me. The housekeeping staff have turned down the bed and switched on the side lamps which I promptly turn off. Now I'm as hidden as anyone who might be lurking around outside. I slide into the window seat and wait for my eyes to adjust to the darkness. Such a glorious night. What a pity there's a murderer out there with evil in their heart. Nellie's young, innocent face once more fills my mind, followed by Maria's exotic, effervescent beauty. Both attractive young women. Their faces hover in front of me as the words loop in my mind. I replay the conversations I had at sundowners and dinner. There's a common thread here. I can feel it in my gut.

The Beatles' lyric drifts back to me . . . 'look for the girl with the sun in her eyes.'

And she's gone!

They're all gone . . . Could that be it?

Staring into the night with renewed intensity, I picture the perpetrator outside, lurking and hiding in the shadows. I whisper to my imagined, unseen killer, "You have no idea how well I see in the dark."

Now, I had to find the evidence to prove it.

CHAPTER TWENTY

A LOUD BANGING ENTERS MY consciousness, stirring me from a restless sleep. "What the hell?" My bed is strewn with notes and files from before I fell asleep.

More banging. "Diana, wake up!"

My head reels and I stumble to the door, dread squirming in my gut. The moment I see Geoff's face, I know. "Mimi," I shriek, and push to go past him.

"It's all right. She's okay."

"What happened?" I dash back, throw on a robe and scuffs, and grab my walking stick.

"I'll explain on the way."

By the time we burst into Mimi's room, I'm beyond panic. She's on the bed, a stack of pillows propped behind her with Hamers holding an ice pack to the side of her forehead.

"Dear god, what happened?" I take Mimi's hand and notice mine's trembling more than hers.

Her gray eyes meet mine and before she speaks, tears appear. "You were right, Diana. Somebody tried to kill me."

Guilt lurches in my stomach. "Oh, Mimi." I reach over and gently lift Hamers' hand holding the ice pack. A bump the size of an orange swells from Mimi's temple. That she wasn't killed by the impact amazes me and by the look on Geoff's and Hamers' faces, they agree.

Mimi clutches my hand and I smile, grateful that she's alive "What happened?"

"It was such a beautiful night, I decided to take a bath on the balcony."

The urge to admonish her for her foolishness is replaced by my relief that she's still alive. "Go on."

"Well, I was just lying there with my eyes closed, meditating, and I thought I heard something. When I pushed up to see what it was, someone hit me."

"Clubbed her is more like it." Geoff's aside is barely audible.

"That's when I shone the torch down this way from where I was on the top of the ridge and saw someone on Mrs. Kramer's balcony with their arm raised," Hamers says. "I sounded the alarm and ran down as fast as I could. But whoever it was ran off. By the time I got here, Mrs. Kramer was moaning but conscious. I brought her inside, got some ice onto her head, and ran to find the Senior Constable."

I shoot a terse glance at Geoff who says nothing because he knows damn well I'm furious. Furious that he all but admitted that tonight wasn't about catching the killer but luring them out. But my outrage will have to keep for now. I stroke Mimi's hand. "How does your head feel?"

"Actually, it feels okay. I've got a killer of a headache coming on though."

"Bad choice of words, Mimi." I angle a brow at her and rise from the bed. "I'll get you some painkillers."

"Ha! bad choice of words, Diana," she retorts. Her sharp wit is intact which makes me feel better.

I head to the bathroom, and for the first time since I answered my door tonight, the knot in my shoulder eases.

"She's lucky." Geoff stands behind me, his concerned expression reflecting in the mirror.

"You think?" I'm seething. "Someone just tried to kill my sister-in-law. And what are you doing about it?"

"Timson has secured the homestead and is taking statements."

"But what are *you* doing about it?" All the tension from the last few days and Mimi's near-death escape starts to erupt. "Are you just going to stand here or are you going to get out there and do something?"

"I'll head down there now with Hamers. I expect you'll be staying here for the rest of the night?"

"Of course!" I know it's not his fault but . . .

"I'll leave you to it then." He exits without another word.

With my hands gripping the sink, I draw three deep breaths. *You've done this before, and you can do it again. Pull yourself together woman and get this bastard.*

After a decisive nod, I fill the glass, grab the tablets, and return to play nursemaid.

Mimi takes her tablets and when she confirms she's feeling up for a chat, it's time to find out why she was targeted. "Where's that sketch pad Maria gave you?"

"Over there on the table with some pencils."

I return with the pad and a pencil, pull up a chair beside her bed, and flip to a clean page. "Right. You're going to tell me everything you remember about any conversation you overheard when I wasn't with you."

Mimi's eyes bug open. "You're kidding me?"

"Not in the least. You've heard something or seen something that you've given no importance to but it's deadly important to the killer who thinks you know what you don't know. In fact, whatever it is nearly got you killed tonight."

"I'm not sure if I can do this now . . ." There's a genuine plea in her voice and eyes.

I soften. "I'm sorry, Mimi, but let's at least begin."

"But how will you know if it's important if I don't?"

"Trust me, Mimi. I'll know. That's what they pay me for . . . to know things." I force a smile and Mimi begins.

★ ★ ★ ★

BACK IN FRONT OF THE mirror. This time in my own retreat and the reflection staring back at me is a fright. The hot shower has helped restore my energy but done nothing for the bags under my eyes. At least, Mimi's sleeping while Timson stands guard at her retreat. I drag a brush through my hair. No luck there either. My artfully styled platinum-blonde hair now hangs lank and lifeless. I rub on some foundation, a couple of circular strokes of blush, and a few licks of mascara. Perhaps a bright lipstick will make me look better, but I think better of it and go for a soft pink. Who cares? What I must do today has no bearing on my appearance. After pulling on some jeans, hiking boots, cotton shirt, and jacket, I grab my walking stick, laptop, and folder of notes, and head off. To my left, the bower bird busies himself at his nest. We're kindred spirits, he and I. Both with an eye for detail and an unstoppable determination. His to attract a mate. Mine to catch a killer. To my right, the helicopter rests on the lawn with no sign of her owner. Good. The place is empty. I skirt up onto the veranda and am thankful Andrew's not raking leaves. At the corner, I listen for voices or movement and when I'm sure there is none, I hurry along the veranda, past the office, and into the library.

I'm greeted by Geoff's crisp blue gaze. "You're up early." Sporting a bright smile, he's a welcoming sight for my tired eyes.

Like a prodigal child, I slink over to the table. "I'm sorry about last night. I . . ."

He holds up a dismissive hand. "Forget it. You had every right to say what you did. I'm just pleased Hamers got there in time. How's Mimi?"

"She's sleeping. Timson's on duty." I slide my laptop and folder onto the table and slip into my chair beside him.

"Good. How about I get us a couple of coffees?"

"It should be me making the peace offering this time."

"Nonsense. Two piping cappuccinos coming up."

By the time he returns, I've arranged my notes in strategic piles on the table. Pages from Mimi's sketch pad that I taped together run the length of the table indicating the timeline of events and marked with days, dates, and times.

"Shit. You must have been up all night doing this?" He hands me the steaming cup topped with a thick foam, and I'm in heaven.

"Not just me. Mimi as well."

He lifts an inquiring brow.

"Let's sit on the sofa, and I'll explain." While we drink our morning kick-starter, I give him a quick precis of what Mimi told me last night.

"That's why Nellie came to see me. When she overheard the name, she couldn't believe it. She was about to tell me, but she thought it was too much of a coincidence as well." I place my empty cup on the table, wishing I had another one.

"It's a helluva coincidence."

"I know but when Mimi said she overheard it as well. Same people, same name, it has to be right."

"Still, it's a mighty big stretch from suspicion of being overheard to murder."

I nod. That thought had kept me awake most of the night. "Look." I motion to the table and Geoff joins me. I talk him through my notes and how the pieces of conversation fit together. "See. This was Tuesday at sundowners. This was Wednesday after lunch and this is what Mimi overheard yesterday."

Geoff inspects each event on the paper timeline. "There definitely seems to be a connection. The timeline fits. But it's a long shot."

"I know. Even for me, it's a leap of faith. There's only one way to be sure. It requires your police contacts and investigative work to confirm my suspicions and find the connection."

"But even if you're right, it won't prove murder."

"I know, but a good cop told me a couple of years ago, whatever your gut tells you, pull the thread."

Geoff grins, obviously guessing I'm talking about John Nash. "Go on."

"I have a feeling that if we pull this thread, the whole thing will unravel."

"Well, it's the best we've got so far. Let's get started then. What do you need?"

While Geoff sends multiple emails, I stand at the window, ruminating on the case. I can't shake the feeling that there's too much going on here. Too many loose ends. On the lawn, Dale cranks up his chopper and the blades reluctantly come to life. A small amount of throttle coaxes her further. Reticent, the machine rocks side to side, until he thrusts harder and she obeys. Like a shaman, he guides her upwards, levitating above the ground. With a slow bank to his left, he pilots her away from the homestead to their destination. "Where's Dale off to?" I ask.

"He's going into town to fetch the doctor for John Torrens."

"Where was he last night when Mimi was attacked?"

"At the staff quarters having a drink with one of the nature guides from the station."

"Did you get any further with the Peter and Dale thing?"

"Not yet. But I expect a response by tomorrow. If not, I'll chase it again."

The chopper flies higher, again reminding me that I need to take a helicopter view. Keep my head in the clouds. Closing my eyes, I imagine Dale's flight path to town—over the orange-tinted, corrugated road that leads from the homestead, above the plains of biting, yellow spear grass, and lifting further still above the isolated oasis of Jackaroo's Waterhole where I found Nellie. In my mind's eye, I hover there, searching for clues, searching for the loose ends. "Geoff, do you believe in fate?" I ask, my eyes still closed.

"What? You mean everything is pre-destined and we're merely pawns in some game of god's?"

"Not exactly . . ." To be honest, I'm not sure what I mean myself. I open my eyes and stare into the distance.

"Then what?"

When I turn towards him, he's got that confused expression that most men have when I come way out of left field. "That if you look hard enough, you'll find what you're searching for."

"Absolutely. That's what police work is all about."

"Which means nothing is a coincidence . . . really."

"I'm not sure I agree with you, but I get your point."

"Can you spare Hamers later this morning to take me to Jackaroo's Waterhole?"

"Yeah. I guess so." He's obviously still puzzled but obliging.

"Good. Thanks."

"Another hunch I take it?"

I nod. "And if this one's correct, we may just find what we're looking for."

★ ★ ★ ★

THOUGH GILLIAN AND AMY DO their best with offers of refreshments, little can persuade the guests of their safety. Even Tony looks decidedly uneasy as he paces in front of the fireplace. The Torrens shrink into the corner of the sofa, almost like small children suffering from family trauma. On the other sofa, Peter seems to have lost some of his petulance, while his wife hugs close beside him. I suspect Trish has a good shot of something in her coffee which probably isn't her first and won't be her last. But by her shell-shocked expression, the alcohol is having little effect on calming her nerves. Sitting straight-backed at the bar, Jo's the only one keeping it together. She rests her hand on the folder I entrusted to her, obviously not letting it out of her sight. *Good.*

Geoff speaks before anyone has the chance. "Thank you again for your patience last night. And for your statements as to your whereabouts when Mrs. Kramer was attacked."

"Do you have any idea who did it?" Sylvia's voice cracks, dry as tinder.

"I'm not at liberty to say at this stage."

"But you told us last night that we were safe." Kristen's voice rises in pitch.

"I said everyone should stay indoors. Unfortunately, Mrs. Kramer was attacked while on her balcony."

"Holy smokes. You can't keep us prisoners here while some lunatic kills us off one by one." For once, Tony's outrage is understandable, and the other guests agree.

"We're hopeful of solving the case in the next day or so."

"Hopeful?" John stands, his tone indignant. "Is that the best you can do?"

"I'm sorry, Mr. Torrens . . ."

"The police are always bloody sorry, but they never solve anything. Bloody useless in my opinion."

"John, please, sit down." Sylvia tugs at his hand but he flicks her away.

"I could teach you a thing or two about police work." Spoiling for a fight, he clenches his fists and makes toward Geoff. I rush in the best I can between them. In the distance, I hear the saving crescendo of the helicopter.

"The doctor's here now," I whisper to John so as not to embarrass him. "Why don't we go and meet him?"

He snaps back as if from a dissociative episode, focusses on me, and relaxes. "Yes," he says in an apologetic tone. "Let's go meet the doctor."

Sylvia darts into his other side and we head for the front doors. The last I hear is Geoff instructing no one to leave the homestead for any reason without his permission for the rest of their stay.

On my return, everyone's vacated the great room except Jo. She remains alone at the bar, an air of quiet resolve about her. I scan the room to make sure no one's eavesdropping.

I prop onto a stool beside her. "How are you holding up?"

"I'd be better if I could get some sleep. Hamers snores like a freight train."

It's not the answer I expect considering Maria's death is so recent, but Jo is an INTJ through and through. She'll keep her emotions under check.

I eye the folder but say nothing.

"From what I can ascertain, you're correct in your suspicions." My eyebrows shoot up in delighted surprise. "I'm still waiting on some of the respondents to get back to me which I assume they'll do tomorrow. But I've got what you're looking for." She pats the folder and smiles, a sinister thin-lipped smirk.

I place my hand on hers, a gentle, compassionate gesture. "Are you going to be all right with this?"

She doesn't flinch. "Yes. Don't worry about me."

"You're not going to do anything that will jeopardize the case, are you?"

"Trust me, Diana. I'm a by-the-book kinda person. You just do what you promised, and I'll keep out of the way."

"Thank you, Jo. Come find me tomorrow once you have everything."

With nothing but a nod, she takes the folder and leaves. Though she's given me her word, I'll have to watch that she doesn't crack under the pressure like John Torrens. The closer we get, the more is at stake, and if I'm correct, tomorrow will reveal the rest.

CHAPTER TWENTY-ONE

THE POLICE FOUR-WHEEL-DRIVE fishtails in the loose sand around some of the sharper corners to Jackaroo's Waterhole. Hamers drives rougher than Hayley but I expect she's as capable behind the wheel as she is on foot. Up ahead, the fluorescent police crime scene tape shrieks its incongruence against dense dark green vegetation.

Hamers turns off the engine. "We'll have to get out here and walk." As we alight the vehicle, she hands me a couple of plastic evidence bags and gloves while pocketing a set for herself. "What is it we're looking for, Mrs. Daniels?"

"I'm not sure, but . . ."

She follows my gaze. "What's he doing here?"

Before she strides over, I say, "I'm sure he's doing no harm. Leave him to me."

She flicks me a skeptical look. "Very well, but . . ."

"I'll bear all responsibility and advise the Senior Constable of the same."

"Very well." After I explain what we're looking for, she sets off to find evidence, while I wander over to the intruder.

"What brings you here?" I ask the enigmatic figure holding court on the top of the picnic table.

Tommy George's intense gaze lands first on my walking stick, and then on me. "Your ankle is nearly healed."

"Yes. It is. But I keep the stick just in case." I lift his gift in appreciation.

"For your ankle or for protection?"

His cryptic replies are like trying to finish a crossword with only half of the clues. But in all honesty, not only do I depend on the stick's support, I have also rehearsed a couple of 'thrust and parry' moves with it . . . just in case.

With his back to the waterhole, he sits cross-legged, his spear resting across his lap, his focus on the far ridge. "You find Nellie's killer yet?"

"Not yet, but I have my suspicions."

"Good. We must catch Waiwera soon before the evil spirit kills again." He's correct about that. Time is of the essence.

"You're not supposed to go beyond the police tape, you know." I nod to the bright yellow tape.

"Plastic tape won't stop Nellie's killer. Won't stop me either. I come to get closer to Nellie. Here, where she died. She will tell me who did this to her."

I didn't disbelieve him because I know there's evidentiary research relating to supernatural occurrences of this sort after people were deceased. "And has she told you anything yet?"

With the spring of a feline predator, he leaps from the table to the ground onto his haunches. He reaches for me to join him. Another feat of magic with a recovering ankle, but I struggle down. Drawing artful designs in the sand, he begins, "My Nellie has returned to the spirits in the sky." As his finger traces a bright sun in the sand, I'm reminded once more of *Lucy in the Sky with Diamonds*. The song that's been with me since I first arrived, with its lyrics about the girl with the kaleidoscope eyes popping into my mind on first meeting Nellie. "She waits there," he points to the sparkling sky above the far ridge. "She waits until we find Waiwera. Then she can be free."

We both gaze into the heavens, him communicating with his dead granddaughter and me hoping my hunches are correct. Tommy George and I aren't that different. Though we may come from different cultures and lead different lives, we both possess the same desire for justice, the same compulsion to find the truth and bring treachery to full account. I reckon to the outside world, we make an odd pair of friends, the sacred old man, and the city-slicker businesswoman. But Tommy George and I know that race, culture, and lifestyle have no bearing on the dispense of justice.

The sun glides higher to its noon position, scorching the land, and I like to think, firing our faith to find the killer. In front of us, the spear grass crackles, and Hamers appears like Doc Graham from a *Field of Dreams*, holding an evidence bag.

"I think I found what you were hoping for." Across her face, a proud smile cuts a wide swathe.

As she draws closer, I glance at the old man and, in unspoken agreement, we stare at the sky and say thank you to Nellie.

★ ★ ★ ★

BY THE TIME WE DROP Tommy George off at the Durack tree and return to the homestead, it's mid-afternoon. With evidence bag in hand, Hamers marches off to the library while I head for the shower. The novelty of being covered in red dust every time you leave the homestead wears thin. With no one in sight, I set a steady pace up the pathway, pleased to be alone with my thoughts.

"Yoo-hoo, Diana." Sylvia strides towards me, waving for me to stop. "Sorry, but I just wanted to thank you for getting the doctor for John."

"How is he?"

"Much better. The doctor prescribed him some Valium. He's resting now."

"I'm pleased." She worries at her hands, reluctant to leave. "Would you like to walk with me to my retreat?" I offer.

"That would be lovely. Thanks."

We fall into step at a leisurely pace. "Why did you choose to come here? To El Kwestro homestead?" I ask.

"To be honest, I can't remember. I think we heard someone talk about it at a dinner party a few years ago. Then when everything settled down after Stephanie's death, we just decided this was as good a place as any."

I push a little harder. "No other reason?"

She frowns at me. "No. Why? Should there be?"

"No. No. Of course not." I shrug off her concern. "We're just trying to piece a few things together."

"When do you think this will be over?" Her question is more a plea than anything else.

"You'll be able to leave very soon I think." My smile seems to reassure her. "Well, here we are. This is my retreat. Would you like to come in?"

She casts around as if looking for something or somebody. "No. That's all right. You must want a shower." She glances down at my boots. "You're covered in dust. Anyway, I better get back in case John needs me. I'll see you later."

Watching her retreat down the path, I'm again impressed by her ability to cope under stressful circumstances. Those ESFJ qualities have served her well. She'll need them even more shortly.

★ ★ ★ ★

AFTER A GLORIOUS SHOWER, I'M a new woman on a mission up to Woollybutt. "Timson." I nod at him, and he steps aside to allow me access. "Anyone come up here today?"

"No, Mrs. Daniels."

"Not even housekeeping?"

"Not a soul."

"Why don't you take a break for a while. I'll be here for at least an hour. Come back then."

"Thanks, Mrs. Daniels." He wastes no time hightailing it back to the homestead.

I open the front door and tiptoe inside in case Mimi's sleeping, but find her propped up in bed, sketching.

"How's the patient?"

"Diana." Sounding bright and cheerful, she tosses her pads and pencils aside and reaches both arms out for a hug. "I've been so bored stuck here under lock and key."

I lean in to inspect the egg on her head. "My goodness, that's huge. Have you seen it?"

"Yes. It's horrid. And my eye is turning the most hideous shade of purple."

"But at least you're alive," I remind her.

"I guess so. But what's Aaron going to say when he sees me?"

"That you're bloody lucky I expect." We giggle about her husband's likely witty comments about her appearance.

"So, what's been happening while I've been in quarantine?"

I recount my day since leaving her this morning.

"Shit! You're only waiting on a couple more things, and you've cracked the case. That's amazing." And with an English accent, adds, "Well done, Sherlock."

She makes me laugh. "Thank you, Watson." My accent isn't as good which makes her laugh. "Even if what I suspect is true, Geoff's not sure whether there's enough evidence to lay charges."

"Rubbish. It'll stick." Her faith is uplifting. "How much longer do I have to stay cooped up here?"

"You'll stay here with either Timson or Hamers on duty until we've got everything ready. We can't risk another attack."

She groans and follows it with a dramatic pout.

I flourish my arm toward the landscape and repeat her words from our first day. "El Kwestro is seven hundred thousand acres of pure magic." She pokes her tongue at me. "And now you have all the time you wanted to sketch this magnificent landscape."

"All right. All right. But I'm not happy."

"No. But you're alive, and I intend to keep you that way."

★ ★ ★ ★

AFTER TIMSON RETURNS IT'S MY turn to hightail it to the library. I find Geoff, head down, examining the notes and files on the table. When he lifts his head, his ravaged expression speaks of his tiredness though his eyes remain bright and alert. "Seems your hunch was right about Jackaroo's Waterhole. Well done." There's a ring of pride in his voice as he walks around the table to greet me, which bolsters my confidence.

I prop my stick beside the sofa and take a seat. "I didn't find it. Hamers did."

"Maybe so but you thought of it and told her where to look." He perches on the arm next to me.

I glance upwards and think of Nellie. "I had a little help . . ." I explain about meeting Tommy George.

"You're both a little left-of-field for me. But hey if it works who am I to question your methods. No matter. I've sent Hamers into town to get forensics onto it. She'll be back in a few hours I expect."

"Great. How did you go with the statements from last night?"

"They all seem to check out, including . . ."

I hold my hand up. "Don't tell me."

"But there was time for Mimi's attack. Not much, but enough."

"Of course, there was." I ladened the words with sarcasm. "Planned to the last detail."

"How is Mrs. Kramer?"

"She's doing okay."

"Has she remembered anything else about her attacker?" Hope laces his words.

"Nothing. I quizzed her again, but all she remembers is hearing someone come in from behind her on the left, and before she had time to turn around, whoever it was, walloped her. She was too groggy to even see them runoff. The whole thing is a blur, and I doubt it will ever get clearer. Did you have any luck finding the weapon?"

"No. And to be honest, I don't expect to. Whatever it was has probably been thrown away. There's just too much land here and with the river, there are any number of places the attacker could have tossed it."

A surge of tiredness takes me by surprise. It's been a stressful, few days. "Anything else?"

"No, as they say in the movies, all quiet on the western front. Everyone's behaving and biding their time."

I nod at the table. "Will we have enough?"

"Too early to say. After tomorrow, we'll know more. There's nothing else we can do now. Why don't you get an early night?"

"I think I will. See you in the morning." I stand and grab my stick. Though I don't really need it any longer, I've grown accustomed to its reassuring presence.

Geoff's cell phone rings and after he answers it, he waves a hand to stop me. "Are you sure?" he asks the person on the other end. "Great. Can you email me all that now?" He proceeds to give his details and then finishes the call.

I raise a brow in enquiry.

"Seems you were right on that other matter." He taps a finger to the back of his hand.

"I thought as much. But I still think there's more to it."

"Leave that to me. I'll get to the bottom of it. Now go and get some rest."

He'll not get an objection from me on that one. I smile my appreciation and make for the door. This time when I step into the corridor, I'm not alone and nearly collide with Amy coming out from her office. When we try to side-step each other, my stick rattles to the floor, and she swoops down to collect it, while I steady myself against the wall.

"I'm so sorry, Diana. Here let me help you." She hands back my stick which I clutch, thankful that my ankle hasn't twisted in the incident.

I catch my breath. "Quite all right, Amy. I was lost in my thoughts and wasn't watching where I was going." I smile to ease the moment.

"Not at all. I rush out of my office way too fast at times. Let me help you." She reaches out, but I refuse.

"Really, I'm fine. But you could do one thing for me."

"Of course. What is it?"

"Could you arrange for some sandwiches to be brought up to Woollybutt for Mimi, myself, and Officer Timson for dinner? We won't be joining the others."

She looks disappointed. "Isn't Mimi any better?"

"Oh, no, she's doing very well, thank you. It's just that we'd prefer to spend the night in if you don't mind."

"No trouble at all. I'll get someone to bring them up. Would you like some wine or drinks?"

I proceed with the rest of the order, after which, and with more caution, I escape the homestead before someone else catches me by surprise.

CHAPTER TWENTY-TWO

"AND I THOUGHT I WAS an early riser?" Sporting a radiant smile, Kristen wanders into the great room appearing more relaxed than I've seen her over the last few days. In fact, she's more like the young, honeymooner who arrived last Wednesday. "That coffee looks good. I think I'll get one." She turns heel toward the kitchen and returns shortly after. "Do you mind if I join you?"

"Not at all." I nod at the sofa.

She deposits her mug on the table and sits directly opposite me. "How's everything going?" Her tone is casual like she's asking about my most recent excursion and not a possible double homicide.

"We're making progress. And you?" I eyeball her over the rim of my mug.

"To be honest, I'm disappointed the Senior Constable has grounded us. Dale was supposed to fly us to see more rock art today. But we can't go now." I lift my brows but say nothing. She huffs a breath. "Peter and I will just have to hang out around here."

Leaning forward, I lower my mug to the table. "I can't help but notice that whenever you speak about Dale, it's like you've known him before coming to El Kwestro."

"Oh, I've known Dale for as long as I've known Peter. They're old friends."

I try for a poker face but not sure I succeed. "Really?"

"Yes. They only see each other a few times a year. But every now and then, if Dale's out our way, he'll drop in for a drink or they'll go out for dinner. Just the boys."

"I see." I dare not take my eyes off her while she sips her coffee.

Just as I'm about to find out more, someone calls my name. "Excuse me, Mrs. Daniels. Ready when you are." Looking her professional best, Hamers marches up and stands beside me. Her timing couldn't be worse, but there's nothing for it now.

"I'm sorry, Kristen. Officer Hamers is giving me a lift to town. It was nice talking to you. Have a lovely day."

"Thanks, Diana. You, too." The sunlight twinkles in her eyes. Sweet girl.

Side by side, I walk with Hamers to the front doors, delighted at an INFP's willingness to share.

After a few pleasantries, Hamers concentrates on her driving while I gaze out the window at the relentless terrain of dry, scorched earth. Everything here struggles to stay alive, to drag moisture from the ground, to hide from the blistering sun, even in winter. Yet I know once the wet season begins and the rains come, the landscape transforms into a verdant green panorama of life. The ninety-minute drive turns meditative, and as the plains speed past, my thoughts travel alongside them. The image of a circular walking labyrinth flashes on the marquee in my mind. So many curves and dead ends leading nowhere. That's how our progress this past week has been, down one path, only to back-track and start again. But I know there's one walkway that will lead me to the heart of the labyrinth. To the dark heart of whoever is responsible for what's been happening at El Kwestro. Though I have my hunch as to who it might be, I'm not sure yet. Still, we're close, and when the last couple of outstanding items are finalized today, we'll know for certain. And like the wet season, justice will rain down leaving the innocent to flourish, if only in memory.

★ ★ ★ ★

"THIS IS IT, MRS. DANIELS." Hamers edges the vehicle into the curb. "How do you want to proceed with this interview?"

"I'd prefer to begin and then if necessary, you can step in in your official capacity."

"Suits me. I don't think you'll have any issues getting the information you need."

"I think you're right. After all, it's a simple question that only needs a yes or no answer."

"Righto. Let's go."

It takes little time to explain to the owner of the business the reason for our visit and to elicit the answer. As suspected, it's a negative. I check off another entry on my mental ledger, and we depart.

"The next stop isn't going to be this easy," I say, sashing my seatbelt.

"I know the suspect. I think he'll crumble like a biscuit when we show him the evidence." The gleeful anticipation on her face elicits a smile from me. "But this is police business, Mrs. Daniels. He's going to be charged. So, I'll handle it."

"Of course." I wouldn't think of taking that pleasure from her.

"But feel free to jump in at the end if you need anything."

"Thank you."

She angles me a keen look. "Ready?"

"Absolutely."

When we enter the premises, Officer Hamers' foreboding presence and stern gaze nail our suspect. His degree of anxiety ratchets up immediately, and I know my hunch is correct. Though his denials are delivered with an affronted attitude, it takes little time for him to 'crumble like a biscuit.' Hamers reads him his rights, slaps on the cuffs, and we transfer him to the police station and leave him in the capable hands of another officer.

"That's two out of two, Mrs. Daniels," Hamers says as we ready ourselves for the drive back.

"Indeed, it is." While my stomach does a happy dance, my mind double-checks its ledger, searching for any loose ends or unanswered questions.

Hamers takes a series of turns leading to the highway, and in no time, we're speeding to El Kwestro. "I don't want you to name names, but do you know who's behind all this now?"

To be honest, I'm a little surprised that the person hasn't come into clear view. I glance up to the sky and silently hum

Lucy in the Sky. Am I missing something? *Come on Nellie. Help me out here.* But still nothing. The only thing I can do is trust that when the time comes, all will be revealed. Narcissistic by nature, murderers love the limelight and it's this self-obsession that often brings them undone.

Not wanting to dampen Hamers' spirits, I say, "Sometimes the right person has to pay for the wrong crime."

She shoots me a sly smile and nods. "Agreed."

While Hamers drives on, I avert my gaze out the window. There's another sixty-minute drive before us which gives me plenty of time to reach the heart of the labyrinth.

★ ★ ★ ★

"WHERE ARE WE IN RELATION to the Durack tree?" I ask after about thirty minutes.

Hamers points ahead. "The turn-off's just up here a bit."

"Can we go there?"

She shrugs. "Sure. But why?"

"I have a hunch Tommy George might be there."

She gives me a skeptical look with an exaggerated cock of her brow but obliges. I'm uncertain as to why Tommy George would be at the tree, but since it's not too far out of our way, I figure it's worth a try.

The corrugated dirt road worsens which slows our approach to the enormous upside-down tree stuck in the middle of nowhere. The landscape's rare beauty, isolation, and magic never cease to impress me, more so now because Tommy George comes into view, propped like a brolga on one leg at the tree.

"I'll be damned." Hamers slows the vehicle to a stop. "How did you know?"

It's my turn to shrug. "I don't know how I know. I just do."

When Tommy George's eyes meet mine through the windscreen, he gives me a nod but doesn't move. Once out of the car, I lean into my stick and walk over to where he stands in the only piece of shade for miles. A lingering sense of loss hangs from him like a heavy cloak.

"How are you?" I ask.

He remains motionless, holding onto his spear, his dark eyes drilling into mine. "You found my Nellie's killer."

"I'm not sure." I grip the walking stick he gave me, suddenly realizing that we're bound by some force of nature coursing through the wood. Is that why he gave me the stick in the first place? As some sort of ancient magic that only he knows how to interpret. Tiny pinpricks of unease crawl over my skin that give rise to a spontaneous shudder.

His mood momentarily lightens, and he smiles as if reading my thoughts and feelings. But the seriousness quickly returns, and his lips pull in a tight smile. "You found Waiwera."

"I think so."

He unfolds his leg. "You have," he says with far more certainty than I feel. "Evil spirit cannot hide now." Without hesitation, he steps off toward the four-wheel drive, leaving me to scuttle behind him.

★ ★ ★ ★

HAMERS SWINGS INTO THE DRIVEWAY and nods toward the homestead. "Something's going on by the look of it."

Up ahead, Geoff seems to be doing his best to calm the situation with considerable arm-waving and head-nodding. I scan the group for Timson and breathe a sigh of relief that he's not there. Hopefully, he's still standing guard at Woollybutt, keeping Mimi safe. As we draw closer, the raised voice of John Torrens reaches us.

"I don't care what you say, Senior Constable, I'm leaving. I'm not staying here any longer. Do you hear me?"

Beside him, Sylvia pleads for her husband to calm down, but he shakes her off. The three of us slip out of the vehicle, and while Hamers joins her boss, Tommy George and I loiter on the edge of the commotion. Geoff acknowledges us with a tilt of his head before returning to the situation.

"I'm sorry, Mr. Torrens, but no one is permitted to leave."

"I've been through this before, and I'm not going through it again."

I notice John's hands clenching into fists at his side.

"Please, John. Come back to the room and take the sedatives the doctor gave you." On the verge of tears, Sylvia gently tugs at her husband's arm.

"No, woman. Leave me alone." He snaps his arm, sending her stumbling backward into me.

She folds into my arms. "Oh god. What am I going to do?"

"Leave it to the Senior Constable. He'll sort it out," I say, rubbing sympathetic circles on her shoulders.

"You seriously don't think my wife, or I had anything to do with this terrible business?"

"It's not that, Mr. Torrens . . ."

"Then what is it?" he bellows. "I don't understand why Dale can't fly us into town and we can leave from there."

Amy intervenes, "Perhaps if we all went into my office, we could discuss this. Maybe the Senior Constable might change his mind and permit you to leave . . ."

Geoff shoots her a death-stare. "I won't be changing my mind. Now. That's the end of it, Mr. Torrens. Officer Hamers will escort you back to your room, and I suggest you take your wife's advice and the medication that the doctor prescribed."

In the blink of an eye, John shifts his weight and swings a punch at Hamers. His arm hovers mid-air like a slow-motion movie, but before it has a chance to connect, he crumbles in the middle from the quick jab Geoff administers.

"John!" Sylvia leaps from my arms to comfort her husband, while Hamers stands primed in case he wants a second round.

After catching his breath, John threatens to lodge an official complaint over Geoff's behavior before he's escorted to his room flanked by Sylvia and Hamers.

"Shit!" Geoff drags his fingers through his buzz cut, then turns on Amy. "No one is leaving here. Have you got that?"

Her chin lifts. "Yes, Senior Constable. I've got it."

"Good. Now off you go."

She snaps a turn with the same curtness as his command and stalks inside the homestead.

I try for levity. "My, you've had a day by the looks of it."

"Don't start with me."

I know his bark is worse than his bite. "You look like you could do with some good news."

A huge breath escapes his chest. "I sure could." He faces Tommy George. "How are you holding up?"

He cackles a sarcastic sound. "Better than you."

"Yeah. Yeah. Come on then." He strides off in front of us, while Tommy George and I exchange a smirk and bring up the rear.

★ ★ ★ ★

ONCE IN THE LIBRARY, I sit on the sofa, motioning Tommy George beside me. We both place our props to the side, and like eager schoolchildren unable to hide our amusement, we watch Geoff. "You first," I say. "How did all that start with the Torrens?"

He leans against the table, arms folded, face frowned. "I heard it from here." He nods to the window that opens out onto the homestead's main entrance about twenty meters away. "John was demanding Dale fly him into Kununurra. He's was getting heated, so I dashed out front to calm things down."

"Aside from not being permitted to leave, why didn't Dale just take the job? Do it on the quiet, rather than turn it down," I ask.

Geoff reaches behind him and fists a handful of keys in the air. "Because I've got the keys to every means of transportation that's here. No one's getting out of here unless it's on foot." His grin says it all. Smart move.

"I wondered why Dale was hanging around near the chopper. Hoping you'd change your mind I expect."

"Yeah. Well, they can all live in hope." He dumps the keys on the table with a loud crash.

"So, Nellie's killer is here? Now," Tommy George asks.

"Yes, sir. We believe so," Geoff replies.

"We need to go through a couple of things firstly though," I say.

Tommy George stares at me hard. His look of vengeance is the same as the one I've seen on John Torrens' face. He wants to confront Nellie's killer and administer his own form of justice. But that's not going to happen.

"I'll get Hamers to organize something for you to eat and drink while you wait," Geoff says.

"No need. I'll be outside until you're ready." The old man rises and with spear in hand, leaves the library. Both Geoff and I go to the window and watch him head for a nearby tree under which he resumes his one-legged pose and waits.

Geoff shakes his head and with admiration in his voice says, "He's got the constitution of an ox and the focus of a fox."

"Agreed. He wants Nellie's killer to be arrested. He's not leaving here until it's done."

"I just hope he doesn't take matters into his own hands with that bloody spear. Do you think we should confiscate it from him?

I bark a cynical laugh. "Are you going to try and take it? Because I sure as hell won't ask him to give it up."

Geoff's mouth twists in frustration. "No. I guess not. But I better make sure Hamers and Timson keep an eye on him. The old bugger's as quick as a snake, and he could throw that spear before we could make a move on him."

I feel a little sorry for Geoff. Not only has he the case to contend with but also an unpredictable, skilled, and respected elder seeking retribution for his granddaughter's murder.

We return to the table. "Righto. What happened with you and Hamers in town?" he asks.

For the next couple of hours, we paw over evidence, folders, and charts, and review emails and interview notes until we come to the final pieces.

"Did you get that email we were expecting?" I ask him.

He nods, and I share my morning conservation in the great room with him.

"Has Jo been in to see you yet?" This is the last piece we need.

"Yes. She sent this through."

I lean over his shoulder while he opens the emails she'd forwarded to him. We scroll through them one-by-one, each telling the same story. I flop into the chair beside him. "Is it enough?"

He rubs a hand across his bristled chin. "To be honest, it's pretty circumstantial. And there's a helluva lot of coincidence here."

"But life can be like that."

"True." He finishes with an unconvinced nod.

"So, what are we going to do? We can't leave Tommy George standing out there for the rest of his days?"

The Senior Constable stands to his full height, flexes his muscles, and tilts his head from side to side. After a final glance out the window, he faces me and says, "Let's catch us a killer."

On a deep inhale, I push myself up from the table to stand beside him. "Let's do that."

★ ★ ★ ★

MIMI AND I STARE AT her reflection. "I can't go down there looking like this."

It's not the bump on her head that's the problem. She can pull a few tendrils of hair to conceal that. It's the massive purplish-black patch that's engulfed her eye that shocks the onlooker. "I look like I've done three rounds with Mike Tyson."

She does. "Mimi, if it hadn't been for you, we would never have solved this case. You have to come down." She pouts at me. "Besides, Timson will be with us, and you're not staying here by yourself."

She huffs out a breath. "All right. But I'm not happy."

I don't blame her. "Listen, let's see if we can't conceal the color with some make-up." I rummage out a concealer stick from my makeup purse.

"You know what'll happen. My eye will end up the color of chartreuse. I'm an artist, remember? I know what happens when you mix colors."

I can't help myself, but I laugh out loud, and thankfully she joins me. We laugh so hard we cry tears, which increases the swelling around her eye.

When we regain some composure, she snatches the concealer from my hand. "At least let me do it." She applies her craft with a deft touch and within no time, the concealer has helped, though she's right, her skin tone is a strange yellowish-green.

"That's much better," I say, trying to sound convincing.

She rolls her eyes at me in the mirror. "It'll have to do." Another smirk. "Okay, Holmes. I'm ready." She hooks her arm through mine. "Let's go catch this killer and then have a well-earned drink."

We walk back through the one-room retreat and pause for a moment. Across the gorge, the landscape lays serene, untouched by time. Nothing seems to have changed for millions of years, yet in six short days two young women have been murdered and the lives of so many have been, and are about to be changed, forever.

"For Nellie," I whisper, imagining her dark, dewy eyes.

"For Maria," Mimi adds.

As the door closes behind us, Mimi stops and faces me. "Are you sure you know what you're doing?"

"Not entirely. But I made a promise to Tommy George."

With my walking stick on one side and Mimi with her painted eye and egg-shaped bump on the other, I set off to expose the killer of the outback.

CHAPTER TWENTY-THREE

THE SUN'S SLOW DESCENT HAS just begun, bathing El Kwestro in an eerie, luminescent light before its dramatic transformation into a blood-red sky. As requested, the long table stands in the middle of the lawn like a boat set adrift in a sea of green. The staff carry in two extra tables and position one at each end at right angles and the lone boat becomes a gigantic U-shaped staple pointing toward the low rock wall at the end of the lawn. Since Geoff needs to keep his wits about him in case of trouble, I'll conduct the meeting and this set-up is my preferred formation—fifteen suspects, five on each table, me in the center, and three officers stationed at the back. I think of Tom who was so articulate when he litigated his cases in court, hoping his words will come to me now. Everyone is here, murmuring anxiously under the mounting pressure. Even the birds chatter as if anticipating a storm. And a storm there will be.

To my left, Tony and Trish stand close to each other, holding hands. Perhaps they've found a new appreciation for each other because of this drama. John Torrens possesses a glassy-eyed gaze and is noticeably more at ease. The sedatives are working. Beside him, his champion and wife, Sylvia keeps a firm grip on his arm. I admire her tenacity and devotion. The Pullmans stand furthest away on the lawn, arm in arm, watching the sunset, oblivious to the other guests. They're in the honeymoon spirit. Near the pool, Jo gives me a nod and turns away. Though she appears staunch in her convictions, I fear her resolve may be tested this evening. Under the far tree at the pool, Tommy George stands like a statue. If I hadn't been searching for him, he would have been easy to miss. I wonder if anyone else even knows he's there. Andrew's off to one side, looking nervous and forlorn. On the other side, I spot the tell-tale glimmer of a lit cigarette and spy Dale sucking back his addiction in his insouciant manner. Amy wanders around with a tray of hors d'oeuvres and a tight smile, but her offer meets little interest. Gillian and Chris Richards loiter close to Officer Hamers and Timson, while it's obvious that Cameron, the night chef, feels out of place in this group. He's a behind-the-scenes sort of guy.

Freshly shaven, showered, and uniformed, Geoff marches towards us. "You ready?"

"I think so," I say, despite my nerves speed knitting in my stomach. "Is everything set?"

"Ready to go." His eyes sparkle, sending a zing of electricity through me.

"Okay." I clap my hands together and give them a rub. The gesture brings a spontaneous smile to my lips as I remember that Detective John Nash used to do the same thing as his power practice. Funny the idiosyncrasies we pick up from others. I give my collared shirt a tug, collect my walking stick leaning beside me, and make for center stage on the lawn.

Geoff and I have spent time planning the seating arrangement of the fifteen guests, and now he, Hamers, and Timson escort everyone to their seats. To my left and starting closest to me, Mimi, Tony, Trish, Dale, and Jo slip into their assigned chairs, after which Hamers takes her position behind them patrolling that quadrant of the lawn. Across the top table, Peter, Kristen, Tommy George, Sylvia, and John take their seats, under Geoff's guidance, who then joins me at the front. To my right and starting furthest from me sit the El Kwestro staff, Gillian, Chris, Amy, Cameron, and Andrew. Once everyone is seated, incessant fidgeting of glasses and sipping of pre-dinner aperitifs replace the last remnants of conversation. My gaze does a slow sweep of the concerned, frustrated, and curious faces, before coming to rest on Geoff beside me. Though his demeanor is official, there's a bemused twinkle in his eyes. We stare, straight-faced at the suspects, their restlessness rising. Many a stakeholder has cracked in boardroom meetings due to the prolonged silence and anticipation caused by the meeting leader and it's a tactic we employ this evening. With the bloodied sunset behind us creating a superb theatrical backdrop adding to the drama, the scene is set. Though I'm not a religious person, I say a silent prayer that the evidence is enough and that the murderer will break under pressure.

Geoff opens the proceedings. "Thank you, everyone, for your patience over the past few days and for your cooperation in changing your plans to remain at El Kwestro.

"We didn't have a choice." Though peevish, Peter's comment lacks his signature intensity.

Geoff ignores him. "We've gathered you here this evening to give you an update on the case."

"What?" Tony sounds affronted already. "You still don't know who killed these girls?"

"Shush, Tony." Trish jabs him in the ribs, and I notice a bottle of water rather than alcohol in front of her. Perhaps she's replacing her addiction with assertiveness. A good choice if she is. He scowls at her but says no more.

"Oh, we know, Mr. Wilson." Geoff's assurance leaves no doubt that the killer is among us and all will be revealed. Another good tactic because sideways glances, agitated whispers, and chair fidgeting increase. "I'll let Mrs. Daniels explain." Before anyone has time to question him further, Geoff strides to the back of the group, leaving me the master of ceremonies like the ringmaster in a circus. And in many ways, that's how I feel. The audience, the performers, and the wild animals must perform on my cue, except none of us have rehearsed this particular routine, so anything could happen. All eyes are fixed on me, some fascinated that this middle-aged woman is going to reveal a killer, some skeptical that I'm capable of the task, and some, like Mimi willing me to get the show on the road and nail the bastard. And of course, there's the killer who's planning their next move, ready to leap from the fray like an escaped tiger.

After taking a deep breath to calm the excitement swirling in my stomach, I begin. "We have here a mastermind." A slight pause for effect. "In crime as in life, there are those who are blessed with critical thinking skills far superior to the average person. This gives them an unfair advantage and as such, their success rate is higher than most." As expected, my opening remarks capture my audience's curiosity, and all fidgeting stops. *Excellent!* Now, I have a baseline from which to gauge everyone's behavior. Once I check off each persons' posture, I proceed. "We have here more than the murders of Nellie Walker and Maria Loukas. We also have the attempted murder of Mimi Kramer." All eyes turn to her with murmurs of sympathy. "And the attempted murder of me." The murmurs rise to match the increased tension I purposely triggered.

"What do you mean?" Kristen asks.

"At Amaroo Falls. Someone deliberately pushed that rock from the ledge above in the hope of hitting me. Probably hoping to kill me."

"But I was there with you," Kristen says. "We didn't see anyone, Diana. Who was it?"

"We'll come to that soon. I can assure you, though, it was all masterminded by the same person who killed Nellie and Maria and tried to kill Mimi." More murmurs and sideways glances.

"My god, that's terrible." Gillian drags a hand across her face, leaving behind a few extra worry lines. "Why here? Why at El Kwestro?"

"That was the first question that needed to be answered. Why would someone intentionally murder Nellie to begin with? Then why kill Maria. It's obvious why the killer wanted me out of the way . . .

"Because you were getting too close," Mimi says.

"Yes."

"But why Mimi?" Kristen again.

"Because the killer thought that Maria might have told Mimi something. Something that might implicate them."

"And did she? Did Maria tell Mimi something?" Tony asks.

"As it turns out, no." I pause and eyeball the lead suspects, but as expected not a flinch. "Back to the original question that this entire case hinges on, why kill Nellie Walker?"

"Because my Nellie was a smart girl." Tommy George speaks with deep affection and pride. "She suspected someone of doing something wrong. That why's Waiwera killed her."

Sylvia swivels to face him. "Who's Waiwera?"

"Evil spirit," he replies. "He took my Nellie from me and now he must pay." He glances at his spear laid on the table in front of him, and I suspect like me, others sense an ugly promise in his words.

John's frown matches those of the other guests. "Sorry, I'm lost. Are you saying Nellie was killed by an evil spirit? And not by someone here?"

I explain, "We're saying that someone here with evil intentions killed Nellie."

"But why? She was just a young innocent girl. Why would anyone want to harm her?" John's voice softens as if in memory of his daughter.

"Because she'd overheard something about the murderer without even knowing its significance. Not until you and Sylvia arrived."

A gasp goes up.

"What do you mean? We didn't have anything to do with Nellie's death."

"Why would we want to hurt Nellie?" John and Sylvia scramble to defend themselves, talking over each other.

I wave my hands up and down. "No. You had nothing to do with her death, but your presence here and our conversation on Tuesday at sundowners set in motion a sad and unexpected chain of events. At first, the coincidence seemed impossible, however, Mimi's attack proved we were on the right track."

With the sun's final farewell only minutes away, I pause to match its dramatic departure.

"Go on then," John urges. "Tell us."

"Nellie thought she knew the identity of your daughter's lover. The person Stephanie committed suicide over when their relationship broke up." And with that, the sun drops from the sky like a stone, and John springs from his seat, ready to kill.

"Who? Tell me who he is? I'll kill him with my bare hands. Right here. Right now."

Sylvia nails me with a withering glare. One filled with horror and disgust that I would put them through this ordeal publicly. But to flush out a murderer sometimes collateral damage is warranted. That's what I'd been trying to convince myself of all day, but I still feel traitorous.

"That's a cheap trick," she snaps at me. "How could you?" She turns her attention to John, and with Geoff and Tommy George's help, quiets him enough to take his seat.

No time for apologies now. I must keep the momentum because the conviction rests with a confession. "It turns out that Stephanie's lover, identified only in her diary as Ace, is here at El Kwestro." More outrage and shock, but I press on. "Nellie overheard us when you mentioned the name Ace" — I glance at Sylvia— "last Wednesday after lunch when she delivered our drinks down at the pool. She came up to my retreat that afternoon seeking my advice. Unfortunately, she didn't tell me what it was she wanted my advice on, except some hypothetical situation of overhearing something of importance. I begged her to confide in me, but she said it would keep, and she'd talk to her grandfather the following morning."

Even from where I stand, I can see a combination of grief, anger, and impatience in Tommy George's eyes. Like John, he wants vengeance and it's clear he believes my long-winded explanation is a waste of time.

Still, I stay the course. "But she was murdered that night. Nellie's murder was opportunistic and rushed. The murderer knew Nellie had heard the nickname of Ace before and that she must be silenced in case she revealed what she'd heard to the Torrens. The incident with the dessert and Peter Pullman's behavior gave the murderer the perfect opportunity. Throw doubt onto Peter for his racist outburst as motive. Then dispose of Nellie immediately after a seemingly crime of passion befitting Peter's violent nature. But it was neither."

"See. I told you I didn't have anything to do with her death." A note of triumph echoes in Peter's voice before he's quickly hushed by Kristen.

I continue, "Though there was only a short lead time, Nellie's murder was planned by a mastermind capable of—"

"I've had enough of this shit. Which one of you bastards killed my Stephanie and murdered Nellie?" Though the emotions waging war in John Torren's mind, body, and soul are acute and chronic, the Valium keeps a lid on him as does Geoff's strong but firm hand on his shoulder.

Ignoring another scathing glare from Sylvia as she consoles her husband, I continue, "On Wednesday evening, the wicked deed was executed. Nellie was lured into a car, drugged, and driven to Jackaroo's Waterhole, where she was killed, and her body dumped. Forensics prove that the rock and the cloth found at the scene were used in her murder. Plus, there's other evidence that we've since collected which points directly to the killer."

"For god's sake, woman, who is it?" Tony's demand is joined by other murmurs of agreement.

"It sounds very circumstantial." Jo's comment comes just at the right time, and I inwardly thank her for her even, measured tone.

"That's what we thought until Mimi overheard a conversation before lunch on Saturday when the nickname Ace was used again. Mimi thought nothing of it at the time, but after she was attacked, I asked her to recount everything she'd heard or seen that day, and there it was. Another mention of Ace."

"You said that Nellie was driven to Jackaroo's Waterhole on Wednesday night. In what car?" Gillian the systems queen doesn't miss a beat. "There were only three vehicles on the homestead that night. Mr. Pullman's rental and the two company vehicles, which were accounted for on the Company Vehicle Register I gave you."

"I'm coming to that. But it's worth noting that the person who murdered Nellie for fear she might expose them as Ace, also killed Maria for completely different reasons."

"This is sounding very complicated, Diana," Amy says, her brow untouched by the confusion in her voice.

"Yes, it's been like trying to catch a tiger by its tail. But in my line of work, I know nothing happens by coincidence. There's always a motivating factor behind every action. And the same was true for Maria's death. It just didn't have anything to do with the motive behind Nellie's murder." I glance at Jo who gives me a slow nod, and I know she's resolved to remain strong. "The motive for Maria's murder was the art."

"What do you mean? The art?" Trish asks, concerned.

"Last Friday night, at the beginning of the Kimberley Under the Stars event, if you recall here on the lawn was a colonnade of canvasses painted by Aboriginal artists."

"Yes. We bought some for our gallery." A hint of pride resounds in Tony's voice leaving little doubt as to his opinion of himself for being a shrewd businessman.

I flash him a tight smile. "I noticed Maria take a particular interest in one canvas called Rainbow Bush Art."

"Yes. We bought that one. What about it?" A tinge of doubt replaces his pride.

"Maria told Mimi and me that she'd been to the artist's studio in Victoria and watched her paint."

"So?" Tony's apprehension increases.

"It wasn't so much what Maria said, it was the way she studied the canvas. And when she told us about the artist's technique, she kept glancing at the painting as if unsure."

"Unsure of what?" This time it's Trish.

"That's what I couldn't work out. Until after she was murdered."

Before the Wilsons have the chance to pursue this any further, Christopher Richards asks, "But are you sure it wasn't an accident. Perhaps Maria fell from her balcony? This whole place could do with better safety measures, but the owners won't spend the money."

"I agree with you on that one, Chris. El Kwestro could do with a serious OH&S audit. However, as far as Maria's death is concerned, the M.E. confirmed bruises on her upper arms indicative of being grabbed. Whoever she let into her room that night, pushed her over the balcony."

The crowd grows restless. Too much smoke and mirrors and not enough substance. I switch tack again. "Then there's the pink Argyle diamond ring that Jo bought from Peter early Friday evening with the intention of proposing to Maria."

Sylvia, Trish, and Kristen chime a sad, romantic chorus toward Jo.

"We've discussed this." Peter sounds offended. "That was a legitimate business transaction."

"It would have been had the diamond been a pink Argyle."

A sharp intake of breath from the assembled guests is barely heard over Peter's indignation. "What do you mean? That ring came with a valuation certifying its authenticity. Of course, it's a pink Argyle diamond. How dare you?"

"The real question is how dare you and Stuart from Top End Jewelers pass off high-grade pink sapphires and sell them as pink Argyle diamonds with exorbitant valuation certificates to unsuspecting buyers."

All heads turn in his direction. Peter clamps his lips together as the truth dawns on him that his partner has given him up. Judgmental stares assail him, including Kristen's whose expression is pitiful. With her honeymoon expectations and hopes of a happy family dashed at her feet, she does nothing to cover her disappointment. "Oh, Peter, you didn't. You promised me those days were over."

Avoiding her gaze, he turns away and says nothing.

"But it's not only Stuart who's complicit in this crime, is it?" A deafening silence descends. "There's a third person. Someone who works as a go-between. Someone who buys the sapphires overseas and brings them back. And someone you threatened over their whereabouts on Wednesday night as blackmail for a bigger cut of the profits, I suspect."

Peter sneers. "That's a lie. Everything you've said is a lie."

"Unfortunately, Stuart's statement implicates you. As does your past juvenile record."

"How can Peter's past have anything to do with this?" Kristen's lingering concern for her husband and the pain he suffered in his past is commendable though misplaced.

"Because that's where he met the third accomplice." I pause and swivel to my left. "Dale Baker."

For the first time, our enigmatic helicopter pilot lifts a brow but is otherwise motionless. I give him a moment in case he wants to say something in his defense but as an ISTJ he stays characteristically quiet.

I return to the crowd. "Peter and Dale met each other when they were teenagers in juvenile detention. Peter for his increasingly violent behavior, and Dale for his escalating fraud misdemeanors. Both became staunch mates on the road to crime, honing their skills and plying their trades into illegal profits. They've kept in touch throughout the years and when the opportunity arose to substitute and sell pink sapphires for pink Argyles, they enlisted Stuart's help in forging the valuation certificates. A neat scheme with a three-way split. That was until after selling Jo one of his rings, Maria got herself killed which warranted a police investigation. Without her death, perhaps the caper mightn't have been discovered. Well, at least, not here or now."

"This is a fantastical story without any proof." Peter tries one last time.

"Stuart has given the police all the documentation needed to lay charges against you both."

Peter casts a furtive look at Dale who sits stony-faced. If he thought his co-conspirator would come to his aid or speak on their behalf, he's sorely mistaken. After the altercation between them that I witnessed, Dale will turn against Peter as soon as they take his statement.

Dale waves his packet in the air. "Do you mind if I smoke?"

My god, the man's got nerves of steel.

"You can stand next to Hamers and smoke there." Geoff instructs Hamers to close in as Dale strolls a few steps back and lights up. Hamers bristles on high alert, ready to jump if he tries to make a move. Geoff's words ring in my ear about Dale being a cool customer. Never more so than now. Though implicated and likely to be convicted, his veneer remains unruffled. But I know, inside he's seething.

"And this brings us back to the Aboriginal art being brokered and sold from El Kwestro—"

"What about it?" Tony seems to intuit the inevitable.

"The canvases you bought believing they were authentic Aboriginal art were forgeries."

Beside him, Trish glances upward. "Dear god in heaven."

I rush on trying to quell the growing disbelief. "On Friday night, when I saw Maria viewing the Rainbow Bush canvas, I sensed something was wrong by the way she kept studying it. And then when I saw her having a serious conversation and pointing back to the colonnade shortly afterward, I knew something was definitely wrong."

"Having a conversation with who?" Gillian asks.

"She brought it to my attention." Amy leans forward and smiles at her reporting manager. "Diana's correct. Maria thought something was off with the painting. I intended following up on it Saturday but with Maria's death and everything else, it got replaced by more urgent matters."

Tony thumps his hands down. "What's going on here? Are you trying to rip me off? I've been buying art from you and paying top dollar and now I find out it's fake. What sort of operation are you running here?"

"Please, Mr. Wilson, I haven't had time to investigate yet. Rest assured, I will get to the bottom of it. I'm confident that the art you've purchased is authentic." Amy delivers her assurance in an exaggerated conciliatory tone, but where there used to be only confidence, now there's a hint of desperation.

He growls, "It had better be, or I'll be suing this whole god-damn place." He slumps back with a huff while Trish shoots daggers at Amy. Suddenly it strikes me that Trish mightn't have been jealous of the homestead manager but wary of her. Perhaps I underestimated Mrs. Wilson and even through her alcoholic fog, she suspected Amy was up to no good.

I say to Amy, "It won't be necessary for you to investigate." I then gesture to my left. "For those who don't know, Jo is a forensic attorney, and she was more than happy to help find who murdered her partner. And as one of the best attorneys in the country, she's turned up certain anomalies."

"What do you mean?" Amy asks.

"She contacted several of the artists listed on the purchase orders of the canvases sold, and they never supplied those paintings to El Kwestro."

Amy interjects, indignant. "I'm sorry. She must be mistaken. Every one of those purchase orders is correct. I can vouch for it."

Jo waves the folder of purchase orders which I gave her on Saturday afternoon. "That's not true. I have evidence here which points directly to Aboriginal art reproductions being sold to overseas buyers through El Kwestro."

Tony's on his feet, shouting at Amy. "I thought you were up to something when you refused to refund those couple of artworks in the last shipment. Giving me some cockamamy story and then promising to sort it out on this invoice. It wasn't until I threatened to tell Gillian that you sorted it out quick smart. I'm going to sue the pants off this place . . ." His arms flail in violent circles.

"Oh, Mr. Wilson, there won't be any need for that. We'll get this sorted out. I promise." Gillian's on her feet, leaning across the table toward him. "I'll personally attend to it."

Tony jabs an accusatory finger at Amy. "I want her fired immediately."

"Absolutely," Gillian says. "El Kwestro will also press charges." She waves at Geoff. "Senior Constable."

Amid the rising pandemonium, Tommy George stands, his voice rising above the hubbub. "I don't care about fake diamonds." Everyone hushes and watches him flick a dismissive hand toward Peter and Dale. "And I don't care about forged art." He half-turns and stares hard at Amy. "Though there will be another form of justice for disrespecting the art of my people." He lifts his eyes and stares directly at me. "I care about who killed my Nellie."

With an emotional burden nearly too heavy to bear, John pushes to his feet and knuckles his fists on the table. "Who the hell is Ace?"

I notice Dale slip his butt into his packet. "Dale, won't you join us please." As Hamers tails him to his chair, I glance at Geoff who nods that all is going to plan.

"Very well." I begin the final step to catching our killer. "My late husband, Tom was a lawyer with exceptional deductive skills. I recall during one of his most challenging cases he said to me afterward, 'The one to fear the most is the one you gave all your trust to.' And this has certainly been the case here and for your daughter, Stephanie." I offer Sylvia and John an apologetic, compassionate look, though I doubt it's accepted in full. "You see Stephanie fell in love with Ace who then ended the relationship breaking Stephanie's heart and tipping her over the edge to suicide. Ace was the one to fear, the one that Stephanie gave all her trust to. However, Stephanie didn't know that Ace was cold, calculating, self-absorbed to the point of narcissism, and capable of evil acts because even though Stephanie's death was reported as a jilted lover takes her own life, Ace never came forward or demonstrated any remorse over the young girl's death. In fact, Ace simply disappeared and started again. The difficulty for the police was who was Ace? They couldn't find anyone who could have been Stephanie's lover or who knew this person. The case went cold until now when by the strangest of coincidences, the Torrens decided to come here to get away from everything to do with Stephanie's death. That's why I asked you, Sylvia, why did you choose to come here, and you mentioned El Kwestro had been recommended at a dinner party. It turns out serendipity has had a hand in your holiday. From my own experience, I know life can be stranger than fiction and that sometimes the wrongs of the past can be righted in the present. And that seems to be the case here. Anyway, Nellie had previously heard someone here use the name Ace as did Mimi last Saturday. Based on my hunches and after much investigative work by our Senior Constable, we found out that Ace was the abbreviation of a person's name, not just a nickname. It turns out that Ace was a part-time tutor at Sydney University, tutoring architecture students like Stephanie." I glance at Geoff and Timson to make sure they're ready while nerves flurry in my stomach. "In fact, Ace was Stephanie's tutor, but campus records identify her as Amy Catherine Emerson."

"You mean our Amy? El Kwestro's manager?" Cameron shoves his chair back away from her in disgust.

"You, bitch!" John lunges like a cheetah in Amy's direction but Geoff and Timson grab him within three strides.

"It was you? You were Stephanie's lover?" Sylvia's on her feet, screaming in disbelief.

Then the truth hits John like a freight train. By his response, I suspect it's a truth he never knew. His daughter was a lesbian. Sylvia reaches him as he crumbles to the ground, heaving deep heartfelt sobs. An undercurrent of moans and recriminations murmur through the other guests, while Amy sits straight-backed, her face frozen. With spear in hand and his eyes impaling her, Tommy George remains stationary, waiting for his prey to make the first move. Amy doesn't flinch but presses her lips tight together, and as she sets her jaw for a fight, her underbite becomes more pronounced. She's tough, hardened to the core, and I wonder what happened in her life to fashion such malevolent cruelty. Her expressionless face masks the exit strategy she's concocting, but I know she's not going down easy.

She turns to me and through clenched teeth says, "I didn't kill Nellie."

I match her deadly stare with one of the sweetest in my repertoire. "Really? Would you like to tell us then who did kill Nellie?"

With the drama of an ESTJ in full command of the situation, Amy rises to her feet and lifts her arm to point across to the other table. "He did."

"What are you doing?" comes the shocked response.

Now I have what I want. At last, when nothing else could faze him, Dale is on his feet.

Everyone including Tommy George and John turn their attention to Dale, while my eyes never leave Amy. A clever move on her part to throw her accomplice under the bus. The move I hoped she'd make. Sly as a fox, she edges backward using the chaos as her smokescreen. She's so intent on ensuring no one notices her slow escape, she doesn't see me shadowing her in parallel.

When she makes her run, Mimi cries out, "Diana. Be careful."

The adrenalin kicks in and my legs pump. For the past few days, I've been rebuilding my strength. My walking stick has been the perfect ruse, giving the false impression I'm still incapacitated. I can see the surprise in Amy's eyes as she skirts me and tries to dart past. She's heading for the edge of the lawn, to the cliff. *Good god, she's not going to hurl herself off?* I push hard into my ankle and though it sends out a mighty scream, I must stop her before she launches to a coward's death. She fumbles a step giving me time to reach out the old, wizened branch, and with the force of a hockey stick slamming the puck, I smack her shins, and she collapses like a stack of cards, while I land hard on my right shoulder. "Shit."

Amy howls obscenities and grabs her shins. "You bitch!" she screams at me. "You couldn't leave it alone, could you." The ferocity of hate in her eyes makes me forget the pain in my shoulder. There it is. Pure evil. Though I've seen it before, it never fails to send cold chills all over me.

Mimi's by my side, helping me to my feet, her gaze never leaving Amy. "Serves you right," she yells at her. "I hope your bloody shins are shattered."

The crowd roars its approval and applauds.

Timson drags Amy to her feet and escorts her, hobbling and cursing to her chair. I turn to find Dale baled up by Hamers next to a spear driven into the ground. No doubt, thrown by Tommy George's strong arm and good aim. Like Timson, Hamers man-handles Dale back to his seat. After Amy and Dale are handcuffed, a collective exhale goes up. With their stares fixed on each other, they share some unspoken pact and say nothing. Like obstinate children, they sit impassive in their chairs. An impressive tactic that I suspect they've employed possibly since childhood to keep them safe from repeated abuse. Whatever the underlying issue, silence won't save them now. Time for the circus to leave town.

CHAPTER TWENTY-FOUR

Geoff waves his hands in the air. "If everyone would return to their seats please." He pays particular attention that John and Tommy George are seated before proceeding. The last thing we need now is a revenge killing. But with Hamers and Timson standing guard over their charges, I doubt anyone will get close to them. And by the hangdog expression on Peter's face, and Kristen's grip tightening around his wrist, she'd sooner drop him herself if he tried anything. I suspect Peter's behavior has challenged Kristen's reluctance to engage in confrontation for the last time, and she's done with being made a fool of.

After Geoff does a final scan of the assembly, he gives me a nod. "Very well, Diana. Continue."

"As I said from the beginning, there's been a mastermind at work here. One with exceptional analytical, operational, and management skills." I nod my head at Amy. "And out of everyone here, Amy has those skills. And because she lacks any sort of moral compass, she'll do whatever it takes to ensure her safety and anonymity. She's the perfect killer—soulless and selfish. She ordered Dale to kill Nellie, so she could have an alibi."

"But how? What about the Company Vehicle Register?" Gillian asks. "The mileage and odometer check out. We went through it together."

"We did. We confirmed that the register wasn't tampered with, none of the readings were changed and the signatures were correct." I glance at Cameron. "Yours and Warren's signatures were correct as was the mileage you signed off. So that left only one person who could have manipulated the data. Amy."

She stares ahead into space, oblivious to the commentary.

"Amy's entry on the register included her trip into town on Wednesday where she claims she visited the photographer for a meeting. However, Hamers and I paid the photographer a visit today, and he denied seeing Amy on Wednesday. Which means either he's lying, or she is. We know he isn't because he was sitting in the dentist's chair on Wednesday getting a wisdom tooth removed. Therefore, Amy lied and added the extra mileage onto her town trip entry on the register."

"Sorry, I don't get it," Andrew says.

"It means that Amy masterminded Nellie's murder from Wednesday morning. She arranged with Dale to take the company vehicle that night, offer Nellie a ride home and murder her at the waterhole. The most important evidence to prove that the company car wasn't involved in the murder was to ensure that the odometer readings matched the register. She knew the register and its signatures had to be clean of any amendments. So, she added the extra mileage to and from Jackaroo's Waterhole under her own trip and used the excuse of visiting the photographer while in town. That way, when she came back from town and signed off the register, she'd already calculated what the reading would be after Dale returned the car that night from Jackaroo's Waterhole and before Cameron got into it after his shift. Thus, the register had the correct mileage, was signed off with no signs of alterations, and all the readings matched."

"Holy shit." Tony sits bug-eyed. "What a piece of work."

I glimpsed a slight lift of the corner of Amy's mouth. No one else probably saw it, but I find narcissists can't help but feel proud of their sinister achievements. Maybe Amy filled her face with Botox not only out of vanity but as a fail-safe measure to conceal her treacherous emotions. Tony's correct. *What a piece of work.*

"I told you I saw Dale lurking around on Wednesday night." Peter waggles a finger at his mate with obvious glee.

"Yes, but I suspect you only did that because you tried blackmailing him. You saw him and Nellie leave together on Wednesday night and by Saturday you decided it was time to get a larger share of the fake diamond business, so you made it clear to him what you knew."

Geoff interjects, "In fact, count yourself lucky, Pullman, that we cracked this case when we did. Otherwise, you would've ended up being the third person murdered."

Even under his bushy beard, Dale's mouth lifts in the same way as Amy's. *Cut of the same cloth*, my grandmother would say.

"You have no evidence to support any of this conjecture," Dale says without emotion.

"But we do. Officer Hamers found a cigarette butt of the same brand you smoke at the site where the murder took place at Jackaroo's Waterhole. Though you're normally fastidious in collecting your butts, this time you missed one. And we expect it to be a direct DNA match to you."

Dale makes no comment, but I suspect he wishes he gave up smoking a long time ago.

Just as I'm about to pick up the thread, Jo asks me, "And what about Maria?"

My heart goes out to her. She's kept her promise by keeping her emotions under control. Now she wants justice for the woman she loved. I smile at her, hoping she can feel my gratitude and respect during this terrible time.

"Poor Maria. A talented artist with a great future. She and Jo came here especially for the Kimberley Under the Stars event, but I suspect something about Amy caught Maria's eye from first sight. In fact, Jo became a little jealous because she often saw Maria looking at Amy. Perhaps Maria had seen Amy on campus during her time there studying art. We will never know for sure. But we do know, thanks to Amy" —I smile, thin-lipped in her direction— "that Maria spoke to her on Friday night about her concerns that the Rainbow Bush art was a reproduction. By then, Amy had already masterminded Nellie's murder, and she couldn't afford Maria to expose her. But this time, we believe she did the deed herself. Maria unwittingly let her into the Chamberlain Suite, probably moved outside under some pretext, where they struggled, and

Amy pushed her off the balcony. It was clumsy and risky because Maria may have survived the fall. But she didn't, and once more, Amy walked away scot-free. By now, having successfully gotten away with murder, twice, only strengthened Amy's belief in her criminal invincibility and genius. So, attacking Mimi based on an obscure suspicion that she might know something was nothing but sport for Amy. She took an early mark on Saturday night and while Cameron finished up in the kitchen, she crept up to Woolybutt and while Mimi was in the outside bath, violently hit her on the head. If Hamers hadn't been close by and seen what was going on, she might have killed her. It was certainly Amy's intention."

Cameron gags a groan. "God. We drove home together that night. I had no idea."

I could almost see his skin crawl with revulsion. "Sociopaths are hard to pick, Cameron. They walk among us, and we never know."

Whether it's the chill or the thought of what I said, several guests shiver and rub their arms.

"But who threw the rock over the ledge at Amaroo Falls?" Kristen asks, again.

"I suspect it was orchestrated by your husband and Dale. They were each other's alibis in that both were missing which meant it could be either-or. But that also means they could be in on the attack together. I suspect it's the latter."

She turns to her husband. "Peter!" He averts his eyes.

"Hang on a minute. Why on earth would Dale do what Amy tells him?" Trish asks.

Others chime in similar sentiments, wanting an answer.

"This is the lynchpin for the diamonds, the art, the murders, the attempted killings—for everything. Amy was the mastermind for it all." I direct my next question to Peter. "Tell me, whose idea was it to substitute pink sapphires for Argyle diamonds?"

He looks my way begrudgingly and inclines his head in Dale's direction. "His."

"I see. You trick your clients, and he supplies the goods."

I turn toward Dale. "And where do you get the sapphires from?"

Nothing.

"I suspect it's Indonesia. The same place you get the Aboriginal art reproduced by local artists who are wizards at copying anything. You pay a fraction of the cost for both the sapphires and the art and ship it all back into Australia through the parochial port of Darwin. A lot easier than through a bigger capital port. Am I right?"

Still nothing.

To Amy, I say, "And if I'm not mistaken, you wrote in your Sydney University submission that your last posting was in Indonesia at a university there."

More gasps and murmurs.

"Amy has the contacts, she masterminds the various businesses, and Dale finds the accomplices to help along the way. It's a great business model. Reminds me a bit of the infamous Ma Barker."

Both Amy and Dale turn to me. I take a long deliberate pause, and in that moment, I know the jig is up. As do they.

"Dale Baker is actually Dale Emerson, Amy's younger brother." The crowd erupts, but I raise my voice louder. "He was listed as next of kin on Amy's university admission." It's now that the guests realize that Amy and Dale both have red hair. They're staring and pointing at them, looking for similar features.

Groaning, Gillian lowers her face into her hands. She's got one helluva mess on her hands and a lot of explaining to do to the owners and stakeholders. I make a mental note to help her out if she wants.

I wave my hands up and down for silence. "Please, everyone, stop for a minute. Take a good look at Dale and imagine him without his beard. There's a distinct family resemblance. We have a photo from his juvenile record, and aside from the obvious red hair and recessive gene, he possesses the same underbite as his sister. Hard to see hidden underneath that beard. But it's there."

"How the hell?" John shakes his head.

"Amy, Ace as she's called by her younger brother, has always been the mastermind. The one who protected them. It didn't matter what lengths she had to go to or asked her brother to do, they were loyal to each other, and only each other." And I wonder what shared horrors they'd endured as children that led them to this life.

"This whole thing is unbelievable." Poor Gillian reminds me of one of my past clients who discovered their top employee had embezzled hundreds of thousands of dollars. I can all but see the guilt settling on her shoulders.

"There was nothing you missed or could have done," I reassure her. "Your systems, no matter how efficient, were no match for the likes of Amy and Dale. I suspect they've left a trail of deceit and destruction behind them, not just here but in other countries too."

All eyes were on them, and if looks could kill, sister and brother would have been struck down some time ago. But true to form, Amy and Dale remain unscathed by people's stares and opinions, whether unspoken or not.

"Right. Get them out of here." Geoff barks the order to his officers who assist the suspects to their feet.

Mumbles of appreciation that it's all over rise from the guests while shoulders relax and backs slump. Just as the atmosphere shifts, Tommy George and John unexpectedly spring from their chairs leaving Geoff to assess the greater risk and choose his target. He signals me to intercept John while he tries to block Tommy George from reaching Dale. Geoff gets to his mark before I do mine, and I overhear Tommy George laying down some incantation on his granddaughter's murderer. In front of me, John's too quick and cuts in front of Amy and Timson before I arrive. His hands wrap around her throat in an instant, and he shakes the life out of her while she plays ragdoll to his hate. Screams echo. People rush over, and John is restrained before he ruins his life. Amy straightens and appears unmoved by the whole attack. But then again, if she was willing to commit suicide, she'd happily die at the hands of someone else she broke. Life isn't of much consequence to her. Power is the prize.

With Christopher and Andrew holding him firm, John strains to kill the woman whose malevolence destroyed his daughter. Tears stream down his face, and in one final contemptuous act, he spits at her feet followed by a litany of curses.

Amy's dead stare travels down to the ground and returns to meet John's loathing, and then without visible emotion, she strolls off on her hand-cuffed exit up the lawn with Timson in tow.

Jo steps in beside me. "Dear god, that woman *is* evil."

"Indeed, she is."

Confused and shaken, we congregate in a tight group as we watch Amy meet her brother at the top of the steps, before walking side by side, into the great room.

"Right. You're with me, Pullman." Geoff claps the cuffs on Peter before he has a chance to protest.

The handsome young man beseeches his new wife with a lingering gaze, but Kristen folds her arms and shakes her head. "I'm sorry, Peter. I need time to reassess. I'll come to the police station in the morning."

A tough decision.

Geoff tugs at Peter's arm. "Right. Let's go." The pair follow the others and into the two police cars waiting on the driveway.

Gillian steps up. "Why don't we go into the great room where I can fix everyone drinks while Chris and Cameron whip up something for us to eat?"

Tony is the first to agree. "Good idea." He reaches out for Trish's hand, and they set off after Gillian, the chefs, and Andrew.

"Come on, John. It's all over now." Sylvia hooks her arm through her husband's and guides him up the lawn. They look shaken but vindicated. Now the healing can commence.

When Jo goes to Kristen, she nods in understanding and Kristen heaves a sigh. Without a word, the two of them walk together sharing a common, yet tragic bond. Both have lost the loves of their lives.

"You did it." Mimi's bright voice chimes in my ear as she gives me a squeeze. "You really did it."

I stare straight ahead, my lips barely tilting a smile. "I can't believe it."

"I can." Tommy George flanks me on the other side, spear in hand. "You have magic, Diana. Nellie was correct when she said you and I are the same."

"She did?" I look into the old man's eyes, sensing his spirit.

"Yes. She knew. My Nellie always knew. It was her gift and curse."

"Nellie in the sky with diamonds. The clue was singing in my head from the day we arrived."

Mimi's brow crinkles in its familiar pattern. "What are you talking about?"

I laugh a small brittle sound. But still, it's a laugh. "Come on, I tell you all about it."

And as we proceed to join the others, I explain how Nellie reminded me of the girl with kaleidoscope eyes, her face floating in the sky, guiding me to the clues.

CHAPTER TWENTY-FIVE

By the time Geoff strides back into the great room, we've got drinks in hand and the atmosphere is decidedly more relaxed.

"Right, they're off with Hamers and Timson to the station," he says. "And I'm officially off the clock. Make mine a beer please, Gillian." He nails her with those aquamarine eyes and within no time, he's enjoying his icy cold draft.

"Have you decided what you want to drink yet, Diana?" Gillian asks.

I hesitate, remembering the promise I made after Nellie's murder. "Can you make me a deadly kiss please?"

"Of course."

"The same way as Nellie used to?"

"Yes. I taught Nellie how to make that cocktail originally, so it'll be identical." She pats my hand in understanding and sets to work with the ingredients.

The twelve of us group at the bar, some standing, some on stools. Like emperor penguins huddling from the sub-freezing temperature, our proximity is comforting. Mimi stands just behind me, holding a bag of ice on my shoulder. "Some holiday this has been," she quips. "Playing Watson to your Sherlock, nursemaid to your injuries, and almost victim to your killers."

Laughter rings out. Though a little forced, it lightens the mood.

Glancing back at her, I smile. "You're the best Watson, nursemaid, and survivor a woman could want."

"Yeah, well, we're off on an all-day excursion to the Bungles tomorrow, a sore shoulder or not. Gillian's organized the flight so be prepared." Her no-nonsense tone makes us laugh some more.

"I'll be ready at the crack of dawn," I confirm, and add as an olive branch. "I'll pay."

"Of course, you'll pay." She leans forward and plants a sisterly kiss on my cheek to more laughter.

"Now we can get on with our holiday." I'm so pleased she's forgiven me.

"You bet," she says to which the others agree.

Jo steps into my left side. "Excuse me, Diana, can I ask you a question?"

"Sure."

"How did you know? From the very beginning. Before the murders."

Mimi interrupts, "She just knows things. Always has. Used to drive her husband, my brother Tom mad. But I've rarely seen her wrong."

Jo shakes her head. "I understand about your hunches and such like, but what made you think it was Amy before Saturday when Mimi overheard Amy called Ace."

Gillian slides my deadly kiss in front of me, and I nod my thanks. "I remember the first night of our arrival. We'd done the Chamberlain River excursion that afternoon, and Amy had us on the lawn for sundowners. John started talking to me . . ." When I smile his way, I notice the mask of grief from his face has lifted. There's a peace settling on him which I hope will last. "You told me about Stephanie, and you mentioned Ace from her diary. That's when Amy clapped her hands and called us up for dinner. I thought nothing of it at the time, but after, when I pieced the timeline together, it occurred to me that Amy was standing near us, right there at the beginning. I suspect she overheard John mention the name Ace firstly, then Nellie heard Sylvia and I talking about Ace, and then Mimi overheard Dale call Amy 'Ace.' The coincidence was too much not to consider."

"But how do you remember all these details of what you see and hear?" Trish asks.

"Observing people is one of my superpowers. I've been doing it for decades in my business, so it comes second nature to me. Wherever I go, I'm assessing people and situations."

"So, you've been assessing all of us all along?" Kristen sounds apprehensive.

"Too right she has," Geoff pipes in. "And she's bloody good at it too."

By the mixed array of stares directed my way, it's time to divert attention. "Sylvia, John, please accept my apologies for putting you through all that just now. We couldn't forewarn you because we needed your instinctive responses to help expose Dale and Amy."

Sylvia raises her wine glass. "Apology accepted. Thank you for discovering who Ace was. Now, we can finally move on." She turns to her husband. "Can't we, John?"

He kisses her on the cheek. "Yes, darling. We can."

"Come to think of it. Amy always reminded me a bit of those expressionless white, mouthless faces of that rock art we saw on our way to Amaroo Falls," Kristen says.

"Indeed, her face was the mask she hid behind, physically and psychologically."

"Thank you, Diana." Tommy George's voice floats toward me from the other end of the bar. Like John, the old man wears an expression of relief. "You found Waiwera, the evil spirit who killed my Nellie."

Geoff says to him, "We'll try to move the case along as quickly as we can, sir. I know you'll be wanting to see justice done."

An enigmatic smile graces the old man's face. "Thank you, Senior Constable. No doubt, Great Spirit will also tend to it. Now Nellie can go to our ancestors."

"Indeed." I raise my glass. "To Nellie, the girl with the kaleidoscope eyes."

"To Nellie," everyone chimes.

And as the first delicious sip from the lavender-colored cocktail touches my lips, I sense her soul whisper a final good-bye before she joins the Great Spirit in the sky.

★ ★ ★ ★

AFTER A LIGHT BUFFET AND once the other guests depart, Geoff stands. "I'm going to head off now. I'm dropping Tommy George at the Durack tree on my way back to town."

"But it's dark out. Will you be all right?" I ask Tommy George.

He casts me an indulgent smile. "Of course, I will. This is my land, day or night."

I offer him the walking stick. "You better take this with you. I don't need it anymore."

"No." He shakes his head, slowly. "It belongs to you. You claimed its magic and it worked for you. It is yours now."

A tingle rushes over my skin. "Thank you, Tommy George. Thank you." Delighted to keep the stick, I rub it with deep affection, not as a souvenir but as a reminder of the power of this ancient land.

"Here, you'll need this as well." Geoff opens his wallet and flips out his business card. "To go with Detective Nash's and the collection I'm sure you'll collect over the years." He chuckles and his eyes blast blue as I pocket the card.

"Thank you." I open my arms and embrace him, and as expected, he gives great hugs.

We all exchange a series of good-byes and promises to keep in touch, but I know that after Nellie's funeral, everyone's lives will return to normal and contact will become sporadic. But that's a good thing. Everyone's future deserves to be happy and free of the taint of past evils. Time to move on.

★ ★ ★ ★

"THIS WAY, LADIES, WATCH YOUR step." Gillian walks in front of us, guiding our steps with torchlight.

Mimi and I returned about an hour ago after a day trekking the Bungles, one of the oldest and strangest geological formations in the world. Flying over them in our light plane, they reminded me of hundreds of giant red beehives, crammed side by side on hundreds of acres of dry, arid land. On foot, they're towering, striped, sandstone domes weathered over twenty million years, which meant we walked more today than we have the entire holiday. Now with my aggravated ankle and cranky shoulder, we tail Gillian onto the perilous dining ledge to dine under the stars for our final night.

We cling to the low stone wall and edge our way around.

"If you sit here, Diana." Gillian pulls out the chair, and I slip in, but only after she's tucked me safely into the table do I relax. Even if I want to visit the toilet during the meal, I'm not moving.

She holds the other chair at an angle. "Mimi, you're here."

Mimi slides in with much more confidence than me. "Thanks, Gillian. This is perfect."

Gillian pours the wine and says, "Right. I'll serve dinner shortly. Enjoy!" With a pivot, she mounts the stone stairs and disappears up the lawn.

"Look up, Diana. The stars are magnificent. Millions of them. We don't see anything like this in the city."

She's right. Out here on the ledge with nothing but the stars as an endless canopy the world takes on a serene meaning. Murder and mystery vanish into the night. "Yes, it is breathtaking."

Mimi lifts her glass. "Despite everything, this has been a terrific holiday. I'm so pleased we came."

I mirror her salute. "Me too. It wasn't what I expected, but it worked out in the end." We smile and sip the lingering aches away. In a short while, we're settled into our perch above the gorge, enjoying a sumptuous dinner.

"Excuse me, Diana." Jo sits on the wall behind us. "Sorry to interrupt but I'm leaving early in the morning, and I wanted to say goodbye."

"That's perfectly all right. How are you?"

"Actually, I'm doing okay. I need to get back to work. Keep busy. You know. It'll be hard without Maria, but life goes on."

"Keep in touch, won't you?"

"I will. Thanks again. To both of you." With a final sad smile, she too disappears into the night.

"She's a lot softer than I gave her credit for," Mimi says.

"I learned that people can sometimes be like chocolates. They may have a hard exterior but inside they're soft marshmallow. I think Jo is a lot like that."

Mimi drops into an English accent. "You're a clever one, aren't you, Sherlock?"

"Elementary, my dear Watson. Elementary."

EPILOGUE

Six Months Later

"LOOK AT THIS, MIMI. THIS just came through from Jo. You know, Maria's girlfriend from El Kwestro." The email brings with it a flood of memories and my eyes travel to my walking stick propped in the corner of my home office.

Mimi strolls over to my desk, her face and hands tipped in leftover paint from her latest painting. "Is it good or bad news?"

"Read for yourself."

Hello Diana and Mimi,

I hope you're both well and not getting into any more mischief 😊 I wanted to update you on what's been happening since I left El Kwestro. My role in Maria's life, aside from loving her with all my heart, was to help with her career as an artist. Maria was such a talented painter, and I knew one day she'd be recognized for her amazing gift. So, on my return home, I decided to enter one of her paintings into that new contest, the Hadley's Art Prize. And it won first prize – $100,000. I know you'll understand that I was elated and devastated at the same time. But there it is. She won. I'm using the money to set up the Maria Loukas Artists Foundation where promising artists can apply for grants to help them in their studies. I know Maria would approve. It's a way to honor her memory and for me to continue in my work of supporting her. But the strangest thing is, the subject of Maria's painting that won was A Boat on the River. If I'm not mistaken, that's the first lyric in Lucy in the Sky with Diamonds. The song that haunted you, Diana, at El Kwestro and helped solve the case.

How very serendipitous. You've made a believer out of me. 😊

Regards to you both
Jo Arnold

"Well, I'll be damned. Good for her," Mimi says, with a nod and a smile. "At least, Maria's legacy will live on."

"Yes. And it will help Jo heal."

We pause a moment, rereading the email before Mimi swivels my chair to face her. I notice she's wearing one of her cheekiest expressions, gray eyes twinkling. "By the way, when are you going on your next holiday?"

I know what she's getting at. "Soon. Very soon."

"Dear god, give me strength."

And we both erupt into fits of laughter.

THE END

DIANA DANIELS FAVORITE RECIPE FOR A DEADLY KISS

Stir rose liqueur into a mixing glass with ice cubes. Discard any surplus liquid.

Add your favorite vodka to the mixing glass and stir for approximately 12 seconds.

Add Violette liqueur to the vodka and stir till opaque in color.

Take a martini glass from the fridge or freezer and atomize all over with the rose liqueur.

Julep strains the contents of the mixing glass into the rose-scented martini glass.

AUTHOR BIOGRAPHY

Diane began her career as a schoolteacher before moving into the entertainment industry as a choreographer, director, event manager, dancer and actress, working in television and live theatre, and managing multi-million-dollar productions.

Following her onstage career, she spent many years as a stress & life skills therapist, keynote speaker and presenter, appearing on national radio and television under the pseudonym of the Goddess of Love.

For her outstanding contribution to the arts, Diane was awarded the 2019 SBAA International Women's Day Leader Award for Leadership in the Entertainment, Creative Arts and Media Industry.

She is an award-winning author of contemporary, genre-busting romance, suspense and mystery novels. Her intuitive insights into human behaviour are woven into her casts of characters, heightening the intrigue in her storytelling. Set in exotic locations, her stories are packed with emotional punch and feature empowered heroines who live life to the fullest, much like the author herself.

Connect with Diane

https://dianedemetre.com/

AWARD WINNING AUTHOR

> " . . . Dare to dream bigger than ever before, dare to forge our own path no matter how hard the challenges. But most of all, dare to be you and let the chips fall where they may. We are all warrior women with gossamer wings . . . It's time to roar! "
>
> — Diane Demetre

Winner of 2019 SBAA International Women's Day Leader Award for Leadership in Entertainment, Creative Arts and/or Media Industry.

Diane was nominated as a finalist in the ARRA Awards 2018 for Favourite Romantic Suspense, for her novel *Retribution.*

In 2017 Diane won the Romance Writers of Australia Emerald Pro Award for Best Unpublished Romance Manuscript.

ALSO, BY DIANE DEMETRE

EVIL ON THE HIGH SEAS
A Diana Daniels Mystery

Murder, Mystery and Dry Martinis

There's evil on board the luxury expedition ship, the *Silver Galapagos*, but no one suspects it. Except for Diana Daniels, a successful management consultant whose rare insight into human behavior and highly developed intuition tell her that not all the passengers are seeking a carefree holiday. Though still struggling with the recent loss of her husband and honoring his request to scatter his ashes in the Galapagos Islands, she becomes intrigued by a mysterious woman in white who arrives at the port of departure.

After discovering that the woman in white is Celeste Constanzo, widow of deceased Mafia boss, Joe Constanzo, Diana is warned away from the notorious crime family by fellow traveler Detective John Nash. But because of their shared widowhood, Diana finds herself inexorably drawn to helping Celeste when the mysterious stranger confides her fear of being murdered by her three adult stepchildren.

When Celeste, along with five-million-dollars-worth of jewelry disappear after the Captain's cocktail party, Diana is certain that her suspicions have been realized. With Detective

Nash's reluctant assistance, she embarks on her own journey to solve what she's sure is the murder of the woman in white.

But without a body, her theory is impossible to prove. With multiple suspects and only a couple of days until debarkation, will Diana find the jewelry, the body, the author of the anonymous letters, and the murderer who's still on board?

With no other choice but to step up and forge a new single life for herself, Diana employs her exceptional skills and gritty determination to solve the mystery of evil on the high seas.

ISLAND OF SECRETS

Two love stories separated in time. Two women following their dreams. In a paradise littered with painful secrets, will love turn the tide?

1973. Cecilia "CiCi" Freemont has a restless soul and the voice of an angel. Leaving her privileged upbringing behind, she chases her dreams to the sandy beaches of an unspoiled Hawaiian paradise, Harbor Island. But life takes an unexpected turn when she falls for the island's young heir-apparent and her newfound adventure becomes too much to bear . . .

2017. Investigative journalist Tina Templeton has dedicated herself to the pursuit of truth. But when she inherits Harbor Island, her career plans take a confusing twist. Managing the sprawling island estate is tough business even with the help of aging cabaret singer, CiCi Freemont. Especially when a massive ecological disaster threatens to destroy her beautiful beaches — and the responding coast guard captain steals her heart.

As the investigation into the disaster reveals a 40-year-old mystery that could change their lives forever, will Tina find love among the secrets, or will CiCi's painful past dash her dreams on the rocks?

Island of Secrets is an epic love story. If you like generations-spanning drama, characters with hidden pasts, heart-warming romance and intrigue, then you'll love Diane Demetre's powerful novel in paradise.

RETRIBUTION

Winner of Romance Writers of Australia Emerald Pro Award 2017.

She's a ballerina with a dark secret.
He's a retired sniper with a tortured past.
Will they find love or fall prey to a stalker's deadly game?

Professional ballerina Jessie Hilton wraps her battle scars in satin pointe shoes, but there's a deeper hurt that haunts her sleep. When a handsome man steps in to save her from a mugging, something about her hero makes her heavy heart leap. Though her career can't afford distractions, he may be her sole source of safety when she gains the unwanted attention of a relentless stalker.

Ex-sniper Brad Jordan survived his tour of duty, but a tragic accident cost him the lives of those closest to him. With his faithful border collie Whiskey by his side, Brad gets a second chance when he protects the beautiful Jessie from danger. When the ballerina's stalker grows more brazen, Brad's tactical training may be their only weapon against tragedy.

Will Jessie and Brad survive a deadly game or will the assailant destroy their chance at love?

Retribution is a stand-alone romantic suspense novel. If you like tough-as-toe-shoes heroines, second-chance romance, and page-turning plots, then you'll love Diane Demetre's heart-stopping saga.

THE STEAMY SECRETS SERIES

TEMPT ME

One woman . . . Two men . . . Threesomes change everything

When Michele Johnston, a forty-two-year-old ex-dancer from the Moulin Rouge gets divorced, she leaps into her new world of singledom with unbridled passion.

Aided and abetted by three vivacious girlfriends, Michele embarks on her steamy, erotic adventures, but gets more than she expects when mysterious yacht captain Mark Miller unleashes her wanton desires.

Further complicating matters, debonair Greek businessman Nick Stavros arrives on the scene and falls madly in love with her, promising the happy-ever-after ending. But will she give up her newfound freedom? Will she choose one man over the other? Or can she continue loving them both?

Tempt Me is the first stand-alone Contemporary Erotic Romance in Diane Demetre's genre-busting series, Steamy Secrets. If you love strong heroes, hot sex, and feisty heroines, don't miss this page-turning love story with a twist.

TEACH ME

When destiny beckons, what is a girl to do?

At twenty-four, Samantha O'Brien scores her dream job as a dancer at the famous Moulin Rouge, only to arrive in Paris to find her well-laid plans in disarray. Fortuitously, Sam is rescued by the eccentric, tarot-card reading proprietress of Hotel Hollandaise, who cautions that Paris is for lovers, but not always love.

As Sam launches into her new career, she suspects that the show's super sexy, Sicilian stage director, Tony Di Falco is more than just a creative genius and hard taskmaster, leaving her to wonder whether secrets are best shared.

Meeting Philippe Lacroix, a struggling, young artist in Montmartre saves Sam from imploding under the pressure. He introduces her to the city of love, captivating her with his angelic good looks and sensuous touch. Yet the mounting attraction intensifies between Sam and Tony, and their tense, sexually charged relationship threatens to overwhelm them. But the show must go on.

Filled with backstage bitchiness, tough rehearsals, a sprinkling of cocaine and the French addiction to cigarettes, Sam grapples with her new life. Then without warning, her destiny changes literally before her eyes, and she learns that even in the most romantic city of the world, you don't find love, love finds you.

Teach Me is the second stand-alone Contemporary Erotic Romance in Diane Demetre's genre-busting series,

Steamy Secrets. If you love strong heroes, hot sex and feisty heroines, don't miss this page-turning love story with a twist.

TAKE ME

How far would you run to find love?

Aiden Bishop is a successful young lawyer hiding out in sunny Spain to escape unsavoury clients in Australia. At twenty-seven, Ace as he's known to his mates, happens upon a local flamenco club in Seville where he's befriended by Rafael Flores and beguiled by Carla Armando — a famous flamenco couple well-known for their fiery performances both on and off the stage.

With ancestral links to the famous gypsy flamenco dancer Carmen Amaya, Rafael and Carla have mysterious Romani culture coursing through their veins. Sensing Aiden's love of adventure, they invite him on a road trip from the Costa Del Sol to Granada in search of Carla's true Romani gifts. However, as the trip stretches deeper into less travelled emotional geography, long-kept secrets are exposed.

Brimming with gypsy traditions, the passion of the dance, mysterious rune readings and intrigue, Aiden realizes that he may be able to evade his clients, but he can't escape his destiny no matter how far he runs.

Take Me is the third stand-alone Contemporary Erotic Romance in Diane Demetre's genre-busting series, Steamy

Secrets. If you love strong heroes, hot sex and feisty heroines, don't miss this page-turning love story with a twist.

the candidates who I thought were guilty turned out to be as innocent as the day is long. I loved the fact that the book kept me engaged. I want to read more and look forward to experiencing all that Diana Daniels has to offer. I have a sneaky suspicion trouble will come looking for her, wherever she goes.

— 5 STARS, **Jonathan and Deborah Bispham**

This is the third book I've read by Diane Demetre and I was absolutely delighted! What a great read. It has everything: a great story line mixed with sensual exploration; mystery; spirituality and wonderfully complex main characters. Couldn't put it down. Loved Aiden – just gorgeous and every woman's dream. Looking forward to the next book.

— 5 STARS, Deborah Bispham

Demetre paints vividly the atmosphere of Paris and the Moulin Rouge with such detail that it adds yet another layer of intimacy to the story. A wonderful read that we highly recommend.

— AusRom Today

I bought this book and wow what a read! To every young woman it's a must! Life lessons learnt in an amazing story told! Though I had other things to do, I had to finish this amazing story! Bring on book 3!

— 5 STARS

A well-written erotic romance with its share of twists and suspense. Love the characters and the way the author describes Paris and behind the scenes of the Moulin Rouge.

— 5 STARS, Peter Brady

Michele, a former pro dancer, has finally extricated herself from a very unsatisfying marriage, & is ready for a chance to kick up her heels, sexually & emotionally. Intent on a one-night stand, she finds, instead, Mark, a most inventive & attentive lover, something she has never experienced before. As she falls in love with him, against her better judgement, she finds that he has way too many secrets that threaten to derail their fledgling relationship. By the time Nick inserts himself into her life, insisting he is just her type, despite her thoughts to the contrary, Mark has disappeared & bad people are after both him & Michele. Under Nick's protection, Michele finally figures out what she wants from life, in a very good heroine's journey. There's an abundance of very hot sex, & the love of a good man.

— 4.5 STARS, Alberta, ManicReaders

Fast Pace!! Erotic!! Read it in 2 days!!!! What a book Woo Hoo!!!!! Congratulations Diane Demetre, I thoroughly enjoyed your book . . .

— 5 STARS, Amazon

DIANE DEMETRE